VICKY RIVERS

C. P. CLARKE

The characters and events portrayed in this book are fictitious. Any similarity to real persons, living or dead is coincidental and not intended by the author.

Text copyright©2014 C.P. Clarke
All rights reserved.

Cover design by: The Smithy Creative
www.thesmithycreative.co.uk

ISBN 13 -:978-1505600391
ISBN-10: 1505600391

Other titles by the author:

Life In Shadows
Stalking The Daylight
The Killing

POV – A Personal Perspective of the Bible
A Question of Faith
Stories on a Wall

We do not see things as they are.
We see things as we are.
The Talmud

C. P. CLARKE

VICKY RIVERS

PART ONE

SURVIVAL

C. P. CLARKE

1

She clenched the arm rests of the seat with sweaty palms. She'd been sat mostly frozen with her seatbelt tightly round her thin waist. Occasionally someone passing along the aisle would brush passed her or accidentally bump her seat as they tried to navigate the thin passageway. She'd declined the meal that had been offered but had accepted the short bottle of Merlot that came with it; in fact there had been a surprisingly wide selection of liquid refreshment considering the size of the metallic trolley pushed along by the immaculate hostess who was donned in the calming pale blue colours of the airline, her hair tight in a bun and her make-up almost tattooed on to conform with company perfection. She had hesitated over the red or white and in the end had gone for the red simply as it was the bottle held out before her. The leggy air hostess lent slightly across her to ask the portly gentleman to her right, who also appeared to be travelling alone, what he wanted, but by the time he had a chance to answer she had cracked open the lid of the bottle and downed almost half of the bitter tasting wine. He looked at her with concern. She half shrugged her shoulders in response and then ignored them both.

He raised an eyebrow and half shook his head, allowing a knowing look to pass between him and the air hostess.

He had attempted to instigate pleasant conversation before take-off but she had given him a curt frosty reply that said in no uncertain terms that she wished to be left alone - no doubt her demeanour during the first half hour or so of the flight and her studious examination of the flight safety demonstration combined with the intimate perusal of the emergency flight card was sure to have left him in no doubts of her fears.

It wasn't that she was scared of flying; she flew loads, so often she got confused to her destinations, like this one. She thought hard – where the hell was she going this time? No, flying wasn't the problem, it was the crashing she didn't care for, and was so very desperate to avoid going through all the pain of it again.

She watched with pity and a tinge of jealousy the young family in the centre row taking up three of the four seats. Mum, was on the farther side taking up care duties while the two boys, maybe 5 and 7 years old, tried to entertain themselves, occasionally turning around to the seat behind where dad sat relegated on his own to the aisle seat after the snooty woman, so the mum had called her (Talisa would have called her bitchy but could understand the mother's restraint with her language) refused to change seats. The boys leapt up and shook the cushioned headrests and called constantly to dad, an early thirty-something escaping the toils of the work place for that precious two week vacation away with the family, the boys pestering constantly trying to show him what they'd coloured in on the child's pack they'd been given by the stewardess before take-off. Their meals sat mainly untouched piled up on mums tray and clamping her in, who being plump around the mid-drift had never lost the excess from her pregnancy weight and never having regrown her long auburn curls longer than the straight bob she now wore having cut it following the constant tugging she'd endured when the kids were mere babes, those same that had so far grown into loveable rouges with too much energy for a flight of any length as they ignored the repeated requests of both mum and dad not to kick the seats in front of them.

Talisa hoped for their sakes the flight would be uneventful.

The seatbelt sign lit up above her head with a chime which drew her attention as the turbulence began. She shook her head expecting the worst, the glistening brown springy ringlets curling down passed her ears, bouncing as the plane began to gently jolt. Her eyes began to water, not quite enough to roll a tear along her cheek to drip onto her conservative v-neck sweater and striped shirt she wore beneath, but it was enough to cause her to suck in breath and blink profusely. The stewardess began walking up the aisle cautioning everyone to buckle up. She appeared unperturbed by the sway of the plane as though it was a normal and regular occurrence, which of course it was, but to Talisa it was just the beginning.

If it were possible to grip the arm rest tighter she would have, but the white of her knuckles showed it couldn't be done. There was a jolt and a sharp dip as the plane caught a pocket of air but the pilot seemed capable as it quickly regained composure. The picture perfect hostess had to grab hold of the shoulder of a seat this time but still smiled with professional calmness at the worried boys whose energetic bobbing had been stilled by the rising chill from their stomachs as the plane momentarily lost altitude.

For minutes the plane flew along with nothing more than an exaggerated shake and sway of the wings, even further back along the aisle another stewardess was still moving along unperturbed with a trolley collecting up any rubbish. For a brief moment Talisa thought her paranoia was just that, but then there was a loud bang like that of a car back firing only a hundred times louder due to the size of the engine, the sound roaring across from the far wing causing all eyes to snap in that direction, including the stewardess who gripped the front seat of the aisle as the nose of the plane dipped sharply and dragged down to the left by whatever had caused the explosion; a failed engine, a bomb, a collision, who knew, and really right now who cared? Right now at this point in time all anybody cared about was not dying.

The stewardess, Talisa hadn't caught the name on her badge, frankly caring little to get too acquainted with anyone she may later regret remembering, had she been looking back up the aisle she would have seen the trolley come careening along the passage unhindered by the brakes which at that point had been released to move it along manually. The trolley, rolled like a runaway train on tracks of grey plastic arm rests that bounced it back on course as it struck the seats eventually colliding with the slender legs of the leggy blonde who noticed it too late to avoid it completely but in enough time to escape the full impact by throwing herself sideways into the vacant toilet. It clipped her legs side-on scraping tights, flesh, and bone all in one hit as it toppled to a rest beside her, the curtain separating the compartments flapping as she went down exposing the terrified faces of the forward cabin who stared back in two minds as to whether they should unclip and help. One man who was close enough did, something he would regret as he would later find himself flung to the back of the plane, for now he reached her as she screamed out in pain, her screams joined by those of the passengers as the nose of the plane failed to recover an upward momentum.

There was a moment of pandemonium as the tail of the aeroplane seemed to lift throwing the nose down and the contents of the cabin up, with it went the contents of a good many stomachs whose failure to reach for the sick bags in time meant a warm foul smelling splattering was had by most sat behind, especially those at the rear as the chunky vomit sailed over a number of seats as it sped away from the descent of the plane. A laptop loose on a forward seat, no doubt at rest from the fingers of its weary task master who, like most people had slammed his hands to his ears at the sudden pain caused by the change in cabin pressure, took flight and bumped off the overhead storage compartments, some of which had popped open and spewed the contents south hitting hard on the heads of the unsuspecting and already panicked passengers, one was struck out cold - a fortunate occurrence for him as he was spared the anticipated end. The loose laptop, flapping with a gaping mouth of a hungry pac-man seeking a ghoul to swallow up in the maze, eventually slammed down on the snooty woman sat next to mum leaving a gash across the side of her head before continuing its journey. If Talisa hadn't been so sure of the end she would have said this was karma but truly it wasn't comical enough to even break her thin pursed lips away from her clenched teeth.

As well as all the other debris floating about the cabin the flapping of oxygen masks added to the confusion. The masks had dropped with the cabin pressure as the vessel fell into an apparent free-fall. She could picture the pilot desperately trying to regain control in a vain attempt to save all the lives on board, living for real every pilot's nightmare.

Mum ignored the instructions of the safety guide and tried desperately to fit her children's masks before fitting her own, almost passing out in the process before realising the sense of what she needed to do, her futile attempts eventually winning through as she mentally tried to block out all else around her as her motherly instincts kicked in and she reached and attached hers before checking theirs were secured in the proper manner, attempting to hug the nearest with a glance between the seats to her husband behind who was reaching forward around the aisle to hold the backward reaching fingers of their other son.

The only blessing for all was that all the window shutters had been down for the majority of the flight so as it plummeted in free fall no one but those in the cockpit could visualise the end and so could only guess at when the collision would be as they prayed to a god they'd previously ignored.

This was how Talisa pictured it. She didn't bother with the oxygen mask, hoping if at all possible to pass out as she closed her eyes, feeling the heavy sinking of the metal shell as it flipped from a nose dive onto its back, the seatbelt pulling tight and bear hugging her intestines as it twisted once more onto its belly;

everyone screaming; everyone bracing for impact as the plane fell out of control. Then after what felt like an age, in what could only have lasted for a split second, there was a short sharp momentary thud and what felt like the blistering heat of a fireball rolling down the cabin engulfing the plane as white light instantly blotted out all else from her mind.

2

She stared at herself in the mirror. The glass was still misted from her shower which caused her to wipe it occasionally with the palm of her hand to get a clear view before it clouded over again. Part of her felt coy at the image reflected but part of her also felt impatient at wanting to inspect the phantom of herself that threw back through the rising moisture of the vacated shower. What stared back was a far cry from what had terrorised the glass twenty minutes earlier when a different person altogether stood in her place.

Twenty minutes earlier the tangled mop of auburn hair clung to the sticky spittle of crimson that had splatted across her face and dried to mix with the smeared violaceous streaks that had strobed her cheeks in a gush of elated emotion she couldn't contain as she'd climaxed with the painful thrill of his mouth flinching and biting down uncontrollably on her clitoris as she held his head down with one hand whilst she thrust the sharpened letter opener that she'd earlier secreted beneath the pillow through the top of his skull with enough force to push it down into the back of his throat so that it pinned his tongue in position, literally not knowing what hit him as his body jolted and fitted, his fingers gripping her bare buttocks, his nails digging in to add to the ecstasy as she rose her hips up to join his suffocating face between her legs as she relished the death throes of the dead man's five seconds, stifling his cry and any exasperated attempts at protest. It was just as she had planned it. No, it was better.

She'd lay there for a minute or two before lifting his naked corpse off her and removing her blood soaked body from his and stepping across the tiled hotel room floor to the bathroom to peer into the mirror.

She stared into the mirror full of self-loathing at her appearance, a crazed smile come grimace straining through the tear smeared make-up and smudged bright red lipstick, a result of either the over passionate snog she shared with the man she just killed as they'd entered the bedroom and frantically pulled off each other's clothes, or it was from where she'd wiped her bloodied mouth after being slapped, or both. She knew the type of man he was, could tell from just looking at him, he was short and stocky with a short back and sides haircut with a low flattop and wore a permanent scowl, the sort you could imagine from someone who would batter his wife for not cleaning the dishes thoroughly, so she knew he wouldn't hesitate in knocking her around when she suggested some rough treatment and that being slapped as he penetrated her was a real turn on for her.

It wasn't the first time she'd lured a man back to her room for sex and then killed him, but it was the first time she'd killed a man during sex - and she liked it. The time before she had left the poor soul handcuffed to the bed as she'd gone to the bathroom and retrieved the gun from the bathroom cabinet, screwed on the silencer, and calmly walked back to shoot him in the head, his erection still standing proud, clearly expecting more of what he'd been getting before she'd left the room.

She hated what stared back at her but at the same time she couldn't imagine loving herself any less. She had ripped off the wig and wiped the fresh tears that had begun to form as she briefly thought of her long passed mother; not a day went by when she didn't think of her and what she would have thought of what she'd become. She stepped to the shower and let herself be cleansed, not of her sins but of the thoughts that tempted to betray her.

So here she stood now twenty minutes later a different woman staring into the mirror. This was Vicky Rivers: wild, intelligent, unpredictable, fearless, and ruthless. Her hair, her real hair, was cropped short with a straight blonde fringe that washed over her left eye. Her eyes were a startling blue that stood out and often drew unwanted attention for their beauty but she disguised them with a heavy mask of make-up, a ghostly ring of eyeliner and shadow meeting to bridge at her nose as a painted on eye mask contrasting the white foundation she'd brushed on to the rest of her face to smooth out the sharpness of her jawline and high cheek bones, a strength of features she sought to hide as though ashamed. Her eyebrows were plucked thin, her eyelashes short, her ears pulled back tight to her head which squarely sat on a slender smooth neck.

She examined her body, it was strong and muscular, a result of the steroids she used to take, not for performance enhancement or recreation, but medicinal. She was tall too, a height that most women couldn't achieve even with heels, yet her height wasn't clumsy or out of proportion but gracefully carried on pins that would turn most heads as her legs reached up to her firm buttocks. A tattoo decorated the outside of her right thigh, it was high up and not too big to be a distraction from any clothing she would normally wear but its theme bore a meaning in her manner as the black Colt 9mm smoked out into a blood red daisy chain that wrapped itself around the handle of the gun. She had been tempted to get another one of a dagger on the other thigh but so far had resisted the temptation.

She had a firm six-pack of stomach muscles, not too bulgy but flat and smoothly ripped. Her biceps were strong too, telling of a no messing woman but one that could equally carry off a ball gown if she needed or wanted to. Her breasts were an ample C cup and not too saggy so that they held nicely without a bra. Her nipples were pert which distracted from the deep slash of scarring across and below the left nipple from a wound that had almost cost her the breast. She stared down at the breast at a rogue mutant long blonde hair that seemed to sprout from the areola which she hadn't noticed before. She inspected for others before gripping it between her finger and thumb and yanking it out.

She was happier with her appearance now which allowed her mind to settle on the practicalities of what she needed to do. She turned on the television and allowed the late night news broadcast to loudly filter through the rooms to disguise any humping around that she required as she sanitised the scene. She didn't bother dressing for this; it was easier to clean herself off than any clothes she might put on. She moped at the bloody footprints she'd left on the floor with a towel (she would take the towels with her and dispose of them elsewhere). She had been careful with her appearance on booking the room and also on how much she touched so knowing what to wipe down was easy. She bleached the sheets on the bed, inspecting closely for hairs or any other fibres that might give her away, before bleaching her victims genitalia and mouth, cleaning out his finger nails and erasing all evidence that she had been there. Of course it would be easy to put together what had happened, as bizarre a scene as she'd leave it, but that would be at least two days from now, so long as the maid respected the privacy sign she would leave on the door when she left. She was sure the police would figure out the basics of what happened, as for the motive, even she wasn't sure of that.

Everything had been pre-planned. Her fresh set of clothes were laid out carefully in the bathroom, her handbag containing her passport and cash were there too on the floor behind the door. She hadn't needed much for this job and was keen to get onto the next. She'd already been assigned and was expected in Stuttgart tomorrow night.

The news channel rambled on in the background repeating the political wanderings of a government official and his connections to the mob; it was boring and nothing new. She had pulled up her panties and was reaching beyond her back for the clasp to do up her bra when a breaking news headline caught her attention. "Ultime Notizie: Un aereo si è schiantato in America uccidendo tutti a bordo" the female newsreader announced turning Vicky's ear towards the small television set sat propped opposite the bed. She stopped what she was doing and listened without being able to see the screen from where she was stood. A plane had crashed in America killing all on board, although one unofficial report claimed that there had been at least one survivor. It was her. She knew it was. It had to be, she could feel it in her bones.

She shook her head, spitefully kissing her teeth as she did so. This changed everything. They wouldn't be happy, but she didn't care. "I'll get you this time," she growled in Italian as she resumed getting dressed with a renewed sense of urgency.

3

Tomek laughed heartily, a short deep snort filtering through his nostrils as he balanced on the back two legs of his pale wooden chair, the tip of his magazine barely resting on the matching table top as the four of them sat shaded under the wide brimmed ivory umbrella that protruded out into the street. There was a chuckle also from Lenart who had equally been tickled by the story Wieslaw had read out as he spluttered through it attempting to sip at his coffee as his eyes followed the print in the newspaper as he hunched from his seat over the slatted table.

Justyna walked around the table with a steaming jug in her hand and refilled two of their cups and wiped at a spillage Tomek had left when he'd jogged the table with his leg.

"Ah, dobra. Dziękuję," said Tomasz raising his head from his Ipad with a distant smile thankful for the refill. Justyna circled another table within the metal railings of Czekolada's expanded pavement space before retreating back inside the café.

"It has that one in here too," directed Wieslaw barely above a whisper towards Lenart without lifting his head from the newspaper before him, "the one you read earlier about better dads having smaller testicles."

"I'm still laughing from that one," said Lenart with his face lighting up with a broad smile at the memory of their earlier discussion.

"I have one," spoke up Tomek blind to the eyes of Lenart following the firm rear of Justyna as she walked away behind him. He tipped his chair forward and placed the magazine on the table to read aloud. "Headline is: Predicting Your Death - 'Scientists in California now believe, by the use of a few simple tests, they can accurately predict when elderly people will die. A study of 1,189 old people identified 13 'biomarkers' such as heart disease, stress and high cholesterol levels which can be linked to early mortality. A mixture of high levels of adrenal hormones and immune problems was especially risky to people aged over 70, they added.'" He looked up for approval but it was clearly in the balance as heads were wobbling sideways in an uncertain gesture.

"Would you really want to predict when you die?" asked Lenart, a thin man with blonde hair that flopped across his brow and a well groomed fair goatee that didn't really suit him; his pallid blue shirt with faded white vertical stripes hung loose over his black jeans which were out of sight beneath the table, his sleeves rolled up tightly to expose the short blonde hairs on his arms that gave them the appearance of being smooth up to the expensive Timex that adorned his left wrist.

"Why not? Just think if you know what's likely to kill you then surely you'll try and change your habits, your diet, the way you live – wouldn't you?"

Lenart and Tomek paused to consider Wieslaw's viewpoint.

"I think I'd rather it just crept up on me. I don't want to spend my life looking over my shoulder worrying about doing this and doing that because it 'might' kill me."

"Tomek's right," Lenart agreed, "You go to all that trouble and then you step off the kerb into the path of a bus."

"Or Lenart's car!" chortled Tomek looking over Lenart's shoulder and across the road to where Cristian Lenart had parked his car, a green Volkswagen Passat that sat not quite straight in one of the bays opposite that formed a long island of parked cars in the middle of the street allowing traffic to flow either side as the shops around formed a wide square along Chmielna, which ended at the Atlantic cinema and the C&A department store at one end with the St. Andrew's Palace Hotel opposite, and a pasta bar at the other end which backed onto a vacant lot before the shops began again. The empty lot with its broken bricks and discarded rubbish blown in, or thrown in, had stood empty for almost two years and as yet no plans were in place to build on what had been the old car showroom. Today the whole street of Chmielna was fairly quiet for both vehicular and pedestrian traffic considering it was not far from Marszalkowska Street and Aleje Jerzolimskie, the two main roads intersecting the centre of Poland's capital Warsaw.

"What's wrong with my parking, you son of a bitch!" retorted Lenart as he looked over his shoulder at the family car that housed the two child seats in the back which would later be filled with his twin girls once he picked them up from kindergarten after lunch, until then he would waste away his morning as was their regular customary routine as they hovered around their most respected friend, Tomasz.

Once more they bowed their heads to their respective periodicals. It had become the norm, to sit around the table mid-week for mid-morning coffee at Czekolada's perusing the various newspapers and popular magazines for intriguing and humorous supposedly true stories to bat around the table as comical issues of debate amongst themselves. Mostly Tomasz would only be vaguely listening as he worked, not that anyone would ever ask him what he was doing, and in his stead Justyna, or Bronislaw, the café owner, would be drafted in as they busied about attending them or other customers. The four of them were well known and respected amongst the community and often they would be greeted by a familiar face passing, or a car would toot in acknowledgement of their presence.

Tomasz was the reason they were together, allowing them to benefit from the morsels he threw them from time to time as they regularly met for coffee. Not only did he hold them there with his insistence on working away from a desk, preferring to keep a mobile office attached to just one of his many regular haunts, haunts which had changed little since they were young men wet behind the ears but full of ambition, but his dynamic gaze which drew you to him with the strength of a master vampire casting you into a trance was commanding, his enigmatic character one you simply didn't want to part from. They each had their own jobs and families but it was to Tomasz they each held their loyalty.

"I have one." It was Tomek again once more tipping his chair forward and placing the magazine on the table so that his companions could see the insert of a zombie taken from a horror movie. There seemed to be a theme running through the weekly satirical magazine Nie that he was reading. They often found that this was the case with similar stories repeated in the different publications, often almost identical but occasionally taking different, if not opposite, slants on the varying stories.

Wieslaw held aloft the extra-large pages of the Gazeta Polska; Lenart's copy of the tabloid Fakt lay flat on the table with its pages open wide for all to see, his coffee cup centrally placed on the table far from his reach resting on the unopened copy of the folded Dziennik. The two attentive men cocked an ear to listen.

Tomek Bednarczyk was the older looking of the quartet, a look that came from his unshaven designer cheeks and his broad paunch that leant to the wearing of sweaters rather than the crisp tight fitting shirts his friends tended to wear. It wasn't that he was older, quite the opposite, and often his roguish boyish behaviour would betray him as the youngest of the group, for he was the junior to the others by almost three years. He had known his three companions his whole life and had grown up in the rough tangle of grey webbing that caught the winter breeze between what was officially business and unofficially crime, or rather office level misdemeanours, not quite street level robbery but sophisticated enough to be organised, and calculated enough to know whose heads to step on and whose arse to lick when necessary. It was a learned talent, one he felt privileged to have been indoctrinated into.

"The Walking Dead, reads the headline," began Tomek.

"What is the obsession with death this morning?" Lenart chirped.

"Like the series? Zombies, yes? I get it," quietly mumbled Wieslaw as if speaking to himself.

Tomek resumed, "'Could zombies, the stuff of horror films soon become reality?' The article asks. 'Scientists in America...' blah blah blah..."

"America again."

"Humph," agreed Wieslaw with a shrug of his shoulders.

Tomek finished scanning the column and picked up on the basics of the story. "'Using a so-called suspended animation technique, they emptied the dead animals' veins of blood and filled them with ice-cold saline solution to preserve the tissues and organs. The animals had no heartbeat or brain activity and were classed as being clinically dead. The saline solution was then replaced with fresh blood and electric shocks were used to restart the heart. The dogs were unharmed by their suspension and appeared to suffer no brain damage.'"

"Sounds more like Frankenstein," piped up Wieslaw.

"'Scientists in Pittsburgh hope to use the technique to save the lives of people who have suffered massive blood loss, such as battlefield casualties or stabbing victims. They are in talks with hospitals about beginning trials on human trauma patients within a year.' It waffles on a bit more about the dogs being in complete cardiac standstill for hours before they recover... blah blah."

"The bloody Americans are obsessed with keeping everybody alive." It was Wieslaw's turn to take the lead with a vocal concern on the subject. "What happens when we save everyone? Where do we all live? How will we all work? Obtaining immortality is one thing, the quest for it I mean, but globally on a large scale it's not sustainable, surely."

Lenart was nodding at his friend's view point. Wieslaw Raczynski was wiry thin, even thinner than both he and Tomasz and his shirt was almost a clone too, as though the three wore a uniform but of differing shades and colours. He had a narrow chin below a bulbous nose besides which was a large mole. His dark hair was fashionably unkempt in a fringe that rested over his forehead but above his eyes. A wave of cigarette smoke wafted from his mouth floating upwards passed his eyes as he blew it away and reached forward to stub out the butt in the ashtray in the middle of the table. He wasn't the only one of the four men to smoke but for the last half hour he was the only one to light up, Tomek resisting the urge to aide Lenart in his attempts to quit in order to please his wife, who was not so much nagging as manipulative in cunningly drawing her husband under her thumb.

Lenart stared at Wieslaw hunched over the Gazeta Polska, not for the first time thinking that his friend reminded him of a weasel, yet knowing that when he wanted to there could be a rapid and suave transformation when he adopted that skill Tomasz had taught him of having the ability to look cool and slick and confident before all others so that upon inspection they would not be intimately aware he, or any of them, were sniffing the brown nor shafting anyone in direct competition or with influence of the rungs of the ladder they were climbing, or had climbed in the decade or so they had run together since finishing business college.

"Do you think it's true?" Lenart enquired with a hint of scepticism.

"Who are you going to get to volunteer for that sort of stuff? Not me!" exclaimed Tomek rebalancing his chair with a smile. "Who wants to live forever anyway?"

"Bloody American's," muttered Wieslaw tapping off his box of cigarettes on the table as he weighed up lighting another one.

Tomek and Lenart shared a look with a smirk and a raised eyebrow in Tomasz' direction. Wieslaw caught it and waited for Tomek to ask the question.

"He'd know. Wouldn't you Tomasz?" Tomek joked with a raised voice. "You could tell us if the American's have achieved immortality. Go on look it up on your Ipad. I bet it's there."

Tomasz Sikora was the master of all he surveyed, having attained his status through cunning endeavour and devious planning and restructuring of those around him, as such as he had trained to be like minded and who were appeaseable to him, his friends included for they were not outside of his domineering influence. He was smart in both appearance and intellect, ruthless yet sophisticated with a sleight of hand in the commercial world that had allowed him to outplay old time criminals and government officials alike as he operated on a different level, appearing the pleasant businessman, in truth he was just that, amenable to all and courteous even to his greatest enemy. He had come to notice by those with even more power than he had ever hoped to wield and to this he had succumbed, with a head no older than mid-thirties, he wielded in a new age within an ancient and esoteric organisation to which he had been invited into with the devious charms of the devil enticing the selling of your soul.

A slight smirk curled the lip of Tomasz as he felt the teasing eyes daring him to break his silence and access the classified files they suspected him to sit on as he worked alongside them.

"Go on, look it up," Tomek begged again.

Tomasz shook his head unreservedly, not giving anything away, having listened to their conversation but not, hearing but not consciously taking in. He'd caught enough to know it was too close to the mark. A stern slight shake continued to say it was never going to happen, his smile broadening wider than his emotions could claw as he stretched the tension his perturbed mind felt as he wore the mask they could never see through.

He looked away from them through the cigarette smoke as Wieslaw lit up another causing them to laugh at his coyness, Lenart reaching for his coffee and Tomek straightening out his copy of Nie.

The phone ringing in his pocket was a relief he had prayed for, wanting something, anything, to break the awkwardness he felt at turning away from his friends. Tomasz reached inside his trouser pocket and retrieved the phone, knowing the caller from the distinctive ringtone before he even looked at the caller ID on the screen. He said nothing to begin with but tapped a name and a note of half-finished words onto the keyboard on the screen of his Ipad. To anyone else it would mean nothing, but to Tomasz it was a priority.

"Sir, yes Sir, I'll deal with it immediately."

He hung up the phone and turned back to his friends. They had seen and heard and knew the signs. They each gave a nod as they acknowledged coffee time was over for the day.

"Excuse me gentlemen, I have work to do."

4

He exited the four story building with a tilt of his head up to the second floor window with the expectation of Garbriella's head peering beneath the net curtains with a broad smile and wave, but no face pushed up against the closed window, not even Francesco's bouncing mop of hair could be seen. To be sure he stepped out further into the street and craned his neck to see past the concrete overhang of the balcony and the black metal inlay that served as a see through barrier to the window. There were no bars on the windows on the upper floors unlike the ground floor which was secured to deter unwanted visitors and vandals. Still no faces appeared and he supposed Maia was busying them for school. He stepped back around the blue line that marked his parking bay beneath the street lamp that hung tall on its green morbidly drooping neck; he had a love hate relationship with the lamp for as well as keeping him awake at night as it shone through his bedroom window of the humble second floor flat his family rented, it also protected his car which lay beneath it in the otherwise gloomily narrow street. He climbed into his little red Fiat Punto and swung out into Via Francesco Morosini.

It was early but still late enough for the traffic to have built up on Corso Vittorio Emanuele II, the duel carriageway that bridged the gap between home and work. The journey was a ten minute drive, although he had managed the 1.8 kilometre journey in seven minutes in clear traffic before. Carmela would already be there; she always beat him in and usually had a coffee on the go waiting for him as she sat at her desk opposite his, carrying the office whilst he went off trawling for dirt that couldn't be uncovered by an internet search.

He reached the Metro Re Umberto which was one short stop away from Turin's main station Torino Porta Nuova in the centre of the city. He took a left before the road turned into the Corso Vittorio and slid up Corso Re Umberto towards the office. He hadn't got far when he was flagged down by a stationary motorcycle police officer who appeared to be sending cars on a detour round the block. He tried to ask what the problem was but received a smileless grunt in return with a forceful wave of the arm. Doing as bid he joined the tail of the snake that weaved its way around the maze of five storey buildings separated by squares of zebra crossings at each junction and parades of shops at their feet.

The traffic cleared and he swung his little Fiat into a parking spot opposite the Banca Del Piemonte, waved at Celso in the barbers shop as he walked passed and pushed at a door leading to the grey offices above.

"Morning Sergio," called Carmela from behind her desk as he entered the office.

. The business consisted of just one office with two desks, two desktop computers, a laptop, a compendium listed off various camera and surveillance equipment which lounged in boxes by the window next to scruffy looking files and a number of cheap metal filing cabinets. Theirs was just one of half a dozen rented units along the corridor sharing facilities such as the rest rooms and small kitchen at the end of the hallway away from the stairs.

"Traffic's bad today," he said checking the temperature of the coffee sitting on his desk. It was still hot; she must have anticipated his delay.

"The police have closed off part of Umberto and entry into Angelo Brofferio," Carmela stated as she typed on the keyboard. She was going through the emails, not that there were many, there never were. Carmela was in her early fifties, plump, and always wore a deceptive scowl which hid her endearing traits: she was hugely proud of her family and talked often of her boys, both grown up now, and what they were up to, one was getting married in the spring and the other had just become a father making Carmela a proud grandmother; she was also a great organiser and very astute, loyal, and most importantly to Sergio, she was discreet. Despite his much younger age Carmela treated him with respect and affection as though he were one of her own boys.

"Any idea what it's about?"

"No I was going to have a walk round there in a little bit and nose around if that's ok with you.'"

"Of course, yes, please do. Any messages?"

"Two, both from Terzo Accosi."

"Don't tell me he's complaining that I infringed on his client's privacy."

Carmela smirked with her response. "The video footage was of her in the bathroom..."

"Screwing her divorce lawyer! I'll call him back later. Let's let him sweat it out a little longer; he knows as well as I do that if he wants to protect his practice then he'll have to convince her to cave in on the divorce settlement and he'll have to stop screwing his clients."

"Do you want me to call the husband and squeeze

him on the fee, considering we not only proved his suspicions but are likely to win him custody?"

"Carmela, you read my mind, what would I do without you?" He walked round to her and gave her a kiss on the top of her head. She really was the life blood of the company; ok he did all the risky stuff that often tread the tightrope of legality and the boring stake outs that took him away from his family at nights so that he could barely put a crust on the table, but it was a job and one he was good at, but he couldn't do half the stuff required if Carmela wasn't holding fort at the office taking calls, answering emails, doing internet searches and general research for him. Besides all that she was family, not blood related but close enough. She had been neighbours to his parents since before he was born and he had grown up playing with her two boys right up until he'd started hanging with the wrong crowd and going off the rails, still through all that she had bridged a path to his parents who had all but given up on him. When Marco, her husband, had died of bowel cancer five years ago Sergio was in a position to repay her for her kindness by offering her a position in his new venture.

She knew all there was to know about Sergio, who he was, who he had been, and who he aspired to be, and to this end she supported him one hundred percent giving him wise counsel and helping him stay on the right side of the law. She vetted his cases and kept him sane amidst the wrangle of tedious cases that, as a lone private investigator, he delved and embedded himself into, sinking into the darker side of people's lives and uncovering the things that most people tried to keep secret.

"Oh I dread to think," she said looking up at him with a kindly wink of knowing acceptance of his potential both good and bad. "There's some mail on your desk," she said as he walked in that direction.

No sooner had he walked away from the desk than the phone rang and Carmela cleared her throat before answering. "Vannucci Investigations, Carmela speaking."

Sergio was busy shuffling through the small pile of brown envelopes that were sat on his desk when he heard Carmela whispering his name. He turned to see her sat there, a concerned look on her face and her hand over the mouthpiece.

"Sergio, someone asking for Luigi."

Sergio took a deep breath and then signalled to Carmela to patch it through to his desk. He tentatively picked up the receiver, cautiously staring at it as he slowly raised it to his face as if it were the head of a snake he were trying not to disturb as he stretched out its body of coiled phone line.

"Sergio Vannucci speaking."

"Luigi, one of our employee's has, how do we say, gone off the grid. Capisce?" The voice was foreign sounding, Eastern European; he spoke in English which seemed to be the common language whenever they called. He'd not spoken to this one before; the last one had been German almost a year ago and had him chasing around for a scientist; who knew where this one would lead to, but he didn't dare refuse.

"Sì, I understand," Sergio replied in English with a look across to Carmela's shaking head.

"There was an incident at Artua & Solferino,"

"That's just round the corner," he said surprised, his eyes flitting up to meet Carmela's.

"Then it shouldn't be too difficult for you. We would like you to locate a woman named Vicky Rivers. Do not approach her but call this number when you have found her: +48 22389 021."

Sergio read the number back whilst jotting it down on the back on one of the envelopes he'd been leafing through. When he had finished the phone went dead. He looked up to Carmela who had typed the number into the computer as he'd read it out.

"It's a Polish number, Warsaw. Do you want me to try and get an exact location?"

"No, better not, but it looks like I will be going to check out why the police have closed the road."

5

The Artua & Solferino Hotel on Via Angelo Broferio was a large magnificent building built at the end of the 19th century and had managed to retain some of its original decor. The doors were made of massive grandiose wood with impersonal and intimidating brass knobs. The ample stairwell was ordained in white marble and elaborate mosaics. The shelves were made of walnut tree and cherry tree wood to the lift with its antique glass doors. For the last forty years it had been a respectable family run business which had built on a previously impeccable reputation. It sat bridging the Corso Re Umberto on one side and the Via Cerfienza on the other, less than a five minute walk from Sergio's office.

It hadn't taken long for Sergio to gain entry passed the police guard that had blocked off the main road for the emergency vehicles and the crime scene investigators who were busy scouring for clues. He had paid the going rate to a familiar face who worked the local police district, a fee which gained him entry to the hotel and a basic idea of what was going on. There would probably be need of further payment inside but he was fortunate the incident was local and he had a good rapport with the local police department. As he climbed the marble staircase to the third floor crime scene he pondered over how this all fitted in with the person he'd been sent to find.

"Vanni!" exclaimed Sergeant Fulvio Abelli with a pleasant smile and an outstretched hand. The two were old school friends who had both run the wrong side of the law for a while before they both tried to make right their wrongs. They had a lot in common and held a mutual respect for each other's life journey. Sergio was more than pleased to see his old friend running point outside the hotel room. "What brings you in here?"

"Came to see what all the fuss is about, as it's on my doorstep. You never know I might get some work out of it."

"How's Maia and the kids?"

"Good, we're all doing good thanks. How's Francesa?"

"Pregnant at long last, due in December, going to be a Christmas baby!"

"Fantastic news! Congratulations. Do you know if it's a boy or a girl?"

"No, she wants it to be a surprise. You'll have to come round sometime before the baby's born."

"Yes, I'd like that, it's been a while." The door to the hotel room opened behind the police sergeant as a woman in a blue paper suit and paper shoe socks stepped out carrying a camera. Sergio peered over his friends shoulder but couldn't really see much beyond the room other than a swell of bodies moving about. "So what happened here, Fulvio?"

"Most bizarre my friend. The room was rented out to a woman but there is no sign of her. It looks like she brought a man back to the room and maybe he raped her, we're not sure, but it would appear she killed him by stabbing him in the head with a letter opener while they were, you know..., anyway the strange thing is this, she bleached his mouth and his dick. He must have hurt her real bad, eh!"

"Do you have a name?"

The sergeant checked his notes before replying. "Caterina Donati was the name the room was booked under but we're having trouble tracing the name. Angelo Farini is the victim."

"Farini! Didn't he quit local council last year over taking bribes?"

The sergeant shrugged his shoulders, rolled his eyes and wobbled his head all in one swift movement that gave away the confirmation of the identity of the corpse at the same time as saying *'you didn't hear it from me'.*

"Nothing's ruled out at this stage with regards motive. It looks like she picked him up at a local bar; he was regular at the Zelli Wine Bar. He was there a couple of nights ago with a girl but no one's seen him since. Forensic's say he's probably been laying here a couple of days so it fits."

"Is it pretty gory in there?" Sergio asked with a hinting glance over the sergeant's shoulder at the now closed door.

"Yeah, and before you ask no you can't take a peek. Due to the nature of it and the possible connections, you know, we're having to play it by the book. You know the new hard-line regime in parliament with this stuff."

"Political bravado, no one takes it seriously." Sergio was itching for a smoke and felt for the packet on the inside of his leather jacket.

"Maybe, who knows?" agreed Sergeant Abelli looking up at the pencil thin frame of the P.I.

"Do you really think this has mob connections?"

"Honestly, no, I don't think so. I think Farini tried to stick it where it wasn't welcome and she struck out with whatever was to hand. You know he had a reputation?"

"Of course. He's not exactly in the running for man of the year in the popularity stakes."

"Men like him have too many enemies." He brought his level down to a whisper. "I doubt too much resources will be spent looking for her." He gave Sergio a wink as the P.I. snuck a cigarette into the corner of his mouth.

The door to the room opened again as another officer exited, this one in plain clothes but Sergio recognised him and acknowledged the curious caution in his eyes as they caught each other in a moment of double take, the door being closed swiftly to prevent intruding eyes.

"My time's up Fulvio." Sergio offered his hand as he stepped back towards the stairs.

"I'll call you if there's anything of interest," the police sergeant said quietly before raising his voice with an overtly chirpy tone considering the setting, "and we'll have to have you and Maia round for dinner sometime soon."

Sergio made his way down to the hotel's reception subtly trying to get a glimpse of the guest register but it was all computerised. He scribbled down the name Caterina Donati on the note pad he kept in his pocket and then headed back to the office.

6

Some things didn't make sense in Sergio's mind. For starters there were other hotels dotted around the Porta Nuova train station where the Zelli Wine Bar was situated: the Best Westerns Genova, Luxor and Executive, the Urbani, the Liberty as well as a whole host of others, all well dressed and respected hotels in their own right, but at the heart of the Turin's city centre they were constantly busy with an overwhelming turnover of clientele which sprawled out to the quieter more exclusive hotels hidden back from the main thoroughfares surrounding the station. This Caterina Donati had chosen one of the quieter hotels hung further back so he assumed she didn't want to get caught on CCTV at the station, having noted that the Artua & Solferino had no cameras in the reception area nor in the corridors.

He had a hit on the fifth car rental company he called; using his usual line of being Sergeant Fulvio Abelli he was able to find out that Caterina Donati had hired a Renault Clio from Hertz at the airport, booked for a week five days ago. The car had yet to be returned, but then nobody would be missing it for another two days.

A general search on the name turned up a number of women sharing the same name in the general Turin area but none fit the profile of what he was looking for. Facebook had proved, as usual, a great asset in being able to trace people and cross reference their ages, locations, personal preferences, and not to mention their activities at the time. Tracing movements via someone's mobile phone was also a task made simpler thanks to apps on Iphones and Google that enabled location services to track the handset, all he needed was to obtain the phone number and then figure out the password. Fortunately most people proved pretty dumb when it came to setting their passwords and usually left enough information on social media sites for him and Carmela to have a good stab at guessing. In this way the process of elimination was made easier and he had discounted all but two Caterina Donati's from his list, and of those two he was willing to bet neither were the person responsible for the murder at the hotel.

He had a good idea who Caterina Donati was going to turn out to be and he doubted from the name he'd been given and the information about the hire car that she was even Italian.

In his mind she had two options: to flee as far as possible in the hire car and try to leave Italy by another route, or to ditch the car and return to Turin Airport and travel as someone else. Baring in mind she had a two day start on everyone else he didn't reckon much on his chances of finding her.

"Carmela," he turned to her as he often did to sound off his thoughts, "if you had two days head start in a hire car where would you drive to?"

Carmela gave it a moment's thought, turning to the wall behind her and the city map that was pinned there.

"If you were innocently running because of a mistake then I'd say east towards Milano, but if it was premeditated then west over the mountain pass into Switzerland or France, or south towards Genoa and leave the country by boat."

"He said she'd gone off the grid," he said recalling the words spoken over the phone earlier, "so assuming Angelo Farini was a sanctioned target then she had to either have missed checking in or she was supposed to be somewhere else."

"So you don't think she ditched the car and went back to the airport?"

"No, surely they could have traced her themselves as soon as she boarded a plane from Turin."

"Don't you think you should share this with Abelli?"

"Somehow I don't think that would be appreciated."

"I don't like it Sergio." She had genuine concern in her voice. Despite none of these anonymous calls ever having lead them astray, and financially had rewarded them greatly, the jobs themselves and the clandestine way in which they were employed always felt wrong to Carmela, to both of them.

"I know. All I have to do is find her and tell them where she is and that's all." He sounded like he was trying to convince himself, which was exactly what he was trying to do. Never before had he dealt with a murder case, let alone been employed to track down the murderer, and at the same time trying to keep one step ahead of the police and not inform them of what he was up to. Deep down he knew somewhere he was breaking the law, but deeper still weighed down like an anchor tearing at the pit of his stomach was the feeling that not to follow this through would have dire untold consequences.

"Marseille? No, too far. Grenoble? Vicky Rivers...American? Does she sound American to you?"

Carmela huffed and shrugged her shoulders. "Screwed up is what she sounds to me. If she meant to kill him why do it like that? That's just crazy. If that makes her American then so be it."

"So all of the nearest airports are domestic. If I were her I'd drive over the mountains across the border into Switzerland and fly out from Geneva back to America."

"But the guy that phoned was Eastern European?"

It was his turn to shrug but he did it in a way that she read as him going on a hunch.

"You know it scares me that you think like a criminal."

"I love you too Carmela."

By the time Sergio reached his destination it was late evening. He had driven for four hours straight. He had made a number of calls before leaving: one to his wife to tell her he wouldn't be home tonight, she was disappointed but understanding, being used to the often unsociable hours he kept; another call was to his contact in Poland, Tomasz, he'd volunteered his name and Carmela had traced the phone number to a call forwarding service in Warsaw where presumably it bounced on to a mobile somewhere in the city, other than that he knew nothing more about him.

He updated Tomasz on his progress so far and requested more information about his subject, stating that it was virtually impossible to track someone travelling on a false identity without knowing what she looks like. The request was denied. He placed another call to a friend who worked in IT, a regular computer hacker who boasted how he had accessed high level systems and had never been caught. To most people this would have been an unrealistic boast but Sergio had seen the results for himself and had paid for his services to access local government records and the vehicle and licence database. He asked him to run a couple of names or variation of names through the flight listings for the last couple of days for flights out of Geneva and to pass the results through to Carmela. The response was that scanning for particular names was too risky and would keep him online too long but he could rip the lists for Carmela to run through herself; it would take longer but it was good enough.

Carmela had commented on the moronic look he had adopted as he focused on the task at hand, a childhood habit he'd developed of sticking out his tongue and chewing on it when he was concentrating or doing something requiring effort. He adopted that pose now as he peered out of the window of his little red Punto, the light having faded on the outskirts of the city as he circled the car park and eyed the ramp to the lower level.

He was in Gaillard, a suburb of the city, not the busy hub but concrete jungle enough to be called part of Geneva as it sat on the road that rolled down the mountain to rest on a plain before the hills took up again in the north around the great lake. It was passed the too obvious shopping centre at Etrembieres (it was the first place anyone would look so he didn't think she'd risk stopping there) but far enough out along the Route Blanche from the city centre to be overlooked.

There were cars abandoned silently sitting in over ground and underground car parks all over the city awaiting the return of their owners from an extended hard day's labour, or left while their owners socialised at local restaurants, bars or cinemas. None would stand out as suspicious or out of place even if it sat still for a couple of days baring foreign plates. He was on his second roll down the ramp of the third underground car park he'd come across. He wasn't interested in the over ground ones; if it was him he'd want the car to stay hidden as long as possible to give as much of a head start while he picked up another, probably by stealing it from another isolated underground car park where no one would notice it missing for a good few hours.

He was desperate to find the hire car if only to confirm his own suspicions. So far he was just acting on his own best guess and had nothing to back up his theory to show he was on the right track. He didn't know what would happen if he failed to find her; failure to complete one of their jobs was something he'd so far been spared the experience of and he didn't want to know what would happen to him if he turned up empty handed, but he knew that any organisation that could trump the heavy hand of the Mafia wasn't one you were quick to disappoint.

Had he sold out to the devil? Probably, but what had been the alternative? At least now he was a respectable businessman that his wife could be proud of instead of falling in and out of jail as was likely to have happened, certainly if the fate of some of his old gang was anything to go by.

Ok, so maybe now and then he needed to draw on Luigi, but was that such a bad thing?

Back then he ran with the crowd, just a bunch of juvenile delinquents really, at least that's how it started out. He'd argued with his parents a lot back then, a stroppy teenager who thought he knew best, ducking college despite all the warnings that he was too intelligent not to study. Even Carmela, the kindly neighbour, had pleaded with him not to treat his parents so harshly, but unlike his parents she had kept the door open despite her fears of him tainting her own sons with his behaviour. Had it not been for her the way back to embracing his family and a heartfelt reconciliation may never have been possible.

He hadn't been so smart in the manner of whom he allowed himself to be swayed by but he was smarter than most in how he skirted the edges of the group and covered his back and his tracks before committing to something he might otherwise regret. He'd lied about his name and his age, they all did, agreeing as a pact to protect each other and their families when they began to get in deeper with a lower tier organised gang, moving from petty thefts and vandalism for a laugh to stealing cars and street robberies. Even at a low level you knew you were only a small step away from a bigger connection that would lead you as running mule errands for a bigger beast. It started with ripping off convenience stores and anywhere else that didn't have any obvious security. Then they caught the attention of those who claimed ownership of the patch they tread upon, and that connection came all too soon as they were left with an ultimatum to join up, pay your dues, and do as told, or take a hiding and lose some fingers in the process for operating without their consent. It was a harsh confrontation but an easy decision to make under the circumstances.

A year in and he had himself the reputation of being one of their chief scouts, able to identify pitfalls in their plans and research the people and places that had been identified as possible targets to loot and rob. He had respect, but it wasn't a respect that made him feel comfortable or proud, instead he felt slightly ashamed and, as much as he hated to admit it, wondered whether his parents had been right all along. He'd been desperate, he'd never wanted this. It had all started out as a laugh and then as an easy way to make money, he had never dreamt of being involved in high level crime, let alone the mob. He sought for any opportunity that would give him a plausible excuse to bow out. He played through scenarios of exit strategies that would appease the hard crooked noses of the chief whips that scourged with the menacing bone talons of the flagellum, or at least had the potential to if you didn't tow the line. It was a discipline order more stringent that any military, for you knew that no laws protected you and going awol wasn't an option, for the gangs had eyes and ears everywhere, and by operating under the umbrella and sanction of the families you were ensured no hiding place for any that crossed the line. It was unheard of to be allowed a reprieve and to leave a gang, so no one did so without good reason, for fear was a huge motivator.

It was hardly surprising street crime was relatively low, for those like Sergio and his friends were swiftly hauled into place so that all street level and corporate crime became organised. The police essentially were constantly fighting something that someone somewhere, both high and low amongst their own ranks, was being paid to turn a blind eye to, leaving them to deal with low level misdemeanours and crimes of passion.

And then came the heist. It wasn't his first, but as with all the others he'd been careful despite them all having been given strict instructions not to look into it too much but just to carry out the job to the letter as it had been passed down.

Sergio, or rather 'Luigi' to the gang, and his pals had never been caught. They'd come close once or twice but never actually had their collars clasped, and he wanted it to stay that way. He did the digging on the job like his instincts told him he should, knowing all along that something just didn't feel right.

The plan was a good one, essentially a smash and grab with a few tactical hurdles to overcome, obstacles that were sketched into the plan: a guard was going to get hurt; an alarm was going to be triggered; a hostage was a possible as a failsafe if the police arrived too soon and ignored the payoff; masks, guns and getaway cars were all in place, along with a safe house. What he didn't like (after he'd done his digging around) was why they were being told to grab everything from the front counters and the cabinets near the cash register when there was an extremely valuable item of celebrity jewellery stashed in the safe, a temporary placement en route from Zurich to Milan with a two day sojourn whilst its owner met with financiers in Turin. He smelled a rat. They were being played for patsies and he felt he had to warn his friends without seeming disloyal to the gang.

His gambit was to disclose what he'd discovered by feigning innocence to the boss' in thinking they didn't know about the treasure haul and hope it would be enough to make them hesitate in their plans and change them in fear of what he may know or suspect. To his surprise the plans were kept the same and he felt he had no choice, albeit out of some sense of misguided loyalty, but to warn the others that they were likely to have a uniformed welcoming committee at the safe house whilst someone, most likely an inside man, got away with the real prize for which they would take the fall. He had warned them passionately, pleading them not to go ahead with it, but they ignored him and went ahead with it anyway believing the forceful assurances of the boss.

The heist took place without Sergio as he was held in a locked room under guard awaiting what he thought would be the order for a new pair of boots and a trip to the lake. The boys made it to the safe house unharmed and without incident and the cash and jewels were delivered as planned. The prize remained locked safely in the vault. A million panicked thoughts had flooded his mind then with no conclusion that shone a rosy tint in his favour. He was a dead man.

He hadn't been wrong as it turned out. The jewels went missing when they reached Milan a few days later; a last minute change of plan forced by his admission to his friends. When the door of his locked room finally opened what he was presented with wasn't what he'd expected. A businessman with an offer helping him set up his own investigative company, a chance to go straight, with one condition: to take on and complete any and every job requested by his silent benefactor. Under his sceptical protests he was assured that his resourcefulness had caught the attention of those who were prepared to 'smooth things over' with the mob, at the same time as being implicit in the fact that they were in no way associated with them. *'Don't be so naive as to think we and they don't know who you are "Sergio". You'll know us when we call, for we will call you by your chosen alias, the undesirable mask you have preferred to hide behind. So do we have an understanding, Luigi?'*

He was a victim of his own success, having been too good to dig up the dirt using all the resources and toys they put at his disposal and the initial finance supplied. His new slick and mysterious silent partners (he had tried to trace the unnamed businessman and the clandestine organisation he worked for without success - they were extremely good at covering their tracks) were just as threatening as the hierarchy of the gangland dons, making it quite clear that no one leaves and no one refuses an offer made in kind.

He questioned then, as he did now and had done often since, why would someone do that for him? The only answer he could ever come up with was that he was good at what he did, and even now that proved true as he circled slowly around the hire car.

It was clean, as you'd expect of a hire car, its rental sticker in the rear window and its Italian number plate giving it away. It could sit here for weeks unnoticed, blending in, and lying dormant, a grave stone filling a vacant lot with no family member stopping by with a lonely bouquet of flowers. Others would come and go but no one would really notice this one, not yet.

He was relieved. His nose was good - or at least the Luigi in him still held good and strong. His confidence was bolstered and he stood up straight and let out a long held breath of thankfulness.

Walking around the vehicle there was nothing of note. He double checked the licence plate with what he had been searching for, knowing it was a match but not wanting to misread anything. He peered through the windows not really expecting to see any signs of its recent driver but hoping maybe she left something behind. She hadn't. He considered popping the lock and having a good snoop around but then reasoned that it wouldn't achieve much, and contaminating the suspect vehicle with his DNA wouldn't be a smart move in a murder case. Besides, he thought she was too professional to leave him a clue as to her next move.

No one had given him any facts about this Vicky Rivers but he was getting a clear enough picture of her and how she might operate. She was dangerous in a lethal way, but certainly not, he suspected, the innocent victim that Fulvio and his colleagues would mistake her for. He hoped that he could locate a point of onward travel and be released of his task without having to draw her attention to himself.

7

Tomasz got the call around midday. It was sooner than he was expecting which boosted his confidence in their man in Turin, so much so that out of curiosity he punched up his picture on his Ipad whilst he spoke to him on the phone.

Sergio Vannucci was twenty eight years old, a self-employed private investigator, married with two children - their names and dates of birth along with available identity photographs showed up against each name, a photo pulled from Facebook appeared next to the names of the children showing that someone in Human Resources had done their homework. Sergio had a dark complexion, brown eyes which webbed out in the smile he wore in the photograph, a black caterpillar of a moustache crawled across his top lip below which his chin narrowed and above which his unkempt hair netted bushily on top but was shaved above the ears. He looked slightly older than his years but friendly enough, and wore a trusting face. According to the file he was known to most as Vanni, a simple shortening of his surname, but to the organisation he was known by his gang name, Luigi, the name through which he had entered the employment of the organisation having been identified as a potential asset.

Assets in the form of personnel were scattered across the globe, many constantly active and on the pay role, but others, such as Luigi, were sleepers lying in wait to be utilised when they were needed. In any case all staff were handsomely looked after for their services. In Luigi's case he had been pulled from a spiralling lifestyle that would have ended with him either in jail or lost to a wasted life of pointless criminality, a lifestyle it had been agreed was a waste of potential and just wouldn't do.

"No, we can't afford any more delays...Do you think you can get more information the other end?... I will consider it. Confirm her arrival and destination first..." Luigi had got the last word, an affirmation of obedience allowing Tomasz to end the call satisfactorily.

He checked his watch; he had another meeting lined up at the Rotunda just a five minutes' walk from Czekolada's. It was a meeting he didn't want to be late for but figured he could afford a few more minutes before he had to leave. His coffee was cold as it sat barely touched on the outside table. Justyna had already asked if he wanted it replenished but he shook his head distractedly as he had paced in a quick fire spatter of directions and harsh commands to someone on the other end of a different earlier phone call.

It had been a busy day so far for Tomasz. So much was going on at once: one of the German investors was trying to pull out of a deal with a Russian mining company which he thought was fuelled by their stance on the whole Syrian situation, smoothing it over wouldn't be too difficult once he got to it and applied the pressure but it meant coordinating some capillary companies and drawing their strings in to close the cords of the net on the German so that he knew who truly held the power; on top of that he had this report to assess based on the university paper from the US - that issue wasn't so pressing but still had a deadline, it was pretty much finished anyway but he wasn't one hundred percent comfortable about submitting it just yet; and then there was Vicky Rivers - his orders were to find her and fast.

He fastened his slim fit grey piped suit jacket as he stood and stepped away from the table where he had been sat alone for the last half hour. He had planned on meeting Wieslaw here for lunch but was forced to postpone him till tomorrow so that he could sort out the German rift. He quickly twisted his head around, letting his eyes scan for anyone listening in on his call, satisfied he dialled a number.

"It's Tomasz...She boarded a plane to Mexico City yesterday...our man in Turin was able to access the flight schedules from Geneva. She flew out under her own passport...yes, that's what I thought, but then they are looking for Caterina Donati, no one there is looking for...ye...maybe she is, as you say, getting sloppy. Maybe she has a plan. Has she been assigned any contracts in Mexico?...and there's no outstanding business there?... I know she missed the connection, sir, yes. A replacement was found I trust?... I will see to it, yes sir. I'll keep him on it till you can get someone in place. I've now sent him a picture so he knows who he's looking for and I'll scour her file to see if she has any connections out there...yes sir, will do."

Tomasz hung up the phone knowing that the pressure was on to find her quickly. He didn't like dealing with people in her line of work and he wondered how long it would be before they pushed him to progress to handling her type. He hoped it wouldn't come to that but knew he was getting in deeper than he'd anticipated or ever hoped for, and ultimately he knew too much knowledge made you dangerous so that the fish swimming at your sides became all razor toothed sharks - great whites overseeing the depths of miniscule fish that swam around and beneath them.

He checked his watch again knowing before he looked at it that he was out of time. He would check her file later, it would delay things but at least it wouldn't delay Luigi as he killed the fourteen hours it would take for him to catch up with her.

He gave Justyna a wink and a nod to his cup indicating he was finished as she wiped one of the nearby tables. She smiled back in return as he picked up his Ipad, broadly grinning as though nothing in the world was at fault.

8

Sergio smoothed out his moustache with his thumb and forefinger as he sat nervously awaiting take-off. This was a bad idea. They'd assured his expenses and Carmela confirmed that they had been paid in advance as he booked his seat onto the first available flight out of Geneva International Airport. All he had was his overnight bag that regularly lived in the boot of the Punto and the photo of Maia he had retrieved from the driver's visa. The photo was a few years old and showed his wife in a Mona Lisa pose serenely looking into the camera, her long black curls draped down one side and her lips a luscious red beneath her powdered cheeks. She looked young in the photograph but it was one of those pictures that he treasured with the memories of their earlier years together when they had been dating before the exhausting trials of sleepless nights and crying children had taken their toll.

He had spoken to Maia briefly explaining the situation. She understood and accepted the realities of his work but was naturally disappointed at the short notice and the implications it would have with the kids, but despite her reservations, which were echoed in the tone of her voice only and not in words, she was calmly compliant - she was a good wife and Sergio didn't need reminding of the fact.

Carmela would take care of the office and also check in on Maia for him which was reassuring. He had promised them both that it would only be a few days. He figured he was most likely to be in the air longer than he would be on the ground and promised both women that all he needed to do was locate someone for the client and then return. Maia in her ignorance was satisfied with this, but Carmela, who knew better, was not so convinced and argued the point with him, warning him to be careful of what he was getting into and not to get too close to the woman, for it was unlikely she'd take too kindly to being traced. He'd answered with an affirmative response, assuring her that he knew what he was doing and that everything would be ok, but in truth he wasn't so sure.

The flight to Mexico City was 14 hours and 20 minutes with an hour and a half stop over at London Heathrow. He'd already read through the in-flight entertainment schedule but found it to be disappointing: no films on demand and what was available was mostly stuff he had no burning desire to see. He'd probably dip into the odd film at some point if he got bored but otherwise he hoped to dose listening to the music channels, or maybe he'd read through the free newspaper he'd picked up when he boarded the plane. If he was lucky he'd be able to fall into a deep sleep which hopefully would be marginally more comfortable than sleeping in the cramped cold conditions of his little Fiat as he had done last night.

The plane itself was fairly old and smaller than he'd expected for this type of flight and he'd overheard some of the other passengers saying that this was due to the whole fleet of regular planes having been grounded due to a crash on another Mexico bound flight a few days ago. He recalled hearing something about it but was vague on the details, apparently no foul play was suspected but it was thought to be the fault of a mechanical malfunction.

He calculated the time difference: 6 hours. He thought about the practicalities of communicating home and tried to map out the best times to make phone calls. He also had no money for the other end and made a mental note to change his Euros into Pesos before he left the airport, maybe if he had time he could change it at Heathrow which would allow him to concentrate on the job at hand when he arrived at Mexico City.

He turned his mind to Vicky Rivers, or Caterina Donati as she had gone by in Turin. As he thought about her he tried to get into her skin. The why was an unknown to him, her motives lost to sea, a message in a bottle not to be caught or opened until it washed ashore of some beach far away where he was unlikely to trace it, and really, did he want to? He thought not, that would only lead to more complications and he didn't want the grief that would come with it.

The manifesto Carmela had read through stated that she was travelling under her real name which made it a lot easier for him to trace but made him wonder whether she was wanting to be found or just not assessing the risk clearly. Either way he hoped to catch her trail quickly and report back to Tomasz so that he could get a local to pick up the lead and allow him to go home, assuming the organisation had connections in that part of the world.

The first thing she would need would be a car, but he wouldn't know which companies to search until he got to the airport and could see which ones she was likely to pick. Then there was a place to stay. Her flight didn't arrive until 7.30pm which meant she was unlikely to go far until the next morning. He already had

Carmela trying to search the local hotels in the vicinity of Benito Juarez International Airport. He figured she'd most likely go for a small one, paying cash if she could. Where she would go after that he had no idea, which was where knowing her motives would be of benefit. He could access local press and translate the news into Italian on-line so if she was there to do another hit he might be able to trace a lead, but Luigi had his doubts. If she was going there to kill someone then it wasn't authorized by her employer. In his mind he suspected whatever it was she was there for it was personal - why else would her employer's be hunting her down?

He didn't let it escape his thinking that maybe he was way off base altogether and that maybe she was trying to make a break from the organisation, or maybe she had something to wield over them, but each time the thought raised its head he cut it back down with the sharpened blade of his instinct - Luigi's instinct! She was using her own name - it didn't add up if she was fleeing from them.

He hoped when he got there she was still using that name, otherwise he'd be lost and he didn't fancy the idea of flashing her photo around at every hotel he came across.

He pulled out his phone now and checked the flight mode was engaged and then opened up the text message from Tomasz with the photo attached. She was mid-thirties at a guess, not bad looking with a strong broad jawline and piercing greeny blue eyes that lay buried beneath a mask of dark makeup and a mop of straggly bleached blonde hair reminding him of a young Daryl Hannah in Blade Runner. He could see how she could be an effective asset in distracting male subjects, having the right countenance and nerve to fulfil her missions. He burned her features into his mind and shook his head with a continued uneasiness about what lay ahead.

The no smoking sign came on along with the seat belt sign and he shook his head again. This was going to be a long flight.

9

Another day, the same routine. He was tired today and eager for his coffee.

"Dzień dobry, Tomasz."

'Justyna," he nodded in response as he took his usual seat outside where he could watch the buzz of early traffic pass by. He liked the routine of seeing familiar faces going about the regular patterns of life around him, it gave him a sense of attachment that allowed him to believe that he hadn't become too disassociated from his old life, and should he fall off the greased rung or slide the snakes back to plummet to his start position then he could rest assured he was still a welcome and popular figure back here where it all began. Influential and powerful at times he appeared to be, but the more he delved into this esoteric world of clandestine operations the more he realised he knew very little and that there were tiers of multifaceted levels above him who held and wielded a scythe long and broad with the ability to cut cleaner and sharper than any blade, so invisible were the slicing of the laser activated by a far remote push of a button on the command of an unseen voice.

He'd read enough by now to know he was just small fry being entrusted with greatness and if he succeeded in keeping his cool and his tongue then much more would be bequeathed to him.

"Usual?"

"Please," he politely replied and then watched her saunter off back inside the dark recess of the café.

It was colder today and the sky was brooding with ominous grey patches masking any potential of blue peeking through, but still he insisted on sitting outside.

He opened up the case to his Ipad and punched in his security code and continued reading the file he'd downloaded before leaving home.

He was thankful for the thick black drainpipe coat he wore over his suit, his tie hugging his Adams Apple snugly. He had another meeting later this morning with the German investor whom he felt was on the verge of giving ground to prop up the Russian mine. The mine itself was designed to search for a rare compound which held some unique properties, along with an underground research facility, the true purpose of which was unknown and not clarified in the business plan, in fact it was completely absent from it leaving the German to be, quite rightly, up in arms at the extortionate price of the mining operation. This had been their objection from the beginning and not a political standpoint as he had expected it to be before they'd met yesterday. Tomasz had been entrusted to smooth things over with fabricated figures and false costing's to appease and convince not just the German but all the other investors who had caught the fever of hesitation that was beginning to manifest into a cold sweat with the board.

He had objected at the deviance from his normal role but had been given the strong line of obedience and loyalty that he was reluctant to dispute with his faceless boss over the phone.

Tomasz closed the file he'd opened, minimised it to come back to, opening instead the file he had open a few days earlier, the one that his friends had been so close to in their conversation. It was this file that intrigued him and had him wondering in the night whether there was any relevance in the behaviour of what he'd sent Luigi off searching for.

He checked his watch and made a quick calculation: 1.30am. The Italian should still be in the air, he would have to call him later.

'THE ReSYEM PROJECT' the title read. It was a research project that the organisation had been funding which was an acronym for Reanimated Synthetic Extracelluar Matrix. He scanned the title having read it extensively a number of times already and once during the middle of last night as the implications echoed in his mind until they swam into the whirlpool of distraction that mixed with the Italian situation.

The file Tomasz held, which in its detail was exhaustive, yet withholding any of the necessary compounded information that would allow anyone to mimic their design research, was a headache to read and indeed it had taken him many days to plough through when he had first been sent it, marking its pitfalls and admiring its incentives and potentials. Eventually he supposed he would green light it for further funding as an on-going concern for the organisation but he held off letting them know that for the present as there was an art in the timing and it was never a smart move to show just how quick you could respond to a task, to do so would raise their expectancy levels each time and reduce the luxurious pace in which he preferred to work; besides all that something was niggling at the recesses of his mind unsettling him about it, causing him to delay his response to the report.

He kept the file mainly for reference yet knew that

once he turned in his supplementary report the cyber bullies of the organisation would sweep his hardware and remove any trace of it. There was no point in copying any files he was privy to as they were able to search his system commands and trace any copies that he may have made bringing his loyalty to the organisation into question - and that was something he had no wish to do; people like Vicky Rivers were employed to take care of any such people.

He looked over some of the most recent findings of ReSYEM as Justyna brought over his cappuccino and almond croissant. He winked at her with a smile.

"Are the boys coming?"

"No, not this morning, maybe later." His smile was broad and friendly enough to be mistaken for genuine interest in her, but he wasn't keen - not anymore. He had courted Justyna's older sister when he was younger and when Justyna herself was still a school girl; there had been a fleeting moment when he had considered engaging her interest now that she was older and had filled out, but her lack of ambition was a real turn off for him, as it had been with her sister; no matter how attractive the girl he couldn't bring himself to lower himself to someone who was satisfied working as a waitress at a café for the rest of her life. He could use her for sex but that would ruin his daily service and make relaxing at Czekolada's awkward and force him to find another café to frequent. He could get plenty of girls for sex so why upset the apple cart?

She was still keen on him, that much was obvious, and it didn't hurt to lead her on a little now and again for the purpose of a pleasant daily table service. He watched her blushing smile back at him as she turned and wandered back inside.

It wasn't his job to question motives, nor to query the minds of those who paid his bills. His job was to spot what stood out, good or bad, and simply highlight it and where required smooth things over with his charming portfolio of manipulation. Some things he spotted he sometimes wished he hadn't and would try his best to ignore, or if unable to would try to forget as soon as practicable. It was what he saw now as an emerging pattern in the open file that troubled him with its almost tangible link with his other charge.

It could, of course, all be coincidence: he had read the ReSYEM Project file, coinciding with the lads teetering on the verge of the truth in their curiously harmless discussion the other day, causing the whole subject to play on his mind, and then the timing of the assassin going missing and the links he saw there. All coincidence? Maybe.

He opened up the file he'd earlier minimised, taking a bite out of his croissant as it loaded and expanded to full frame on the screen. There were a number of photographs depicting the changing image of Vicky Rivers, but essentially it was the same person: troubled, no family, psychotic, a highly skilled and determined individual who held no particular alliance or loyalty but remained on the regular payroll either through fear and obedience or a subconscious need for protection. He wasn't sure which and much of what he surmised wasn't written down in the file.

She was renowned for things grand with a reckless modus operandi that had the powers that be on the edge on their seat with a cleaner on call to mop up whatever she consistently left behind - yet despite that they let her alone as she always delivered, always hitting her target even if it did mean taking on an unprecedented amount of collateral damage. There was a long list cataloguing her achievements which decrypted page by page as he scrolled down so that the information wouldn't be lost to anyone should his Ipad fall out of his possession.

There was an emerging pattern of high casualty disasters, bombs, and crashes all happening in the vicinity of Vicky Rivers, or soon after she had been at any particular location. Vicky had been in Boston when the marathon bomb went off, targeting a runner but having nothing to do with the bomb itself, purely coincidental - or so it seemed. There were a number of light aircraft incidents that she could claim credit for and one commercial passenger airline that had angered the organisation. There were train derailments where conveniently her target's body would be found amongst the wreckage. She seemed to have a knack for making use of the natural too, ensuring that her target would end up as one of the many victims of an earthquake or a flood, she simply taking advantage of an easy disposal and minimising her risk in the process. Then there were the other mass killings where she was present yet with no determinable justification - had she caused them for a convenient cover for her hits or were they something else? No wonder the upper tiers were getting jittery, if she was being this reckless then sooner or later it would lead back to them and that just wouldn't do for any of them.

The file painted her as unbelievably psychotic and a liability.

The only thing about Mexico recently that he could

see was the flight that had crashed in the desert en route to Mexico City from LA, but she'd been in Italy at the time. Vicky had spent a week in LA putting to bed a systems architect who had designed a number of mines in Russia for the corporation. She had managed to ensure he was caught in the wildfires that had swept the region at the time, also ensuring his data burnt with him in his home. There was a note of concern marked on the file to keep her under observation (something that had yet to be put in place and no doubt someone would lose a pay cheque over) following an incident in LA where she'd been pulled out of the water by lifeguards who claimed she almost drowned swimming after someone off the Santa Monica pier. Her 'mark' and reason for being there had already been taken care of so it was uncertain who she was chasing and no body was found floating nor washed up on the beach later. Naturally she had fled the scene by the time the police arrived but the LAPD report that had been filed stated that she had struck wildly at the lifeguards screaming that the woman she was chasing wasn't dead.

How many incidents like this had gone unreported, Tomasz thought. The only reason this one was recorded was because in her delirium of almost dying and having to be resuscitated she had given her name in answer to the lifeguard's standard questions to bring her round and focus her mind.

Tomasz wondered why they hadn't pulled her and terminated her contract by now. Reading her file was grim and terrifying and he shuddered at the thought of the company that the organisation sheltered and which by association he too worked alongside. He surmised they still valued her as an effective asset, that or they were running short on good quality assassins. It was clear enough though from the file that the organisation was, and always had been, well aware of her unstable mental state.

The LA incident was a month ago. *Who was it she had been chasing?*

He could see a pattern of destruction which read clearly off the page as nothing more than a crazed killer who enjoyed her job a little too much, but in his mind Tomasz couldn't shake the feeling that the pattern he could see linked too closely to the ReSYEM Project and wondered not so much what was in the files but what was absent from them and whether he wasn't being given the full story.

He took a sip from his cup and another bite from his croissant. He checked his watch again eager to place a call of warning but knowing he needed to wait. Pacifying the German was his first priority for this morning and he needed to concentrate on that and not allow himself to get distracted by what was happening on the other side of the world.

10

His plane landed at Benito Juarez International Airport at 5.30am. He was exhausted having slept little on the plane and having gained himself a crooked neck from his multiple attempts to get comfortable in the inflexible seat on the journey from Heathrow. The passenger in the seat next to him, a British middle aged woman travelling to see family, had tried engaging him in conversation. He exchanged pleasantries well enough but felt quite smug when he was able to claim his poor English meant he couldn't continue their quaint little chat, and fortunately she didn't speak any Italian and so he was spared an agonising flight of interruptions, though he could sense her discomfort and burning desire to speak to someone but being trapped in the window seat her frustration was vented into incessant fidgeting.

Carmela had phoned during the flight and left a message for him with the details of a possible hotel that had been booked in the name of Caterina Donati, but the hotel's logs showed that she had booked out yesterday.

· It worried him that she was reverting back to using the alias; if she used more than one then he'd lose track of her for sure.

He zoomed in on a car hire company at the airport he thought she'd most likely aim for, the one he would if he were in her position. He was spot on and the two men behind the desk confirmed they recognised her from the photo on his phone but explained in slow broken English that they couldn't give out any further details of her booking. He nodded his understanding and proceeded with his own booking, eager to be out of the terminal building to light up a cigarette.

He placed a call to Carmela to let her know he'd arrived and to give her the hire company details - she would do the rest and call him back when the information came in. It was early afternoon in Italy so there was a good chance she'd get back to him quickly with the information he needed.

Following that he called Maia to reassure her he was ok and to check that all was well with them: the kids were at school and she'd just got in with the shopping. The phone calls done he quickly got his bearings and headed for the hotel.

Carmela's searching had paid off. The Hotel Residencia Pontevedra was no Hilton, sitting south just two miles outside of the airport. It perched uncomfortably off Avenue Norte in the district of Panititlan, a largely commercial area bordered by a number of trading estates and warehouses that serviced the airport and the city alike. It was a clean enough district but not a place you'd chose for an extended stay as there was nothing locally to visit and it was too close to the airport to shut out the noise of the planes even through the double glazing. He could see why she booked it, probably driving around till she found somewhere suitable: there was little in the means of residential houses to bother her and the frequent heavy rumble of goods vehicles coming and going to mask her activities as an ant among giants, and again there were no cameras, which considering the city's well known high crime rate Sergio was extremely surprised about.

Lying on the bed now he was tempted to catch a couple of hours sleep but knew he needed to walk the area around the hotel searching for clues. When he arrived he had parked up outside, eyeing up the cars sitting vacant in the lot to the side of the hotel, a few were rentals but mostly they looked to be the battered carriages of local workers who used the hotel's parking lot as secure off street parking. There were a couple of beaten up old Fords parked in marked bays which he surmised belonged to the hotel staff, which gave him hope to the accessibility of the pockets he would need to fill for information. He checked his wallet and tried to ascertain how much in pesos he would have to part with to find out what he needed. It turned out not to be much, which he was thankful for.

There was a greasy overweight looking chap on the reception desk who sat with his mouth open and his tongue lolling moronically out of his mouth. Sergio was ashamed to think that he'd been told often enough of the same pose he pulled when he concentrated and fought hard not to be judgemental. As it turned out the man had a broad smile upon seeing him and was extremely friendly and was keen to do anything to please his new customer, and he even had a good grasp of Italian, which was more than a surprise and a great relief. Sceptically he tilted his head at the mention of his previous guest, tilting his head like a bemused dog, but at the extra cash bonus being offered for a room for the night his smile returned and he became ever so chatty, even offering Sergio her vacated room now that it had been cleaned and made up.

Yes, it was definitely her in the photograph, very striking in appearance and having stood out for her pale skin and blonde hair which was shorter, he said, than in the photograph. Yes she had stayed for two nights. No she hadn't left anything behind. No she didn't have anyone with her. No she didn't say where she was going next (he thought she might have mentioned going north but he had trouble understanding her accent, but generally she barely said anything to him). Yes she did have a car and happily he provided the registration number but had no record of the make, stating that because the car park was to the side of the building he hadn't seen her in the car and hadn't bothered to venture out to look for himself.

Sergio had thanked him for his kindness and retired to the room where, after a quick double check of what was present (there was an ashtray on the dresser and no 'no smoking' signs in view) and the view from the window (a warehouse loading bay), he had collapsed on the bed, ashtray in one hand and cigarette in the other, so far satisfied with his progress but unsure of where to proceed from here.

Vanni, Vanni, Vanni, he thought to himself, *think, what would she do next? What would Luigi do?* But he couldn't think; without knowing her motives he was in the dark as to her next move. He would have to go out to scour the street like a beggar splashing her photograph around and hoping the workers nearby spoke Italian or maybe a little English. It was a long shot, too long for his tired mind to compute.

11

He was back at Czekolada's. It had only been a few hours since he'd left but in that time he had achieved much with the German and dissected and pierced with his scalpel with the precision of open heart surgery the internal thinking of his patient, pulling back the skin and clamping it in place as he unveiled the pumping vessels that bled out in a gush of fear as the reluctant reticence over the mine deal was laid bare. Damage limitation was now the goal as it became apparent that third parties had been spoken to; other investors had been included in conference calls to discuss the improbabilities and concerns and now it was Tomasz's role to get a cap on it and prevent the overflow bubbling into a frothy mess across the table of financial contracts that were yet to be signed.

He had called the guys in last minute for a lunch meeting to bounce ideas and splash instructions to those of his inner circle that he trusted. Wieslaw and Lenart were both there but Tomek was across town on other business and unlikely to make it, but that was ok, for what he needed would be sat around the table with him.

He briefed them on his problem as they waited for their lunch order and allowed it to stew on their minds as they tucked into the delicacies Justyna brought them. They ate in relative silence, each busying their minds: Lenart and Wieslaw pondering how to inventively tackle and persuade the rogue investors while Tomasz sat with one eye on his food and the other on the open file on his Ipad as he switched his mental channel over the far flung fantasies of the ReSYEM Project and the curiosities that plagued the quest he'd sent Luigi off on.

He wished no ill will towards Luigi, in fact having read his profile he seemed quite a likeable sort of guy, straight up and trying to earn an honest living to support his family - a real nice guy, no longer the Luigi of his past having left that side of him behind to embrace the Sergio that would no doubt soon seek to break away from the hold that the organisation had over him; maybe he would try to relocate or try to renegotiate and bargain for release based on his achievements they'd demanded of him. But whether they would let him go was another matter. Tomasz himself had yet to see in his short term of employment if they had a compassionate side. He hoped so, for his own sake, and for that of his friends should it come to it, for as detached and two faced as he clothed himself, in reality he wished no one any real ill will.

Through a mouthful of food Lenart mumbled an idea of a sweetener, another business opportunity to give the investors something bad to examine to make the mine look more appealing in comparison. He'd spat some specks of bread across the table as he spoke and reached for his napkin to wipe at any mess, checking his casual thin blue shirt beneath his wide collared brown leather jacket which he'd been reluctant to remove feeling a chill that the others seemed to miss; he would have been more comfortable sat inside but dared not suggest it unless his friends too showed some discomfort - it made him wonder as to whether he was coming down with something one of the twins had, a cold maybe, either way he'd been up most of the night with her. He dabbed at his goatee with the napkin.

Tomasz gave a nod of approval and gave space for Lenart to expand further on the idea. When they were fresh out of college Wieslaw and Lenart had both pitched for the same job and were both shortlisted to the final three but during the process Wieslaw had grown cold for the company and had his eyes set on something grander, so they had colluded together on the required presentation ensuring that Lenart's was outstanding and Wielaw's mediocre, a little unfounded rumour spreading about the third candidate and Lenart was secured the job. Lenart reminded them of this causing a smirk of proud remembrance to light Wielaw's features.

"Digging up some dirt should be pretty easy," Wieslaw mumbled.

"And creating a shadow project using one of the shell companies should be relatively simple too, although it might take a bit of work," Lenart added. "Give me a couple of days to set it up and we can play it by the end of the week."

"Is the German married?"

Tomasz nodded. "With kids."

Wieslaw smirked. "Give me his details and I'll do a search on his web browsing, it usually turns up something nasty and embarrassing. Arrange a meeting with the investors for early next week and in the meantime we'll play havoc with their minds," he suggested with his head tilted towards Tomasz but his neck hung forward in its almost permanent position that rolled his shoulders into a grovelling hunch.

"Drop whatever else you've got on, if you can, and I'll look after your loses." He said this with a wink knowing that the two friends would gladly abandon their regular work for the sort of compensation Tomasz would transfer directly into their bank accounts. "You'd better let me know if there are any problems," he added and the two men nodded in response and continued their meal, all three thinking about the sweetener to be offered the German that would end ultimately with a sour taste. They would brain storm it together in silence and chip in ideas as it came to them, in this way they would leave the table with a solid plan of action to work upon. Tomasz felt relieved that he had such a reliable team to call upon.

"You going to tell us what that is?" Wieslaw hung a lazy finger at the Ipad and the open screen Tomasz had absentmindedly placed on the table, maybe subconsciously he wanted them to ask, he wasn't sure.

"It's nothing, just a project I've been asked to look over," Tomasz' tone was dismissive enough as he switched the screen off but there was enough of a hesitation in his voice for both his companions to raise an interested eyebrow.

"Come on, share, you know you want to." Lenart was close enough to allow his playful tone sing across the table yet be able to keep it hushed enough from prying ears.

"Leave him alone Cristian, you know he can't talk too much shop or he'll be answerable to those upstairs."

Wieslaw knew which buttons to push and the idea that Tomasz was answerable to anybody was a certain back straightener. The shroud of infallibility and supremacy amongst his peers, or at least the image of such was interconnected with his playboy ego and to undermine that by suggesting that he were answerable to anyone and hadn't yet climbed the dizzy heights of the ladder right to the top was refutable, no matter how much truth lay in it. He knew Tomasz well enough to know to play on his vanity, especially in a public setting among peers.

"It's not that I can't tell you...it's just that..."

Wieslaw and Lenart both darted smiling, winking eyes at each other, so brief that Tomasz missed it as he stumbled over his excuses why not to share his information with them.

"...it's complex and sensitive. Besides if you let it be known that I'd told you anything your life could be in danger."

Lenart laughed.

"No, it's true. You don't know what they're capable of. They could be listening to us right now; it only takes a click of a button to remotely open the microphone on your mobile phone or your laptop..."

"Or your Ipad," chipped in Wieslaw.

"Precisely."

"That's being a little bit paranoid don't you think?" scoffed Lennart. "Well, if you're not allowed to tell then we can't help you, can we? Assuming it's something you'd want our help with?"

Tomasz let out a deep sigh and drew in a heavy resigned breath, his mouth opened to speak and the other two systematically leant forward to hear what was to be said.

The cutting chirp of a telephone sliced the words before they could get life and both Lenart and Wieslaw knew they'd lost their chance. Their curiosity soaked in a pale of water they sat back and returned their minds to the occupation of dealing with the German.

"Sir, yes sir...it's been taken care of... I've got some of my local team on it so we'll have a result quickly...no sir, they know no intimate details and they are totally reliable and trustworthy." His eyes widened at his two friends whose heads had tilted upwards in his direction as he raised a finger to his lips to emphasise their discretion. "The other matter? I...yes I'm still waiting for verification...yes sir."

The call ended abruptly with a crease ruffling the otherwise smooth brow of Tomasz' forehead.

"Trouble?" asked Lenart.

"Ask me another time," replied Tomasz, thinking now that the ReSYEM Project was more important than he realised.

12

The turquoise tinted water crashed in with a torrent of a repetitive swishing as it drew a blanket up over the sloped stepped rocks, recessing to a regular sliding roll back up and over smoothing the rough sharp edges until its gradient defeated it, trapping some in pools and crags to feed the miniscule life that survived there until drowned again by the later rising tide.

It was an ideal spot for surfing and as she looked out she spotted a couple of brave souls paddling slowly around the rocks of the headland aiming for the breakers that edged into the deeper bluer waters away from the treacherous battering of the sunken landmass.

The sun sparkled a myriad of diamonds off the rippling waves speckling the blue with silvery white which met foaming to the yellow along the shoreline further up. She shielded her eyes with the fingers of her hands, tasting the dryness of her lips with her tongue and wondering aloud to herself with no one to hear the question on the deserted stretch of unrecognisable coast, "Where the hell am I?"

It was late in the day, nearing four in the afternoon she guessed, not that she knew for sure; she never wore a watch but had a tendency to know the time instinctively. The line of travel of the sun in the sky probably helped and the shadows cast through the trees. The rest was a guess, as always.

There were ants crawling along the branch where her hand held back the trees, big black ones, she didn't think she'd ever seen bigger anywhere before. She moved her arm away before any found a new path up the thin line of weak pale flesh, closing the curtain of green across her view.

A dry wooded path lay before her with grey brown dead leaves scattered on the parched earth along with some fallen twigs mixed with a speckling of green growth that told her the land was foreign and that it wouldn't be just the people that would be of a different nature to what she was used to, the natives, she figured, were most likely to be of a darker skin and a complicated tongue.

A few trees hung out like skeletons stripped of their greenery by the wind swept in from the sea, save for the odd branch. Some jutted out at an angle from the incline of cliff as it rose away from the rocks below reminding her of happier times when she hung one handed from the side of a lamppost posing for a photograph on a long forgotten Dublin street.

There was other wildlife too: birds she could hear but not see, cicadas she thought she could make out in the distance clinging to the trees, the rustling of leaves in the undergrowth as she passed by, lizards or snakes maybe, she couldn't tell but her ears were alert to all. She could smell the wood and the freshness of the sea and the faint smell of smoke and the aroma of food further inland informing her of a settlement of some sort nearby. She didn't want that; she had no desire to be around people right now. She could follow the coastline for a while and get her bearings, if she wandered long enough on her own hopefully her memory would return and the fear of facing the population would dissipate - she hoped.

Talisa had no memory of getting here, but that was

nothing new. It was often the case after an incident that her mind would go into shock and she'd wander far both mentally and physically. There would often be a logic to it as even her unconscious thoughts sought to protect her. She recalled the crash but little afterwards, her mind struggling to reattach the fragments of flashing imagery that she couldn't be sure she wasn't inventing to fill in the gaps. She had a vague image or memory of a parched desert landscape. Had she wandered that far towards the coast? She had always been a fast walker; her favourite mode of travel where she could escape into her own thoughts as her feet carried her who knew where.

She watched the trees swaying back and forth in the ferocious wind, buffeted from the sea like players catching a baseball in a giant glove, the hand swinging back before flinging it forward again into play like a catapult aimed at a stampeding army. There were dark clouds building on the horizon and the gaining wind spoke of an impending storm to break the pleasant calm which beautified the shoreline. She looked down once more at the surfers and could see the hesitation as they sat on their boards staring up at the sky. They would soon make for land she was sure.

She felt a sharp pain she couldn't account for, like someone stabbing her in the kidneys like someone was sticking pins in a voodoo doll made in her image while she slept. It was almost the sharp twang of a damaged muscle grating as she stood still. It wasn't just the kidneys that hurt, her abdomen was tender also and as she concentrated her thoughts on it she suddenly doubled up in pain as tight cramps gripped a fist of tissue on her intestines and twisted viciously. She cried out in pain as she dropped to one knee, her hand feeling the clammy sheltered earth beneath her fingers. It lasted only a few moments and then subsided. She took a breath and slowly stood.

There were many things she thought the pain could have been: injury from the crash was the most obvious thing to spring to the forefront of her mind; then there was the probability of that whatever had been done to her was having side effects, her body finally weakening and slowing to repair itself - she had long suspected this would happen eventually, but this last crippling spasm confirmed the real cause. She had no supplies on her, no handbag, and no purse. She would need to find a bathroom and steal what she needed. It wouldn't be the first time she'd been forced to break the law to survive, and she suspected here in this foreign land she would have to do a great deal to get her by. She thought about the smell of food she'd scented moments ago and rethought her plans of avoiding life and walking aimlessly along the coast, but storms, hunger, and period pains had a tendency to change one's mind rather quickly.

She shifted gear and momentum, her mind set to beg, borrow or steal whatever she would need to get by.

She gave thought to her appearance, with no mirror she would have to guess at how she would be presented by the feel of the grime on her straight nose and drawn cheeks. The thin lips of her paltry mouth felt intact, not cracked or bleeding. Her usual, or what had once upon a time been her usual cheeky, naughty, playful expression was long wiped from her face. Her low stature was engulfed in her long bouffant auburn hair that tangled in wind-blown knots in an brusque accent of its own as it told of her haggard journey thus far with its centre parting lost exposing the greying roots and wiry strands of silver that, despite looking young due to her height, made her age hard to judge - early to mid-thirties maybe upon close inspection, but right now with her memory fading she couldn't even be sure of that. The tight tweed jacket she wore was intact as was the knee length charcoal skirt she wore over her bare legs. She didn't recall wearing the jacket on the plane but figured she must have picked up the clothes somehow on her journey, despite being familiar and well-fitting - she dismissed the thought as irrelevant.

She looked into the wash of leaning trees limbo dancing in the wind. She was torn between her practical needs and an overwhelming sense to keep moving. She was certain that once the flight manifest became known they would send someone to find her. How long had it been already? She must keep moving. She must find somewhere where she could blend in, not here, she clearly didn't belong here.

She had her suspicious of where she was now. Her mind was beginning to piece it all together, as a magnet pulling iron fillings she drew her thoughts to her. The course of the plane, the lay of the coast, the vegetation, even her inner compass sent her signals of where she was.

Thinking momentarily about it she knew little of the country except for what she had picked up from friends and colleagues over the years, bits of tittle tattle over the din of clinking glasses and raucous voices over the bar music as the girls espoused their conquests in all the gory details in a blow by blow account that made her squirm with inner disgust as politely and prudishly she had listened in on their holiday exploits. There were places, she was sure, where you could go in every country to blend into the party scene, places where last night's cheap shag was tomorrows blurred face in the distant crowd, easily dodged should you be unlucky enough to bump into him, or her for that matter. She doubted this was such a place, and it would be too close and obvious a place to hide. She would have to go further across country before she could relax and let her guard down enough to live, if only a little.

She turned her feet to the nearby settlement and pushed away from the coast at her back.

13

The plane had come down in the mountains just north of Tepic in the region of Nayarit, a good seven hours drive north of Mexico City. Fortunately he was spared the laborious hours behind the wheel as it was agreed he could charter a light aircraft to Tepic and hire a car from there. It seemed that the locals were all geared up for frequent visitors to the area over the past week as taxis' were readily available at the small, usually under used, airfield that served the city.

Sergio was readily driven in the direction of Santiago Ixcuintla, which was less than an hour's drive from Tepic, at an inflated price he had no qualms in paying, he wasn't picking up the tab so what did he care? Why Tomasz had called him and tipped him to this he wasn't sure. Certainly the faceless Pole had left him little to go on other than a hunch which he wasn't prepared to share. Besides, what did he have to lose? Mexico City had so far drawn him to a dead end. Having canvased the area around the hotel he'd drawn a blank - she just seemed to have disappeared and could, for all he knew, be anywhere in Mexico by now.

He tried to check, as best he could whether anyone fitting her description had chartered a plane to Tepic over the last two days. It was a question he wished he hadn't asked. Of course there had been lots of flights out to Tepic as the world's media descended on the crash site, how else were they to get there? He'd flashed her photo but to no avail, doing likewise when he arrived and then again when he reached Santiago Ixcuintla. From there he needed to pay for a local guide to drive him up into the jagged mountains to where the plane had met its gruesome end. As enterprising luck would have it his taxi driver from Tepic also doubled as a guide for a fee almost double the cab ride, and of course this was one way, if he wanted to come back down to town again it would cost him double - in cash. Fortunately he was getting used to the way of things and had withdrawn enough to cover any and all eventualities and was quick to separate and conceal much of what he carried in case he was robbed. He also found that his ear for the language was quickening and he was conversing comfortably much sooner than he had expected.

The plains around the town were mainly fields farmed out by the town's people and the surrounding villages that were dotted here and there. Fifteen minutes west as the crow flies lay the coast and the warm seas of the Pacific. Forty minutes east lay the jagged ridges that scarred a column along the western edge of the Mexico Plateau that was the beginning of the Sierra Madre Occidental.

Mostly the wreckage was collected up and hauled off in trucks for examination as the investigation into the cause of the crash swiftly got under way, so all that was to view as the day drew close to closing its door in his face were the tents and temporary huts put in place to protect the few investigators still left at the scene and the recovery units who still scoured the mountainside with the use of flyby helicopters zooming in and photographing every space of debris they could pinpoint. There were tourists too; he found it appalling and try as he might he couldn't get his head around those that had spent the time, energy and money to gawp at what was left of a mass funeral pyre.

Dragging on cigarette after cigarette he carefully scanned the faces of those that strode before him, as he had done ever since touching down in Mexico City, but none resembled her. He flashed his phone before all who cared to look at her picture and found words were not necessary for such a question, but to each no positive answer was given as he littered the area around the crash site with his butts, trampled beneath the footfall or blown with the desert dust as the wind picked up over the mountains. It was a waste of time and he was reluctantly feeling the urge to abandon the chase and book the next available flight home. At least now he could complain that Tomasz was clearly holding out on him, surely sending him to the crash site meant that there was something he wasn't being told.

He spied out his drive come guide and nodded his wish to return to town, tossing his final butt before climbing in the car. He would need to pick up some more smokes before flying out again. If he was lucky he could get back before the sun set and not have to spend a night up here if there was a plane ready to take him back to the capital.

It was as he passed through the fields around the town that he realised that he had been out of cellular reception as his pocket sprang to life with the vibration and wild chime of exclamation that signalled a message. He reached for the phone and picked up his voicemail, it was Carmela, she had taken the liberty of running checks on the flights out of all the regions Sergio passed through (a task much easier to do it appeared in this end of the world than it was at home as the security protocols in the smaller airports proved rather lax - something he suspected was on purpose to encourage the open passing of pesos for information). Vicky Rivers had caught a flight out of Tepic not four hours ago - he had probably crossed her as he arrived.

Carmela's message was brief but informative. She was heading back to Mexico City but with no intention of stopping there for she had booked an onward flight. At last he was catching her up. He wondered whether she had driven the hire car to Tepic, probably he guessed by the length of time she'd spent here. He wondered whether he'd be able to find her car at the airport, not that he expected to find any clues there as to why she had come all this way. All that mattered to him now was finding out where she was going.

He gave instruction to his driver to head straight back to Tepic and would pay extra for a speedy journey - this pleased him greatly as he pushed hard on the pedal and drove like a demented maniac, smiling broadly at a prosperous day's pay. Sergio, having already ditched his own hire car at the airport first thing this morning was now racing on her tail eager to close the gap.

14

The penthouse apartment was a mere two minutes' walk from Czekolada's on Szpitalna. It wasn't a tall building, a puny five stories that gave a meagre view of the square below as the junction of roads merged into a wide platform for pedestrians and vehicles alike. Opposite rose the ten storey block of squalid and cramped flats that stood above the ever popular Sphinx Restaurant and Bar that was a hub into the early hours and which even now he could hear rising up to his window as he stood in the spacious and modern living room that he'd had converted two years ago (having been in a kindly position of persuadence with the chief of the council's planning department). It had been a top floor of four large flats which now consisted of three, with each of his rooms expanded to his crisp and bright immaculate taste. It was ridiculously too big for a single man, but he liked to party (much to the annoyance of his few immediate neighbours) and the space was just right to accommodate the groupies and associates that tagged behind him collecting the crumbs from his ever filled and constantly polished table. There was nothing in his apartment that spoke of age and not a speck of dust was on show as he paid for a housemaid to clean and do his shopping on a daily basis.

Tomasz stood by the window overlooking the evening traffic and the dance of lights that wisped back and forth across the city like fireflies busily buzzing from tree to concrete tree. He could see into some of the flats opposite, the tower block forming the point of a triangle which bled back to the north side of the city hiding Poland's administrative bank behind. He had no desire to peer into the flats; he had done so often enough in the past, spying curiously on the unsuspecting occupants from the darkness of his pad - the blonde on the third floor was his favourite, a nymphomaniac if ever he saw one, constantly putting on a sexually explicit show in the hope she was being observed. There were other persons that peeked his interest from time to time but tonight he cared little for any of them.

The street lights shone below, misty globes lighting the footfall of social traffic and hiding his abode in the darkness above.

He stood with his slim line blue shirt undone to the waist allowing his taut finely cut torso to breathe the warm air of the apartment. He held a glass of whiskey in one hand, an Irish malt he had taken a liking to on a visit to the UK a few years ago. In his other hand, glued in its almost permanent position was his Ipad. The screen showed a map, one of his design as he plotted the course of the organisation's activities. The mining and ore business he realised was not independent to the chemical and research arm of the corporation as his map overlaid markers of secret facilities and mines one on top of another and drawn together with a coloured line as he linked each to its relevant business strand. He didn't know the connection between the need for the mines and the chemical and bio facilities, he simply assumed there was a particular mineral needed for whatever closed book project was draining the company millions.

He was desperate not to put two and two together

but he couldn't help himself, jigsaw puzzles had always been his thing as a child, piecing together the bigger picture. He'd moved on to more elaborate puzzles and conundrums as the years went on, a gift that allowed him to see into the corporate world's defences and strategically dismantle and rebuild the structures to his own design and profit.

Germany was on the map, so was South Africa and Kenya; Australia, China, and Russia were there to no surprise; moving west he could see a number of offices in Europe which he had prior knowledge of, administrative mainly but key points on his map nonetheless. If he overlaid Vicky Rivers' travel dossier he wondered how many more points would interconnect, certainly Boston, Los Angeles, and Alaska were on the map; he had linked (or thought he had - he was guessing at the private jet that had gone down on route to Washington) at least three murders to her already, four if you included the most recent one in Italy. Now he had marked Mexico too, but from what he could see the company had no business interests there, not in an office or facility anyhow, which left him only one conclusion: she was chasing a ReSYEM subject.

He rubbed his forehead with the back of his hand, careful not to tip his glass and spill his drink. If he was right then either she was acting alone or she was receiving orders from elsewhere within or from without the organisation.

He wondered whether he should speak up with his suspicions, then doubt crept in; it wasn't his place and if he alluded to something above his pay grade then there was a real danger he would put himself in the firing line. Of course there was a chance it could also place him in line for promotion, but was it worth the risk, and did he really want to embed himself deeper than he already was?

He figured that he was best keeping a low profile with his thoughts but the curiosity was eating away at him. How much did he dare tell the Italian, Sergio? He'd begun to think of him by his real name now, a mistake he knew as he grew attached to the person he pictured behind the name and a conscience grew and a sense of responsibility for his safety chewed at his ear. Now he was beginning to understand why he'd been instructed to call him Luigi and to have minimal contact, but he was beyond that. How else was the man supposed to do his job and find her if he didn't have all the facts? How else was he supposed to stay safe? But then safety was not their concern; if he turned up dead it would simply be another bread crumb to follow.

He thought that if he could figure out what Rivers was chasing he might be able to push Sergio in the right direction ahead of her and at the same time warn him off any impending danger.

He shook his head at the moon winking between the clouds as the soft mellow globes of light reflected off the inside of the window. "Dumb ass!" he said aloud, "You're the wrong man for this job, Tomasz."

What do I know? he thought to himself. *I mean for real, what do I really know?*

He knew a man was dead. He knew who had killed him but not the reason why. He knew that the killer had gone off the grid and the company wanted to find where she was. He knew that the company invested in mining and research facilities as well as about a couple dozen other business and political interests that he knew of. Everything else was circumspect and assumption.

Oh, and he knew the ReSYEM Project.

But even that was grasping at straws. For all he knew it was purely coincidental. His mind was filled with the jargon of the research and he was admittedly in awe of the results, if not a little intrigued and tempted to the lure of what he suspected drove the board to invest their billions into.

The project itself had extrapolated years of research carried out at the North Carolina State University and the University of Pittsburgh in Pennsylvania, enhancing their findings in a completely new direction based under tight security at a privately rented laboratory in the Irvine campus of the University of California. The report he sat on highlighted it all in fine detail, with the exception of any technical data that would be required to verify the report as anything other than a theoretical paper.

The original research was based on post-World War II experiments into battlefield skin grafts, failed experiments that sparked a plethora of ideas. ReSYEM had focused on the 'extracellular matrix' - the stuff that remains if you strip away the living cells from a blood vessel, an organ or a bit of skin. This supportive frame structures the detailed shape and solidity of the host body, basically holding things together like an organic scaffolding system. Regenerative medicine researchers at Pittsburgh had used animals to take an organ and strip it of native cells then used what remained, the dormant chassis, as a template on which to load on new stem cells, recoating the matrix with live flesh. They found that the matrix was then able to draw in structural proteins and molecules: collagen, elastin, fibronectins and integrins to build specific cells, then by manipulating the stiffness or rigidity of the cells they could be turned into fat or muscle or even bone, this special matrix then forming blood vessels on top providing oxygen to nourish the new organs.

This part of the research was of no great secret and had been widely published in the mainstream scientific journals. There was obvious interest in its potential applications from a wide spectrum of industry, not excluding the US military who were bouncing up and down at the concept of decellularised body parts: muscles, bones, organs, all of which could be experimented on by mainly using the destroyed limbs of US marines rather than the general populace of roadside accident victims; their own hand-picked willing participants for human trials would be accountable and relied upon for their silence whereas a civilian would always be a liability should results fail or have unexpected side-effects. Early results from the Pittsburgh animal trials showed that cells taken from the same subject and replanted onto the stripped down area seemed to systematically know where to repair and how.

The problem the official research team had encountered came when the subject itself was inanimate. The test subject needed to be placed into a temporary stasis of inactivity, inducing a kind of temporary death with all vital organs, including the brain, showing inactivity which made it increasingly difficult for the researchers to monitor any lasting effects on the cognitive processes upon reanimation, and as a result completely ruled out any potential for human trials. Another problem was that during the induced state the regrowth was slower than hoped and would thus increase the trauma the longer the subject was forced into the temporary state of death.

. Despite the implications the military was still willing to sign off on human trials, actively seeking out terminally injured servicemen to volunteer for a chance of extending their lives in a high risk medical experiment that relied on them basically to undergo an induced death. Yet even their research was limited and slow and under the stranglehold of financial restrictions in a time when the country's economic outlook was grim and the purse strings of the military budget were being squeezed. They had taken the research to a test facility at Edwards Air Force Base just northeast of Lancaster, California. It was the stuff of science fiction: the military keen to create super soldiers who could repair themselves in the field, or even better not be killed at all. This wasn't cloning, it was very different; there were no copies of the original subject being created as this process only allowed the cells to be regrown within the original body, having to be part of the original live subject to begin with. To be able to avert a patient from perishing altogether in, say a fire, the speed in which the regrowth occurred was an essential part of the experiment, yet in all cases the acceleration was still way too slow. In a case of an explosion however, where the patient's body parts were separated into multiple locations, results found that only parts attached to the main section of the body survived and that separated limbs or body parts would perish as would normally be expected. By accident it was discovered that where the head was severed from the neck no regrowth occurred at all as though there needed to be a conscious link between body and mind.

This area of the research had stumped the military scientists working on the project, who were all sworn to secrecy by an airtight legal contract that gagged them all and robbed them of any ownership of either their research or the project results. The financial crash and the long drawn out conflict in the Middle East drew a sharp end, or at least a temporary halt, to the military's dabbling in search of a biological super soldier.

Little did the military know that the original ReSYEM Project was still continuing with private funding under cover at UCI.

At UCI it was thought that somehow the synthesised matrix was capable of communicating with the unconscious mind on more than a pure physical level and to this end the research had been on-going, and in this the organisation had been particularly interested in as it indicated that the mind held a greater power over the body than previously thought leading to questions as to whether it could exist as a separate entity altogether: immortal without the complications and hindrances of an imperfect bodily casing prone to damage, disease and death. The organisation, or those at the top of it anyhow, sought immortality, and this was just one of their major projects which they ploughed their millions into as they attempted to attain the exalted height of the gods and to be gods themselves.

ReSYEM, through much trial and error, had created a synthetic matrix which was then implanted into the dormant animal trial subject to replace and supersede the natural matrix so that eventually the reproduction being copied was a growth of biological laboratory design rather than the natural order of things. This had worked well with the initial experiments allowing a second phase to proceed to human subjects, yet here not all went to plan.

Of course, as with all scientific experiments the results weren't perfect, and likened to all clinical trials and medicines was prone to side effects, effects which the company was keen to hush up and brush under the carpet, hence the file being regularly re-evaluated for its viability and security protocols as nobody wanted to take responsibility for the all too permanent fatalities that had already occurred during the course of the research, not to mention trying to explain why certain test subjects were being detained due to growth abnormalities such as elements of short stubby hands stretching down from an elongated jaw-line, or a knee joint attempting to grow on an upper thigh, or finger nails like scales layering the backs of hands, just a sample of the failed processes that littered the pages of the report, but mostly the main concern was with brain damage as it appeared that given time of days to a few months all the subjects presented with symptoms akin to strokes, major debilitating ones in most cases. It was something the hybrid synthetic matrix seemed incapable of repairing, leaving researchers stumped once again at the intricacies and mystery of the human brain and questioning the capability of the mind to overcome the difficulties of an imperfect body.

In the summary the project manager, in promoting the achievements and expectations of the project, had voiced that it wouldn't be long before you could pre-order a designer body in much the same way that plastic surgery could manipulate appearance, only this method would be much more potent: the preferred 'made to your own particular specifications' synthetic matrix implanted with the aim of transforming your body into a whole new you. You could easily picture the marketing campaign as the bill board posters lit under neon lights and the television advert exclaimed it as the next best thing, as though it were as simple as putting on your make-up and as optional as clothes shopping.

The military would have an interest in this also; it would bring international espionage into a whole new age and give a new meaning to double agent. Even on the black market criminals would have a slice of the cake as they switched identities on demand and whenever necessary to carry out a crime or evade capture. You could even retain the option of keeping the original coding of the natural matrix so that you could claim back your own body even if it was only for the weekend, and transgender swapping wasn't necessarily out of the question either.

All this would lead to the improbabilities of a chaotic, false and highly corrupt society, unless of course the pitfalls were identified early and the legal framework put in place to regulate it all and to quell the inevitable fears and protests of the militant ethical brigade, who no doubt would propagate their campaign of objection through the press in order to manipulate the many who could quietly voice their distrust over dinner or bitch about it over a pint in the pub but didn't actually have any clout to change the outcome, for that power, as in all things of corporate importance, was held and influenced by those with deep pockets, and they would always back whatever pinched at their own personal and vested interests.

Tomasz saw all these pitfalls and had highlighted them in his report, how many of them would be taken notice of he dared not guess at, for in the end he had no real idea as to the aims and ideals of those who wished to own society and form it, either for the greater good or for themselves.

Part of him felt like Isaac Asimov drawing up the rules and laws of robotics for a future generation, only the robots were dressed up in human flesh, potential zombies where the mind could be removed or controlled within a perfect reanimate cell formed at the bidding of those in power and sold to others as a plaything.

The potential future of the human race looked grim through the half-filled whiskey glass he swirled in his hand.

He wondered what it felt like to be put into stasis for the procedure. Was there a white light? Did they dream? Did they remember? The report didn't say, but he was sure that another report was out there somewhere echoing the compilation of near death experiences and its medical and psychological effects on the human body and mind; no doubt the report would go further in extrapolating ideas for further cognitive and biological research. What was it like to die? he wondered. He pondered whether Vicky Rivers sought the same answer and wondered whether her conscience, as murderously depraved as it was, was more morally sane than those they both worked for.

He looked down through the window at the scurrying figures, cockroaches beneath him, surviving in a class of their own, and waiting to be trampled upon by the boot of aristocracy. What gave him the right to judge? Wealth? Intelligence? His social circle? Take away his privileged position and the insight and protection of his employer and what would he be?

He shook his head knowing he would be no different to everyone else scuttling about below, and knew morally whom he would prefer to stand with.

For the first time he doubted the ladder he was climbing, staring down at the slippery back of the snake and wondering how many of them already had their DNA altered by the hand of the ghosts of Mars or whatever mask the organisation presented itself as.

15

There was no river in view, plenty of sea but no river other than the one she sang about. Her tune, the one she sung and hummed in remembrance of her name with the fondness of a nine year old cradled in the arms of her mother, having her hair stroked and occasionally her tummy tickled as they spent quality time out of ear shot of Jonathan who often grew jealous of his older sister hogging 'me time' with their mother.

Well, you can drown me in the river, tears for the river, I'll weep a river for you

So her mother would sing. She remembered it as a song she had sung to her father upon adopting his name, but that had to be wrong for the words didn't match the love they shared that was imprinted on her mind, so she ignored the meaning of the words, loving the melodic flow of the tune that had been sung down to her adoringly as a child until the tune was embedded in her subconscious, echoing her name so that she would never forget it or where she came from, nor whom she had loved.

You left me crying, lonely and dying, While you went off wining and dining, As my tears flowed a river over you.

Her brother had a song, not nearly as melodic or beautifully enchanting, his was more energetic and frantic to accompany the hyperactivity of a five year old who could never sit still. They had good fun back then, singing and playing, but that was before things changed. Her mind often froze in time on that moment before, she sitting in her mother's arms staring up adoringly like nothing in the world could ever harm her or steal her away from such love.

She stared out to sea fully aware that she was off the grid, once more having disappeared on a mission of her own. They would send someone after her and she would make her excuses and they would leave her be, or give her another assignment to keep her out of trouble. She didn't talk to them about what she knew. She was too scared of where that would lead. So long as she kept hitting their targets she was confident they would leave her alone, hopefully just thinking she was a scatty loose cannon but dependable enough to do her job.

Had she missed a hit? Where was that? She couldn't remember. She wondered whether she might be in trouble for that one, but then shook her head in denial; she had other things to think about.

She stared out across the cold crisp blue that seemed settled in the blazing mid-day sun. The skinny neotropic cormorants, small dark long necked shapes bobbing, diving with a splash, the jokers of the still waters, or not so depending on where the waves broke over the shallows of sand banks, catching the eye in a sideways glance in hopeful expectation of it being a submerging dolphin, then waiting eagerly for its reappearance to the 'nah na, na na nah' of the cormorant as its slender neck tattled 'made you look made you stare, but you're the fool 'cause there's no dolphin here!' But they were the fools, she thought, as she entertained a tittle tattle competition between herself and the mocking birds, for there, dipping and rising off in the distance were the grey graceful arcs out of the waters, silently cruising in their pod, not feeling the need to rush or splash or jump, just casually going about their day, the sun glinting majestically off their fins as it caught the perpetual moistness.

A movement had caught the corner of her eye and hooked her head to her left along the path that curled inland away from the cliff edge and the swave of wind battered trees that leaned back towards...towards where? Tepic? But she wasn't there; she had left there already, but her mind was still replaying events.

An old man was ambling along, short in stature with dirty plain pasty coloured trousers and blazer that looked thin and comfortable to the point that she wondered whether he ever took them off. She couldn't see his face for his back was turned to walk away into whatever village hid behind the trees but she imagined him to be lined and crimpled with age and tanned by the orb that hung over head. He seemed to have a defect down one side that caused him to limp in a manner that gave the appearance of an abnormal body length on one side. He turned to see her, already aware of her presence and hastening to alert others. He quickened his pace on seeing her devilish piercing eyes beneath the black streak of make-up that levelled a mask above her cheeks and across the bridge of her nose. He tottered off out of view, marching along incessantly like the limbless captain of the Pequod.

"Welcome to the Playa Mujeres," the woman said in perfect English with more than a hint of a strong Spanish accent.

Vicky shook her head as she snapped out of the daydream as she realised she was now front of the queue. She checked in with an air of distraction, eager to replay the memory but not faltering on her smile or manners as she perfectly played her part as she crossed the foyer and headed for the elevator to her room. The doors closed and she was alone to her thoughts once more.

The smell of sea air wafted back up to her nostrils as she searched the tree line for where the old man had gone.

She had followed the trail this far but here she had lost it. It hadn't taken her long to figure that Talisa Hayes wouldn't stick around the crash site, knowing her condition would raise too many questions and attract the attention of the organisation that she was keen to avoid. The coast was the most likely place she would head for and so she had followed the trail, plotting out a likely walking route on a map and then driving as she got into her mind-set and tried to close the gap of distance Talisa may have walked or hitched a ride in the few days lead she had over her.

If there was a village nearby Vicky thought it a good bet she would have gone there. She would be down on supplies and would want somewhere fairly safe to rest, at least for a night before moving on.

The lift doors opened and she turned into the corridor looking for her room number. She fumbled with her bags and dropped the key-card on the floor, grimacing at a twinge of abdominal pain as she bent down and wondered where she'd packed her medication.

She opened the door, humming aloud the tune in her head, and stepped inside and lent against the closed door, blotting out the immaculately dressed room before her as she clenched her fist around the old man's throat as she pinned him to a tree.

His English was non-existent, but that was acceptable as her Spanish was adequate enough. Oh she'd been there alright, and foolishly she'd enquired on how to get across the country, and had even secured a lift part of the journey.

'You left me crying, lonely and dying...,' she sang barely above a whisper as she left the old man for dead without having to risk even entering the village. Now all she needed to do was find her here in this hub of frenetic sun seekers. For the untrained it would be a hunt for a needle in a haystack but to Vicky it felt more like having dropped her keys down through the grating of a drain, she knew they were there but couldn't see them through the mucky grime, and all she needed to do was lift the drain and reach in and fish around. She'd studied Talisa Hayes well over the last couple of years and was confident she knew her well enough to hunt her out and wait for her to surface again.

It was providence that had brought her here and providence would see her through to the end.

PART TWO

PROVIDENCE

1

The first time was five years ago or there abouts, before Jack at any rate. The job had come through a third party, not her usual contact, a reliable soul who appeared and vanished with utmost ease but paid on account and didn't question her methods.

It was a simple job. One target subject. Make it look like an accident.

After watching her for a few days she had come to the conclusion that it was one of those jobs that even an amateur could have pulled off without too much difficulty, leaving her wondering why they were paying over the odds to have a professional take her out. She didn't know the reason, didn't care, and didn't care to ask.

Talisa Hayes, was in her late twenties, Irish, a legal secretary for a small firm in Dublin. She had a small flat in the city but spent most of her weekends with her parents and six brothers who lived on a farm outside of the southern end of the city. One of her brothers, the third eldest, Niall, also lived in the city with his girlfriend, and Talisa was of a habit of spending many weekday evenings in their company. She was a family girl who came from a tight nit Catholic community where the old fashioned ways were still applauded and the debauchery of social hedonism was firmly frowned upon. As a result Niall was the black sheep of the family, going against the conformist views of the other male siblings who ploughed the family field in his absence. Talisa, being the only daughter, was a constant worry to her parents for her decision to live in the city and to socialise with Niall, despite not sharing his views and being, if it were possible, even more prudish than her parents.

Talisa was always the odd one out in a crowd, not for her views for she hid them well, but for her stature and dress. She was short, barely above five feet in height, and regularly wore black or grey suits that hid the curves of her body, along with flat shoes that kept her level and unlady-like in her step. Her sometimes odd behaviour towards the opposite sex, or even sex in general, coupled with her straight bland fashion had sparked more than one or two rumours as to her sexuality, and unfounded whispers of lesbian encounters echoed along the bars in her absence; it was true to say that even her closest friends suspected she was hiding in a closet afraid to step out for either fear of her parents reaction or God's, but most probably both as she passionately revered the strong arm and authority of the church.

She wore her brown wavy locks long (but Vicky had noticed that in her later fretful flight across the globe her style had altered inconsistently as she attempted to disguise herself). She was healthy by all accounts with the exception of a prolonged hospitalisation for what should have been a simple procedure to remove an ovarian cyst.

Matthew Delaney was twenty five, tall and athletic. Being a desirable male among her social circle, and of a few years younger than she, it was well thought by their peers that the pair were mismatched, not that this deterred Talisa who found herself fortunate to have bagged such a catch. She knew that she was quirky, but within her self-professed style and character she was likeable and had a wide social circle of acquaintances (not so much friends, as she often tended to keep her distance from most as she feared getting too close to anyone – Matthew included). She knew of some of the rumours of her being gay and hoped that this relationship would finally put to bed the spiteful tongues that refused to accept her for who she was. She had no idea that her short entanglement with Matthew was nothing but a sham and that she was the victim of an elaborate bar room bet. That being that she had no idea of it until the day she died.

Vicky had observed it all. She had created her victims profile as she would any target, doing her homework as swiftly as possible and collating the facts before striking on a plan of action. Talisa's relationship with Matthew was a coiled spring wound up so tightly that the jack in the box wasn't patient enough to wait for the lid to be opened from the outside. So fiery was it that Vicky was fortunate enough to see it come to a head within a short time of tailing the couple.

A blazing row had erupted outside the petite girl's flat wherein Matthew had indiscreetly outed her frigidity across the street, a few heads turning in the evening light as the street lights flickered on to illuminate their stage. She was a boring and inexperienced kisser who was likely to remain a virgin for the rest of her life in the opinion of the boyfriend who was soon not to match up to the standard of even a friend. He had expostulated loudly that her views were outdated and that all she needed was a good hard shag. It was no wonder everyone thought she was a lesbian, but even dykes weren't as frigid and anally retentive as her. Not only that but that all her friends thought so too which was why they had dared him to get into her knickers and make a woman of her and pull her off the aloof pedestal she had placed herself on.

Stomping into her car, the keys rattling within a shaky hand barely able to get the door open, she sped off desperate not to hear the truth being yelled at her dinky red Mini as she pulled out into the road seeking the comfort of her parent's farm.

Vicky had followed. She had seen it all and had savoured every moment, finding the whole encounter quite amusing, but also seizing the moment knowing she was unlikely to get as fortuitous an opportunity as what was recklessly speeding away from her.

She crossed the river at Wood Quay, driving like a lunatic towards Ballsbridge and out through to Donnybrook. There were a couple of occasions where Talisa, clearly stewing and upset, slipped a gear in anger and frustration so that the engine roared ferociously, its temperament of revs and crunching of gears thundering the strained fiery expulsion spat out through the exhaust into Vicky's path behind, but it was not quite enough to extinguish the flame ignited within the closed confines of the car itself. In her rage of shame and humiliation and guilty sense of betrayal Talisa could have been followed by a fleet of Sherman tanks painted bright red with blue flashing lights and the fog horn of a steam liner and she would have known no different. The road was a blur before her but somehow she navigated it without incident. There were a few close calls admittedly and once or twice she was forced to apply the brakes a little more forceful than she'd at first intended to avoid a collision, all the while aiming for Clonskeagh and the judgement of mum and dad, but that was alright for at least there she knew where she stood.

Vicky was waiting for her chance to overtake. The traffic was too heavy coming out of town but now the streetlamps where growing sparse and the roads were narrowing and the walls of houses being replaced with hedges and stone walls of field boundaries and humps of streams. Vicky scanned ahead at the headlights snaking the path off in the distance and checked too the distance of the nearest lamps behind struggling to keep up with the pace set by Talisa. She dropped down a gear and thrust forward, swinging wide of the speeding Mini ahead and nipping in in front before the gap of the road closed on her. She showed Talisa her demon tail as she blazed away into the distance and disappeared into the gate of a field further along the lane. Vicky had killed her lights and quickly spun the car around in the narrow mud patch of the gate entrance in a hurry to coil back the way she came to play chicken on the single track lane, but with the key advantage of being able to see the oncoming traffic, something Talisa could not in the now blackened tunnel of road. At the last minute she flicked on her headlights to full beam and swerved only slightly to force Talisa in the direction she wanted her to go.

The Mini took to the air as it clipped the edge of a wall, spinning its rear wide a full 360°, smashing the bonnet against the trunk of a well rooted tree at a speed that folded the chassis in two like a slice of bread. At the very least Vicky supposed Talisa's head would have taken a beating numerous times against the cars frame as it pirouetted and then slammed hard into the tree, hopefully snapping her neck with the force, or at the very least crushing her internally as the steering wheel and the car's frame shunted against her.

Vicky waited a few moments for the oncoming traffic in both directions to catch up with the scene and then made as if to move her own car out of the road before switching off her lights once more and casually fading from the scene while everyone else raced to the aide of Talisa Hayes.

Driving back to the city Vicky Rivers sat smug behind the wheel of her car, knowing that if by chance the girl had survived the crash she could easily finish her off at the hospital without raising too much suspicion, for her wounds would be easily life threatening. She thought about the guilt that Matthew Delaney would feel upon finding out the fatal effects of his prank and how, no matter how he tried, he would be ostracised by all and played for as the stooge while everyone else praised the poor dead girl who never hurt a fly.

She drove into Ballsbridge before she turned around to revisit the scene to check on her subject. Normally in an urban area this would be too risky a venture but here it was rural enough for her not to be identified a second time travelling the same stretch of road.

The traffic indeed had stopped short of where the accident was and cars were doing three point turns to escape the holdup and find alternative routes. Vicky parked up about a comfortable twenty cars back in the queue and walked slowly and inquisitively, murmuring to other bystanders in her best Irish accent as the emergency services could be heard far over the hill with their blues flashing in the darkness.

"She's ok," she heard one man shout with a relieved smile on his face as his word echoed along the row of busybodies curious as to what was happening.

Vicky frowned and shook her head knowing this couldn't be the case; the man was mistaken, he had got it wrong. Nevertheless she stepped up her speed to get a better view of the crash site. As she got closer she could see where the door of the Mini had been prised open, a feat in itself, but as it turned out the first car to arrive on the scene was a mobile mechanic with tools fit for purpose in the rear. And to her surprise there stood, or rather half sat Talisa Hayes in a state of shock with her clothes splattered in blood but with no obvious wound to show for it.

Vicky sunk back into the shadows and avoided the wide eyed glare of her victim. She looked across at the crumpled wreck of the Mini and wondered how on earth she had escaped without serious injury.

Try as she might the next day Vicky failed to locate Talisa Hayes. She had vanished from the face of the earth. Matthew Delaney too had gone into hiding, taken in, it was thought, by a sympathetic ex-girlfriend. The family at the Hayes farm now posted the name of O'Hannon at their gate, which they locked firmly from prying eyes and didn't surface for days, although Vicky had spied in her observations a number of dark suited men coming and going a few days after the crash, but her attempts to trace them fell afoul of an urgent call away in search of Jack. The brother Niall, who was by far the most visual, carried on as though nothing was amiss.

It seemed that Talisa Hayes had suitably disappeared

in a situation that perplexed and worried Vicky as she wondered how to explain her failure to her employer, which, as it turned out, she was spared the embarrassment of as her completion settlement was paid at the appointed time with no questions asked.

Since then Talisa Hayes had grown much in the fascination of Vicky Rivers. She opened her file, which had breached out beyond the confines of its binder, and stared at the numerous photos she had of the different accident and crash sites where she had traced her to. Some were innocent, others not so, for Vicky had a penchant for the dramatic, using the mass fatalities to draw out the one, and the torrents of nature to disguise the deaths of many or the few.

The hidden boiler in the bathroom was humming, pipes gently vibrating along the bathroom worktop tapping Morse for the spiders that spun their webs covertly in the corners out of sight of human interference. The sounds usually blotted out beneath the gyrating fan of the walled in fourth floor hotel room. She cocked an ear to it as its tune played beneath the drum and bass rising up from the bar below. She joined the hum she favoured the pipes to be playing as the words echoed in her head. *Well you can drown me in the river, tears for the river,* her mind sang as she began to lay out the pictures hoping that here she would make a last stand against the girl who taunted her with her apparent immortality.

To Vicky it was unacceptable, being an agent that dealt in death, that there could be a girl who wouldn't die.

I'll weep a river for you.

2

The shell of dead road kill by the side of the road on the dusty grass verge was almost impossible to distinguish. It may at one time have been a rabbit or most probably a small dog, one of the many that roamed in packs often straddling sun baked lanes of pot holed tarmac away from the tourist track. Flies buzzed about the carcass, helicopters hovering awaiting their landing slot before touching down briefly to fly off to their next destination further along the mottled clump of fur and gore that had cemented itself into the baked grooves of the road where it would stay until the next heavy rain washed it away, or until enough of it had clothed the passing tyres and worn itself out of existence.

Talisa looked down at the carcass and fought the urge to vomit. She wasn't well and the slightest scent of foul odour was champing to churn her stomach. Part of it she thought was hunger; she hadn't eaten in at least two days as she made her way across country carefully steering clear of the main routes. She suspected, though, that not all that ailed her was lack of sustenance.

So many times she spied La Policía riding along on their motorbikes or cruising along in their cars. She'd ducked from sight each time and often too late but if they saw her they paid her no attention. She hoped that a penniless gringo was of little use to them but feared mostly what she'd be worth if they hauled her in and ran a check on who she was. Occasionally she thought she'd caught glimpse of the black sedan she'd often seen the company men driving; those men whom she'd seen in their dark suits and featureless faces, the ones who flitted into the crevasses' of her dreams whenever she tried to focus on them, the ones who stood behind doors and held her down and kept her shackled but whose names she never caught in their silence as she screamed at the reflection of her own face in their emotionless sunglasses.

There were worse things than the authorities. There were things that permeated through her nightmares into the waking world and hunted her down and tore at her limbs like a raging animal filled with bitter hate and disgust for what she'd become. And what was that? She didn't fully know herself nor understand why, but whatever it was it wasn't finished.

So she ran. She hid. She left her old life behind and when she was able she would stop and weep, crying with the pain and loss till her bones ached and the breath no longer drew in with her sobs. She longed to die, but that no longer seemed an option.

She could guess at what they'd done to her and in her dreams she had screamed at them to tell her, begging to understand the how and why, longing for her old life back. Then they would sedate her and tell her nothing while they probed her and conducted their tests.

How many times she had died she didn't know; she tried to forget, and often did, succumbing to a temporary amnesia which unfortunately didn't last long enough. Each death held its own individual pain. A bullet wound could fester as she felt the slug oozing its way through her veins seeking a way out as it was squeezed between muscle fibres, scraping bone in the search for an orifice to exit. Searing burns blistered her skin; the smell of charred flesh gagging at her throat as her nerves retracted and flinched at the pain of her peeling skin. Hearing the sound of her own bones breaking as she was crushed by a heavy object or by the downward momentum of her body on the solid ground below always choked her senses into a shock she would sadly recover from.

Occasionally she would be spared the pain and the reanimation would occur whilst her mind went blank, she having passed out before the event; this was rare but a welcome way to go, although drowning she had found more peaceful than she had ever expected, once she got over the initial panic of breathlessness that was, sucking in that final breath beneath the water when all became calm as she found she had no need to breathe to be conscious.

Wherever she went, no matter how she travelled, or with whom, she seemed magnetically linked to catastrophe. She cried out to God for compassion and mercy, begging him for leniency for her sins, beating her flat breast until she bruised and her knuckles cracked. Her petitions at first were humble and sincere but anger and rage soon took their hold as she bitterly argued with the god of her parents, challenging him to care and to prove himself until finally apathy blew over like a calm cooling breeze off the mountain and she turned her back on him, and with him the hope of any life she once had.

She had occasional flashbacks of her mother at Christmas time, and moving further back into her younger childhood of her father tossing her in the air and catching her in his arms. She flushed the memories away each time; they were too vivid, too dangerous.

She carried on walking away from the road kill and

towards the tall towers she could see off in the distance bordering the coastline like a line of trees at the edge of a felled forest. That was where she was aiming for, that was where she hoped she could hide, maybe secure a job and a room and blend into the crowd. She just hoped that bitch hadn't got their first.

She was sure to have followed the trail of the airline crash, but hopefully that would have been as far as she got. Talisa had learned enough about her to know she was in the pocket of the same people that had turned her into this monster. She knew that her name was Vicky and that Vicky was obsessed with finding and killing her. She didn't know what she had done to upset the psychotic murderous lunatic but she knew that the majority of her unfortunate events had been at her hand.

She assured herself that this time she had been careful, that there was no way she could know where she was heading, but nevertheless she walked the road fearful, jittery and panicking at every passing car.

Dust blew up in a cloud around her and she felt the nausea rise in her again as she caught a lungful. She winced as it grated dryly on her insides and coughed for fresh air, but none was forthcoming. Her cramps contracted again and she almost bent to one knee in response, knowing that this was no usual period pain, that she had felt this before a long time ago way back when, before they put her under. With the pain she felt hope; if only a rotting death from the inside would kill her once and for all.

3

Giles Montgomery was one of those London psychiatrists that typified that old fashioned stereotype of the English gentry, a professor who submerged himself in a nautilus of hard-spined and bland looking encyclopaedias, swooning gaily at the scent of ancient bound paper that folded dryly as it turned. Yes, Giles Montgomery fitted the image of that quaint old professor, an image he proudly portrayed through the décor of his office as he sat behind his sturdy mahogany desk in a throne-like wooden chair that stiffened his back at all times so that no slouching were aloud, not even from those who sat opposite in a chair more suitably uncomfortable, leaving his patients feeling small and insignificant in the varnished teak that sat half the size and with less than meagre padding.

Parting the piles of files, and neatly placed papers of obvious importance, or declaration of such, sat the triangular block perched like the polished glinting of a suspension bridge atop the wave of grainy brown, a block of mahogany just long enough for his name to be engraved onto the long gold plate stuck to one side so it could be viewed from his clients' seat as they sat down before him. Like everything else in his office, Giles Montgomery was just as quaintly old fashioned.

His manner, right down from his bushy crown of wiry grey that circled his flake strewn scalp, to the overgrowth of dirty brown and silver beard that wore the unchecked flakes of his morning toast, down to the sepia tweed blazer which surprisingly hung above a plain white shirt whose collar was left unbuttoned and missing the picturesque bow tie, held in totality an air of utter aloofness and arrogance that it was undeniable the level of superiority he awarded himself. Yet despite this, and being now beyond the years when he could have (and probably should have) retired, he still drew in a steady flow of clients, mostly recommended wealthy patients unaware he was riding still the heights of many a decades old reputation from the publications in the field that stamped his name across social policy and insight.

He sat reassuring his client in his deep uninteresting (and uninterested) tone of voice that was nothing but condescending, that she was far from mad, that he knew madness, not himself he stressed with a forced chuckle to a line he had repeated far too often, but that he had seen it in many a client and subjects he had studied and he was sure her odd behaviour and ticks of uncontrollable habit were not the works of an insane mind but of a troubled one, and yes he could help her unravel the causes and effect a different result over a period of time and lengthy discussion once or twice a week for the following few weeks. In a dismissive voice he concluded that she could book in with his secretary for their next meeting and any other enquiries such as payment could be directed through her – such things were clearly beneath him, and was that not his privilege and a measure of his success.

He had spent thirty minutes listening to his new client explain her woes and the intricacies of her life, and he had spent just over five minutes summarising what she had said and repeating many of her words back to her as he had written them down on his headed note paper using his gold plated Montblanc pen. Did she feel cheated? Probably. Did he care? So long as he got the respect he thought he deserved, not a darn bit.

He set his eyes down and scribbled some notes, determined not to raise his gaze until she had left the room. Rain was tapping its desire to enter the window through the grey wind that whistled up the drainpipe to the second floor office and drew him irritable as though the fingers of his late wife were tapping her impatience with him on the dinner table as he spoke of their future travels during the retirement he promised he would take. Now three years on and he was lonely and bored, wanting to take that retirement but no longer seeing its purpose as he had no one to share it with - and so he trundled along, growing bitter and regretful with each passing day.

The telephone rang and he answered it in his usual manner of one telling his name with indifference. He listened intently to the inquiry, his mind alert, his eyebrows arching as his back tilted to the strong steep cliff face of the chair behind. He scribbled down some notes as he briefly conversed with his ghostly conversant and then hung up the telephone. He circled something on the piece of paper and then put the pen on the desk and stroked his beard deep in thought, staring at the name of 'Vicky Rivers' he had just written on the page.

4

"Does God exist, Vicky?"

"Whose god? Your god? Which god exactly are we talking about?"

"Well, you tell me. Which god would you like to believe in?"

Vicky kicked back in the chair and laughed and turned her head to stare out the window. A few moments silence followed.

"We won't get anywhere by you closing up. You raised the issue of mortality and a superior deity; I'm merely delving into the possibility that there is someone or something directing your life."

"Directing me to hell you mean!"

"If that's what you believe. But I don't think it is, not truly, or else you wouldn't be here. You want to know if there is anything better for you, don't you?"

"You're full of shit, doc!"

Giles Montgomery smiled and said, "Thank you."

"Ok, say you're right and there is some big bearded guy up there..."

"I never said there *was* a god."

"Whatever. The bastard doesn't exactly care that much for me now, does he? Now the devil I can believe in. Now there's a figure I could relate to. I figure he's got a room all padded out and toasty for me already."

"And you're beyond redemption?"

There was another pause as the two sat across the

Formica desk, he gripping his thin brown beard that was speckled with wiry grey strands between his thumb and forefinger, she piercing his eyes with a blood thirsty glare. He had already removed the letter opener he had accidently left on top of the otherwise bare table as she had entered the empty rented office that he sometimes used for some of his more exclusive or erratic clients. Vicky Rivers was both, having been referred by his esteemed clients that sent some of their more disturbed employees to him for evaluation. It hadn't taken him long to identify her sociopathic tendencies and violent attributes, not that he was surprised in any way for he'd known her way before the company had sent her as a client.

"I don't need redemption."

"Oh, how so?"

"If there is a god, who is to say I'm not doing his work?"

"By killing people?"

"If they were good no one would want them dead."

"Do you really believe that?"

"Some people deserve to die."

"Are we talking about anybody in particular here?"

"Leave him out of it!"

"Who? Leave who out of it, Vicky?"

"I don't want to talk about it old man."

"You know we'll have to at some point Vicky. Tell me, do you think God used him in the same way?"

"I don't understand."

"What he did to you as a child, do you think that was providence? If so what was its purpose? Do you think God was punishing you? For what?"

Vicky didn't answer but threw her gaze to the window.

"Do you think God uses you both? Are you both ministers of providence?"

"Don't you dare liken me to him!"

She kicked back her chair, her long brown curly locks fluttering besides her ears and over her shoulders as she rose to leave. At least he hoped she was leaving and not about to lurch forward at him. He had been on the receiving end of her wrath before and now always made sure he had a table between them and a loaded gun taped to the underside of the desk. She knew about the gun, and so did her employers; it was by mutual agreement that things would be smoothed over if ever it had to be used.

"Out of interest, what are you reading at the moment Vicky?"

"Screw you!" she bellowed as she bolted from the room.

5

To say Vicky Rivers had been one of his most enterprising clients would be an understatement. So much of his life's work had been based around the profiling of her psyche: her troubled childhood, her traumas, her disengagement with life, her health problems, her drug addictions, her promiscuity, and her lack of conscience and care for life itself, be it hers or anyone else's.

His mind could have taken him back to many a point in her life where their paths had crossed but this one in particular had stuck in his mind, the one meeting he regretted most of all.

He could have written volumes on Vicky Rivers, and in a way had written a few, not that anyone would ever know the nameless subject of many a hypothetical thesis was in fact based on the real life exploits of one unbelievable life. She was a gem that he had dropped in the ocean, not once but twice, and here she was resurfacing again.

He had mountains of files on her locked away, files he had gladly buried. She had died to him twice already and thanks to him others had died too. How much of the guilt had chiselled his character over his later years he wasn't sure. His wife, Rachel, had told him to abandon her, not that he ever told her the intimate details, or even her name (patient confidentiality and all), but the recurrence of such an enigma as Vicky Rivers had to be shared in part, if for nothing else than to relieve the burden.

Rachel had warned him that he had begun to obsess over her and that his apparent intrigue into drawing closer to her mind was a dangerous endeavour. She was right of course, she usually was, he thought with regret. Yet still he kept her on as a client. Still he studied her. Still even when she no longer came to visit for her sessions he would trace her exploits and study her patterns and attempt to foil the plans of her mind by unlocking that which held her captive, desperate was he to undo what he had condoned.

Rachel had argued that he hadn't created the monster; he was no Frankenstein. The monster lived before she ever entered his laboratory, which was why she was there in the first place. To this he had no comeback, for once again she was right. Had his choice of words that day been different her killing spree may not have developed with so much lust.

She had left his session that day with thoughts of being of God's right arm and she saw him, Giles Montgomery, as her advocate. He had hoped to draw out her thoughts on religion in order for her to examine the roles of life and death and the fragility of experience, a proven technique he had applied on many occasions with many patients as he manipulated and controlled conversations to draw out the things they had never thought to delve into. Depending on her mood Vicky was known to joke about death and be curt about death, but never to cry unless it was about her mother. Death to Vicky was a regular flippant topic to which he had found it hard to draw any true merit from and he had used the religious theme with her a number of times without her engaging in any serious intent.

He shook his head as he began leafing through her

files for the Polish gentleman from the company who requested a summary report of her history and mental state. The photographs of some of the dead that sat in her file he was ashamed of, for it was he that had planted the idea of providence in her head, and she had grasped at it eagerly to justify her means.

6

It was amazing she could see anything through the glare as the sun sparkled off the sea across the road of the strip of Cancún's main hotel district. Sand was strewn over the tarmac having been blown up from the crowded beach on the far side from where she walked. What she did see was the glint off metal and glass as tourist hire cars and excursion buses sped along in the midday heat. Beyond this the world was a blur as her tongue hung limp and dry; a lizard on a desert dune would feel less parched she thought after her long walk and aimless meanderings familiarising herself with her surroundings. So through this blur how she had spotted her she couldn't fathom, unless of course it was a mirage and her mind was playing tricks on her. In a moment of doubt she puzzled over the city scape and wondered whether if she turned around quick enough it would all disappear from sight and she would find herself strapped into a chair surrounded by doctors testing her and probing her under sedation.

She shook off the feeling and refocused on the car that had caught her attention. She couldn't make out the model but thought it was a dark green colour or possibly even blue, her headache wouldn't allow her to target it properly as she squinted her eyes to follow its journey. She stood still to watch it drive north away from her and marked its position as it turned into a driveway besides a high-rise hotel.

It took her a few minutes to reach the point she thought the car had turned into and spent those hesitant steps doubtfully double checking her senses as she walked towards impending danger.

Talisa had only caught the smallest of glimpses of the driver: dark hair and pale skin, a tourist for sure and one who had only recently arrived for her pallor was yet to wear the dusting of tan that all sun seekers bathed in. Even with a slight side profile Talisa had thought she recognised the ear and nose and strong jawline and cheek bones that were unmistakably belonging to Vicky.

What had she been doing, adjusting the radio, lighting a cigarette? She couldn't be sure, but she had a frozen image in her head, almost a photograph imprinted of the driver snapped against the slopping waves of the Caribbean.

But if it was her, why the hell was she walking towards her?

In truth she didn't know for sure but she tried to convince herself that if she knew where Vicky was holed up and could watch her movements then she would for once have an advantage. The fear of always being on the run and not knowing when someone, an assassin or company agent, would leap out at her left her nerves in tatters so that she would often jump at her own reflection as she walked passed a shop window or caught herself unawares in a mirror. She would often give a thick tree a wide berth and would be suspicious of anyone whose hands looked like they were about to reveal a hidden object from beneath a coat or bag - fortunately here that was less likely due to the lack of attire being worn in the midday sun.

What she would do when she found Vicky she hadn't quite thought through yet as seeing her so soon was so unexpected. Hide and observe, figure out her movements and her plans and then hit her when she least expected it - it was a loosely forming plan of action but one she had never once thought she'd be in a position to enact as running and hiding was for so long her means of survival.

She tentatively turned the corner of the driveway, careful of who was about before exposing herself fully. There was a hotel bellboy smoking to the side of the main hotel entrance which lumbered in a recess hidden back from the road with its pinnacle rising high above trying to catch the distant wisps of white dancing spectral doves in the sea of blue above. The bellboy didn't notice her as she hid behind a dumpster and crouched down with a clear view of the hotel lobby and the expanse of car park where the car was now parked unattended.

***

How slowly time passes when you're stood just waiting for something to happen. Bikini clad girls bronzed up and glistening and laughing under their wide shades carrying their beach towels, books and whatever else necessary to lay beautiful and adoring on the beach walked back and forth without identity or any sense of individualism. There were couples also but these were few and far between as though this particular edge of the resort was where couples baited each other rather than spent a romantic break. She was jealous nonetheless. At one point a group of chiselled young men in bermuda shorts, in their early twenties she guessed and all with loud brash American accents, fell out of the hotel lobby whistling and jeering jokingly after three shapely girls that had just walked out ahead of them. She watched them go from her hiding place behind the dumpster, the smell of the garbage can overdue to be emptied, her eyes and heart discarding the aroma as she pined for a different life.

She'd had it once, or so she thought. She had escaped to Canada and had found herself lost wandering the bitter cold towns of the northern hemisphere, something her thin frame took little to as biting chills gnashed at her bones and stilled her senses so that her thoughts were short to comprehend. It could have been the ideal place to hide had she not found herself there in the deep of winter with little shelter to comfort her. Of Canada she knew little but of what she'd seen on telly: snow, skiing, mountains, and Niagara Falls. The Falls, being a tourist attraction, would provide work, she reasoned. If she could get up enough money she could go elsewhere, maybe get a plane to Washington or Boston or lose herself in New York, slowly making her way south to a warmer climate.

She had always suffered from colds as a child; being slight she came down with every bug to be passed around the school yard and her parents instilled in her that she never had a chance to avoid the plague. It had crossed her mind whether they had anything to do with her current predicament, in all good faith wanting the best for her she was sure, but still, how could they? Her doubt about their motives niggled at her until she cast them out of her life as if they be demons constantly sitting upon her shoulder. She hoped it were coincidence that Vicky had shown up each time shortly after she had made a call home to say where she was and that she was safe.

All those illnesses of her childhood were gone now, now not even a sniffle as she stood naked in the snow - something she had to do only once as she tried to bathe in the icy waters of a lake after days of hitchhiking to find herself in the middle of nowhere, having abandoned her ride of a pimped up old man who in his leering French accent had gesticulated his intention and then, with one hand on the steering wheel, had masturbated in front of her and tried to pull her head down by the hair towards him. She had punched and bit hard and wailed like a banshee until he was forced to loosen his grip and slow the car enough to throw herself out at which he sped off without checking to see if she was hurt.

It was one of the dangers of travelling alone, but it was one she couldn't avoid, and she took comfort in the fact that whatever they did to her she would heal, physically at least.

Her period had come on strong then and again she had been caught out in the middle of nowhere without money or supplies and feeling dirty. The dip in the lake was like being baptised. As she rose out of the water she felt refreshed and awake and ready to start anew. It was then she decided to head for Niagara Falls.

Almost three months she had spent at the Falls, the longest she had stayed in any one place, and it was all down to JP.

Jean Paul confusingly was an American citizen having emigrated from France as a boy and had found work translating for tourists visiting the monumental site in Ontario. On first meeting him she had taken him for a French speaking Canadian, but his accent dipped occasionally into the abrupt and mispronounced vowels of New Jersey. He was a short but not unhandsome man, his black hair and straight nose sharply distinguishing his heritage, his brooding eyes speaking of soulful, deep, and sad thoughts. They were of a similar age and shared tastes in food and music, but most importantly for Talisa was that he was kind and gentle and patient. He didn't once try to pressurise her for sex, though they kissed, and she even let her guard down enough to let him fondle her breasts through her jumper, she moving his hand swiftly upwards if he tried to tug up at her top to get underneath, but he never complained and always complied with her wishes.

She could have stayed in JP's arms for as long as he would have her; she felt safe with him and was soon forgetting the danger she was in.

She understood enough at this point of what had happened to her, having pieced together the fragments of images that swelled up through her dreams. She had searched the internet for company logos and names she caught snapshots of in the peripheral of her nightmares in an attempt to picture the puzzle as a whole, but too many pieces were missing. She didn't know the full story but she knew enough, or at least suspected enough to be scared.

PJ wasn't to know who it was that froze the blood in her veins as they walked along the path at the top of Horseshoe Falls. Suddenly she went the colour of snow and as rigid as ice, halting in her tracks allowing PJ to walk on a couple of steps before realising that she wasn't beside him. Her pause was momentary, but at the time it was a monumental slowing of reality, her mind speeding up in a dozen definitive life changing decisions that ultimately left their lives hanging in the balance.

PJ would never understand what she did next, nor would he ever know that her actions were to protect him and deflect him as a target. Surely if she stayed close to him he would have lurched forward to protect her, but it would have cost him his life.

She was still far off but her strong stature and gait gave her away along the deserted pathway. So many times they had walked off together hand in hand to routes little known to tourists, and rarely of late had she been alone. Thinking on this later she was convinced that Vicky had been watching her movements and waiting for the opportunity where she had few places to run. The path was narrow, fenced over the falls by a thirty foot railing with crushing water on both sides with only a long run behind her as a means of escape, and the stronger, fitter assassin could easily outrun her she was sure.

To PJ she would always be that quirky Irish lass who had crossed the pond in search of adventure; the guilt and suspicion that would fall on him later she often blotted from her mind, except in those moments of weakness when she attempted to put pen to paper to let him know she still lived and that it wasn't his fault. She could never get the words to flow to the page and the paper would always end up crumpled up and tossed aside. It was for the best.

The stop watch of time restarted and Talisa was scaling the railings. Jean Paul rushed to stop her, not understanding, thinking initially she was larking about, but then his voice slowing and rising in pitch with concern as his eyes widened at the rise of her leg as she breached the top bar and perched there, bare skinny legs on the metal flashing her wares and taking one last look along the path before sliding down the far side with tightened fists gripping the bitter cold bars. Over his shoulder he didn't see what was coming, but she did. 'I'm sorry', she whispered quickly letting go to throw herself back into a dive to the torrent of cascading water.

She emerged 180 feet below and further downstream near the Journey Behind the Falls observation platform. As she lifted her head for breath she felt the bones clicking back into place within her but her flesh was numbed to the burning pain which was bathed in the soothing icy current that held her waif frame. Her eyes cleared the water enough to see faces peering into the water searching for the figure that had been seen hurtling down with the water, fortunately they were all looking in the wrong place for she had managed to swim with the current submerged as she came to her senses. Looking up, only one figure remained a tiny panic stricken spec in the distance and she knew then that the chase was on.

She slipped beneath the water again and swam as far as she could knowing it would be dark soon and Vicky would lose her scent in what to her was unfamiliar territory. Time was on her side but how far she would get she hadn't known. Part of her always wanted to go back for Jean Paul but her heart told she would never know that feeling of happiness and security again.

The heat of the outdoor car park was in complete contrast to that day of her icy swim.

A couple of cars had pulled into the car park during

the time she'd been crouched uncomfortably in her hiding place, a bedraggled rat, starving and tired.

A rental pulled in and circled the car park before pulling up close behind the car she had seen Vicky driving, then it found a spot of its own and its driver got out, flicked a cigarette butt on the floor and circled Vicky's car. He felt the hood and stared through the windows, all the while looking around furtively as though he were about to break into the car.

This guy had a lighter complexion than the locals and was much taller too. He was thin and wore a moustache beneath a bush mop of hair that distracted from his face. He returned to his own car and withdrew a bag and then headed into the hotel, stopping to speak to the bellboy who now sat unprofessionally on the steps smoking a cigarette. The new arrival lifted what looked like a mobile phone and showed its face to the bellboy, a young Mexican lad who seemed to care little for his job. He nodded agreement to the stranger and pointed in the direction of the car of interest and then waited patiently with an open palm for his gratuity.

The handful of steps to the entrance were climbed swiftly and the door opened for the new guest with an appreciative smile, perhaps in hope of being of further assistance. The stranger then walked up to the reception desk and appeared to Talisa to book himself a room.

There were many people Talisa thought might want to track this bitch down but she had no idea which group or individual this particular character represented, not that she cared, for anyone hunting Vicky meant that there was an added distraction allowing her to play in the shadows and gain even more of an advantage.

7

The day was drawing to an end and Vicky couldn't help but wonder where Talisa was hiding. She had hoped to come across her by now and was eager to get it over with for they were certain to have sent someone after her by now. She had played in her mind so many times how she was going to kill Talisa Hayes but in every scenario everything failed. The only way she could achieve any satisfaction was to capture her and bind her and bleed her dry, torturing her until the life-force no longer had a will to survive - and then, and only then, would she dismember the body and send the parts to the far flung corners of the globe. The thought of it made her salivate and she rubbed her lips, both on her face and below, with excitement. She donned a thin dress and made her way out of the hotel room and down to the outdoor pool bar hoping she could satisfy the itch she had between her legs.

The sun had faded already and the bar was empty. She was too early and in her haste realised that dinner had just begun to be served in the restaurant and the queues of hungry guests had just fed in to satisfy their empty stomachs on the all-inclusive buffet. Suddenly she felt hungry and knew she would have to return to her room to get her medication.

Another guest was walking along the corridor and passed her door as she exited the lift on the fourth floor, she paid him no attention as she walked up to her door and slid in the key card. She grabbed what she needed and walked back to the elevator, hearing the movement of another door and footsteps. She held the lift doors expecting company but none came.

Dinner was lonely as she watched the people filing in and filling their faces greedily and leaving their marks on the glasses. She loved to watch the odd couples together, some talking dynamically, but most amusing of all were those who barely said a word to each other as though life itself had become such a bore that it wasn't even worth sharing with the person they were living it with, surely it couldn't just be total boredom of each other - they were zombies feeding off each other's indifference to life.

The pain hit her again as she ate and she rubbed at her abdomen and slurped at her table water to ease the dryness on her tongue. The tablets helped and it soon subsided but she was way over due for a check-up and these latest symptoms were a bad sign.

She made her way out after eating to the pool bar once more. It was to the other side of the hotel from the car park, the infinity pool itself sprawling out towards the fenced off road, risen high enough for the merging of the water flowing into the sea if you lined yourself up along the pool edge, so long as no tall vehicles were passing to spoil the illusion.

She wanted to get laid but the meal and the pain had dampened her longing and her mind was settling more on the task at hand. She hatched a plan in her head to wander the clubs and bars looking for Talisa, maybe returning back here later if she didn't score one way or another

8

Giles was sure she had planned Jack's demise an infinite number of times in her mind, an idea that had probably grown steadily over the years like a fungus or a cancer, small at first and barely visible leaving no obvious symptom of its existence as it silently festered in the recesses of her mind. The hatred would have birthed much earlier, once the numbness had worn off and her thoughts narrowed in her confinement till she could contain them no longer. Had it not been for her illness distracting her momentarily then maybe she would have self-destructed much earlier and never developed into the prime killer she was today. Giles had taught her the word 'providence' so that not only was she a killer but now she thought it was her calling - and her primary target was Jack Walters.

She bided her time with Jack, researching him, studying him, getting to know his every tick and mannerisms. She knew what he liked to read and read the same. She knew his taste in the arts, in music and film and so submerged herself entirely in his life. Yet all the while he never knew she existed.

Vicky seduced her subject with tantalising glimpses from afar, attracting him in the one thing he had become expert in - murder. It was to emulate Jack that she became a killer, but now that he was dead she didn't know how to stop.

Only Vicky Rivers knew the truth about Jack Walters, who he was and what he had done to her. Giles knew it in part but only from what he had pieced together from being privileged enough to have known her back story.

Any other psychiatrist assigned to Vicky Rivers would have been stumbling about in the dark as she gave little away in conversation, but he'd known her since she was the traumatised little girl held captive and abandoned in the institution.

Giles, sat now in his office with his head propped up in the cup of his hand as he flicked page after page of her extensive file, dreamt back to the days when he was employed on contract to social services, a spunky and arrogant upstart still wet behind the ears trying to prove himself as he toiled the family cases that circled Surrey's growing pile of failing families in the early 1980's.

A case had come in that had caused a stir across the nation and which involved Vicky Rivers. Giles had nothing to do with it at the time but a few years later he gained work with a government institution for the mentally incapable. The Manor House Hospital in Epsom was an unremarkable building serviced by capable, and for the most part, caring staff. He had no doubt as the years passed that one or more staff were guilty of atrocities upon the patients and that the patients were incapable of resisting or speaking up about their mistreatment. Vicky was one such a victim and had confirmed to him what he had only ever suspected. It was a likely contributory factor to her sexual promiscuity that she had somehow managed to wield to her advantage and unbelievably managed to avoid, to his knowledge, contracting any diseases. Motherhood, due to her condition, had never been an option once she had left the institution, which fortunately wasn't known in the earlier years for if it had she would have been treated little less than a mannequin of young subtle flesh, much more so than she had.

It had always been thought that she was dead. Officially she had committed suicide when she was a teenager after struggling to cope with her family loss and her illness. No one suspected the aid she had from a compassionate staff member willing to put all on the line to hatch a plan to help her disappear upon hearing the news that Jack had escaped.

Giles should have reported her re-emergence to the authorities when by chance she graced his door again, now older and more intriguing a patient, but his curiosity overwhelmed him and his fear of betraying his client too strong. She remembered him and it was maybe that which gave him a window back into her life. Had anyone else received her as a patient she would no doubt have played games in hiding the mystery of who she was and what had happened to her. Her acceptance of him gave him hope that she wanted to be helped; she wanted someone to connect her to her childhood to help her reconcile her pain.

Instead he had planted the idea that God was using her. He tried to talk her out of it, of course he did, but she fancied herself to Edmund Dante, fancying herself the favourite of a deity, a god whom she would speak to and confess all too. Like Monte Cristo, bestowed with riches to enact Gods purposes, she had discovered a talent her god had bestowed on her to enact her vengeance and then to seek a purpose, a justification for it, and looked back on her installation at the mental home as Dante's detention at the Chateau d'If.

She had no deliberate religious allegiance or even a

true faith in the Christian god, or any other, but confirmed in herself that she was committed to a higher purpose and was destined to seek righteous retribution and bring it upon those who had wronged her - and Jack Walters was her singular target.

His end had come fittingly in a quiet and empty church, a bullet through the head as she finally revealed who she was, quoting as she did so a line from one of his many favourite quotes from literature, so she had boastfully retold it to Giles in one of their sessions.

Her killing spree hadn't ceased at Jack, if anything it had intensified as she lusted uncontrollably for the thrill she expected it to give her to fill the empty void within her.

Giles had hypothesised about who she would become upon killing Jack and what would happen to her afterwards, how she would cope with a life without purpose, knowing that the self-destruction that she had escaped so many years ago would finally catch up with her. He gave it a name also, indirectly suggested it at least, and Vicky, hanging on his every word, had nurtured it in the dark corners of her mind.

9

Vicky walked along the stretch of beach for hours, occasionally sitting on the sand to rest her feet as she took a break from playing lioness in the wilderness of clubs and bars ready to pounce on her prey at any moment, rushing through the wildebeest to get to her slight gazelle who no doubt would take to flight leaping for the nearest smoky exit into the dark night outside. The night was good; Vicky liked hunting in the dark.

Her feet were weary and she had abandoned her slip-ons (comfortably disguised to run in which matched nicely with the loose fitting dress that concealed her ghost holster) and had taken the opportunity of massaging the sand with her toes.

There were a few trees here as she came to the end of the strait of reclaimed land where it curved inland to a ragged bay of weather beaten rock. She brushed the dusting of sand that clung to her shins and stepped towards the edge of the water she could hear swishing but couldn't clearly see. Turtles were known to come ashore along this coast to lay their eggs in the sand of the beaches. She had seen a few pitches of sticks tied with tape over ditches dug by their flippers. The locals, she'd been told, often walked the beaches to preserve the eggs from tourists in the hope that they would safely hatch in due time. She looked along the stretch of beach in both directions peering into the darkness for any low lying boulder shapes flumping slowly across the sand. She knew they came at night but so far, like now, and like all else at the moment, they eluded her.

She sighed her disappointment and looked out across the sea and at the brooding waves splashing their annoyance at each other.

Here they are hidden in the depths of darkness blown in by the torrent beast that drives them thus; rabid frothing as they drive home the monster of destruction as it tears away and deposits afresh in unison as the deep relentlessly pounds from the rear offering up its discarded debris as the moonlit hound races in. I can't see you but I know you are there!

So her thoughts swam as she likened herself to the waves and her deity the monster, that driving wind forcing her on.

She gripped her stomach as the pain tightened a knotted fist around her insides. The spasms were increasing and the drugs were no longer slowing its onslaught.

"There's no such thing as pain, only intense sensations," she said to herself aloud through gritted teeth. It was a mantra an old martial arts instructor had taught her as he forced her through blood and tears to keep striking the Wing Chun wooden dummy. She hated him for it but was thankful that he didn't relent on the bargain; she had paid him in kind for the abuse after all, like so many other things, she had sought it out.

There were many things she'd learnt in her early twenties when cutting her teeth and sharpening her claws to learn her craft. Odd quirky things that stuck in her mind like gum on a sidewalk. She remembered being told by Mace, an old pro that had taken her under his wings, that if you wanted to steal a car or rob a house or commit any crime do it during a storm, 'those dumbass police don't want to get wet you see, it's that old saying "a good policeman never gets wet" and India 99 won't be able to fly so no tracking from above.' He'd been a shrewd old bastard and being ex-job he knew how to stay out of their way; but she never did get the story from the cantankerous old git as to why he'd left the Metropolitan Police Service and joined up with London's east end gangs as their hard hitting batter, but she suspected he was just a greedy pig who had slopped his muck too near the gate and his colleagues got wind of him so he baled before he got caught. His greed got him into trouble with his own gang too as he took a back hander to duck a hit, faking the outcome with the inevitable outcome of Vicky receiving her first envelope on someone she knew. She handled it well and without emotion and earned the respect she needed to step up a level.

Vicky's education in her craft was much like Jack's. She had emulated much in him with the aim of overtaking him, excelling where he had failed in order to surpass him and eventually turn back and bite him where it hurt most. Jack had been a loner from the beginning, but Vicky had learned the value of team, not that she didn't like working alone, it was just that she could take jobs he couldn't by being prepared with a team of like-minded players that respected her command. The plane job was a prime example: Jack had been offered it first but had predictably turned it down and Vicky had taken up the reins being prepared to scout the private jet and get her own flight crew on board so that she could take out the two VIP's on board before baling the downed jet. She had put it together swiftly and simply with hardly any planning and on such short notice - the hardest part had been loitering near the toilets to watch a stewardess tap in the 3 digit code into the security door for the lift to the south wing of the staff lounge, once she had access there disabling the genuine flight crew and getting her own team in place was easy. It was a job she was well proud of.

She had picked up a lot of tricks just by observing Jack over the years, not that he ever suspected he had a stalker. Neat and simple tricks she liked the best, like carrying a baseball cap in case of cameras, or wearing a reversible jacket to slip into the crowd, and particularly she liked his propensity to submerge into character to study and subdue his target. There were other things he taught her too: if something felt wrong to him he would walk away (like when he didn't go back for the family photo she'd left him because he'd parked his car too far away - if he had gone back to get it instead of following his instinct to abandon the car then he wouldn't have walked into the church, although on that occasion it had worked in her favour), or if something didn't go immediately to plan he would simply walk away. So why hadn't she?

Did it matter?

She cross examined her reasoning. She copied Jack. Jack had become predictable. She'd lured him to the church. Jack died.

What was Jack's fault, being predictable or following his instincts?

So why am I doing both, being predictable and following my instincts, if both got him killed?

With all that had happened with Talisa ever since that first botched attempt - why hadn't she walked away? Pride? Was it vanity bracing her in its clutches taunting her with the one who wouldn't or couldn't die?

She would not fail! She would not be defeated!

She violently shook her head to dismiss her own misgivings. So what if Jack had gotten predictable. He had walked into her trap. Did she feel better for it, hell no!

She hoped she wasn't making the same mistakes as him.

What if she's second guessing me *now?*

She swept her head over her shoulder suddenly frightened someone was there watching her or lurking in the shadows waiting to creep up behind her.

She thought of Ahab stubbornly pursuant of his prize of the white whale, and Roland of his dark tower, a list of names and historical and literary figures beginning to fill her mind washing in with the waves: Odysseus and his longing for home; Menelaus chasing his disloyal and adulterous wife Helen; Alexander and his thirst for territory and the crown of a deity; Pharaoh and his pursuit of the Israelites; Gollum and his search for his 'precious', the ring to rule them all, all the way to his doom at Mordor. And was that not what they all had in common? An eventual doom.

"But Odysseus made it home and the dwarves got their mountain and the Jews got their promised land," she whispered to herself.

'Yes, but at what cost?' argued the voice in her head.

A shudder went down her spine as the warm night breeze that blew in danced around her a heavy hint of an expectant downpour. She spun round again as though aware of being watched. Again there was no one there but that didn't make her feel any better. She rubbed off the pain in her mid-drift and cast it from her mind - *there's no pain, there's no pain!* The words echoed in rhythm with the crashing waves giving poetic motion to her chant as she turned away from the sea.

She'd had enough for one night and had a strange longing to be back in the security of the hotel.

10

It had taken Sergio almost an hour to re-emerge from his room after his nerves gave way. He couldn't believe he almost got busted. Sure he'd mixed with enough bad boys in his time to have a certain amount of courage and bravado to hold his own in a gang and even now years later would willingly break the odd law as a means to an ends, but he had never meddled with outright cold blooded killers.

He had no idea how to get the hotel door open as he was completely thwarted by the electronic key slot and had stood outside the door wondering how much it was likely to cost to get a spare key from José, the cheeky delinquent bell boy he'd met on the way into the hotel, and then how much it would cost to buy his silence. He had been stood at the door pondering all this when he heard the lift doors open and quickly took a step back and turned to walk away, just in time as he sensed someone turn the corner behind him and follow him along the corridor. He swore under his breath as he heard her stop outside the room and slip the key-card in. He kept walking, resisting the temptation to turn around and look as she entered the room. He had managed to secure a room along the same corridor and calmly made his way there, only then daring to look along the empty passageway between the doors staring out at him through their goldfish bowl lens as he cracked open the door.

From the safety of his room he felt the crotch of his pants to find out just how much had trickled out, it wasn't noticeable but he closed his eyes and allowed his clammy forehead to hit the door.

"Pull yourself together Vanni!" he ordered himself.

He was out of his comfort zone. Tracking people he could do. Watching people he could do. Breaking into the room of a professional killer was most definitely out of his league. What the hell was Tomasz expecting him to find anyway?

Up to now Carmela had been indispensable with providing him information and searching the internet to keeping him on track, how much the business at home was suffering as a result he tried not to think about but it brought home to him just how much more she was than a secretary, she was his guardian angel. She had warned him to be careful of Tomasz and not to take any unnecessary risks and to get his backside home to Italy as soon as practicably possible.

Tomasz wanted him to sit tight and observe and find out what she was up to, who she was meeting, 'get into her room and snoop around', he'd been told, but he couldn't do it. He was scared and he was missing his family.

He etched open the door when he heard her leave again, watching her move back towards the elevators. He stepped out to follow knowing he at least needed to see where she was heading but he failed to get more than a few steps before he back tracked to his room again. She was probably heading to dinner, he argued, and he would see her down there when he went for his own meal.

He sat in his room for the next hour deliberating over whether or not to try her room again but after attacking the mini bar for a beer he decided it wasn't worth getting himself killed over.

He made his way eventually down for dinner but by then she had left the hotel's restaurant. He kept an eye open instead for José, hoping to build on any useful information he could provide and hopefully secure himself an easier access to her room, but he was a no show so he flirted innocently with one of the entertainment team as he made himself comfortable around the pool bar.

He figured the bell boy would start the early shift in the morning and so made a mental note to rise early and try to catch him then.

***

The day had been muggy and humid, even in the late afternoon by the pool when he had arrived, cruising along the poolside and checking out the facilities to familiarise himself with his surroundings and sizing up the likely places Vicky might attend, even then the temperature seemed uncannily uncomfortable, but he had just put it down to his acclimatising. There was no desire to exert much energy in the heat of the day to promote the ooze of damp sweat from the pores that had already begun to seep into the thin shorts and light cotton shirt with its colourful design and obligatory 'Cancun' emblazoned logo which he bought from the hotel gift shop, the shop which sold every possible and needless artefact and memento of the trip from the hideously embossed paperweight and beach towel to the baseball cap and snorkel gear, of course it also sold the essentials such as suntan lotion snacks and the overpriced soft drinks, but that wasn't its main trade, and whether you loved it or hated it a visit to the hotel shop was a necessity and an imperative part of the holiday whether you intended on buying anything or not. For Sergio it had been a necessary evil as he had already exhausted the supplies in his overnight bag and had come ill prepared for the exhausting sun that showered down on him. So happily replenished with a cap, T-shirt, shorts, sunglasses, sandals, and sun tan lotion, he was ready to hit the pool.

He did feel a tad guilty at the extravagance of lounging as if on holiday all at the expense of others, especially as his wife was stuck at home tending to the children, but he felt it was justified as he hadn't taken a break in days and had done a lot of travelling about and was likely to do still more before he was home again; it was a perk of the job - and besides, he didn't have a clue at that point where his target was nor why she was here.

As he sat by the pool there had been a slight wind, or at least the slight sensation of one, in truth it was brisk, evidenced only by the waving trees planted within the grounds of the hotel garden and the flapping beach towels that refused to stay on the loungers without the weights of their charge, the sun cutting through to scorch the already crisp skin of violet and red and slowly browning in a rainbow of pain and flake. He watched many enviously take a cool refreshing dip in an overcrowded pool to cool off before resuming with dog eared books soiled by the damp of their swimming costumes, the books themselves only read by a few as eyes hid behind the shaded lenses as the pages flopped and the eyes drooped.

He thought about returning to the gift shop to buy some swimming shorts but resisted knowing that he wouldn't be able to follow her quickly enough if she suddenly emerged into view.

He watched the unique body shapes of every size, some chiselled and well kempt, others with curves that held no respectability in the skimpy outfits that clung to them, bellies of pregnancy hung on men and thighs of elephants on women yet in all no offence made or taken, all was acceptable, all was normal, the perception of perfect, imperfect, and abnormal as the models cast in plastic melted away into a false façade under the spotlight of the sun.

But now night had fallen how different the hotel gardens and pool felt.

Sitting in a white plastic chair with a slowly warming bottle of beer on an equally synthetic table, Sergio's weariness of the past couple of days seemed to dissipate and a restlessness creased his brow in a wave of haze that hovered more gently than the flies he could see skimming and skirting off the chlorinated edge where one of the hotel's skinny feral cats had left a small deposit earlier on the tiled ledge.

In the heat of the pool bar at night there were couples drinking solicitously in hushed whispers, women walking around in bikinis despite the over pungent odour of deet wafting from others sat around, a few made pleasant conversation with the bar staff, a few gratuity bills passing hands with the drinks as the friendly light hearted banter clamoured above the simmering murmur that hid the birds and crickets and rustling wind as the tempting storm in the distance blew the palms gently, the smell of sea air rising with the waves breaking on the beach nearby. A recorded quartet under laid the scene as it sang out from the small speakers attached to the wooden pillars supporting the thatched roof of the circular bar, the foreign sounds strumming in what in any other setting would have been an annoying and unwelcome cacophony but which here fell easily on ears that allowed it to fill the background along with the waves and wildlife which sank beneath the focus of their attention.

An attendant mopped the poolside whilst silent stargazers reclined back on the sun loungers mapping the constellations or cuddling a loved one in the shelter of the shadows, only noticeable should you wander too close upon the smooching pair. A hue of yellow lights lit the scene allowing enough glint and mellow to soften the stone tile beneath the feet and cast the imperfections from the faces of those sat astride.

In all it was calm, and in his calmness he longed for Maia. He wanted to phone Tomasz and tell him that he had lost the scent and was returning home but knew he had already given over too much information and would have to sit it out until someone else arrived to replace him. Someone would come he'd been assured, but the hesitation of when exactly left him feeling that there was an indecisiveness somewhere along the chain of command and that Tomasz was being held back in acting until they knew exactly what Vicky's intentions were.

How much damage could they do to me? he wondered. A lot probably, was the answer he kept coming up with; whether it was his business or his family he had a lot to lose and he really didn't want to cross these guys.

He had missed a storm before he got here; they were

regular, sweeping in from the sea in a whirlwind, not quite a hurricane, and he could sense there was one brewing, he could feel it breaching the horizon and splitting the sky racing to make landfall before she left these shores. He wanted to flee before it hit.

He lifted his bottle and supped at his beer, staring down the shaft of the glass as she stepped up through the gate from the road, shoes in hand and feet covered in sand, elegantly sauntering across the far side of the pool feeling the light breeze that wafted her thin dress, the light behind her silhouetting her strong thighs and the rigid outline strapped to one that barely caused a bulge. *Is that a knife?* he thought to himself staring up at her broad confident shoulders.

He shook his head slightly and lowered his gaze as she circled round the pool and crossed towards him.

11

Talisa was watching.

She sat in her bedroom, thick blackout curtains hiding her as she twiddled with the pull bar she had used to close them so that they covered the whole wall of the glass patio doors and bug screen that led out to the patio and the pool garden beyond.

She occupied one of those rooms where the poor unfortunate holiday makers drew the short straw of the lottery to suffer the proximity of the space by the bar reserved for the nightly show with the speakers too inconsiderately placed and the volume purposely too loud to afford any decent rest until the early hours when the revellers settled down and the over the top and annoying entertainment staff ceased what they warranted as good family enjoyment, but for which most would not miss were it absent, as it was tonight, and would welcome its continued absence were it omitted from the program altogether.

She had a clear view of Vicky as she sauntered seductively up to the table and seemed to invite herself to join the man sat on his own. It was the same man she had seen earlier looking at the car and Talisa wondered whether they knew each other, but judging by his uncomfortable response and awkwardness in his seat she guessed not.

Had Vicky clocked him watching her? It was a possibility but whether she had or not she seemed to be trying to entice his eyes to admire the parts of her flesh that were mostly covered. She raised the heel of her foot onto her chair so that her dress rose up exposing high up to her underwear, revealing the tattooed sidearm that shot out with the intention of getting him steamed up beneath his collar.

Her tactics seemed to work as he, flustered though he was, remarked on her body art giving her cause to stroke her upper thigh temptingly.

Talisa expected Vicky would get him to buy her a drink at the bar but that didn't seem her game plan, she was being more forward than that as her other hand appeared to move up to her breast and gently brush against an erect nipple, her tongue running along the ridge of her upper teeth. The man choked on his beer and sat upright as he coughed and apologised at his coyness. She brushed it off, obviously eyeing the bulge in his shorts that gave away the excitement he was trying to hide with his face, seductively gripping his hand as she stood and led him away from the table.

12

The doorbell rang and Tomasz put down his coffee and walked to the intercom and pressed the button upon seeing Tomek stood by the door to the sidewalk.

He unlatched the door and stepped back to retrieve his coffee.

"You look like hell," offered up Tomek as he entered a couple of minutes later.

Tomasz motioned to an empty bottle of whiskey perched on the kitchen worktop and then flapped his hand back to his forehead to massage the daylight from his eyes. He turned from the window to face his friend.

"What, no invite for me?"

"I didn't have a party, and no, before you say it, I had no girls over either."

"Drinking alone? You want to talk about it?"

Tomasz shook his head. "I've just got things on my mind. What brings you here so early?"

"You don't know?" Tomek shook his head mockingly. "Turn on the news channel."

Tomasz did as bade and the 85" 3D screen burst to life in an LSD explosion of colour at the far end of the apartment. Music blared out from the music channel that threw up a Dutch band that were breaking big on the European pop scene. He found the right button on the remote and switched it over to hear a newscaster interviewing a colleague reporting live from the aftermath of what appeared to be an explosion. He read the tickertape update that scrolled along the bottom of the screen to brief him on all the information he hadn't yet gathered from the live report.

"Shit!"

"I'd have thought you would have got a call."

"Where's my damned phone?" Tomasz began hunting the apartment in all the usual places he habitually discarded his mobile phone. It had rung a couple of times during the night but seeing it was the office and not Sergio, the latter being predominantly on his mind, he had chosen to ignore the calls that he wasn't in a sober enough mood to pacify in the hope that his clear head of the morning would avail him of a reasonable enough justification for avoidance. He only vaguely remembered turning the volume off as he fell into a deep slumber on his oversized bed.

He emerged from the bedroom with the phone in hand, his face aghast at the number of missed calls.

"Have you missed the German?"

"And others. He's the least of my worries."

Tomasz dialled a number and held the phone to his ear.

"Yes, I know, I'm sorry, I've only just heard... of course...I'll deal with it. I may need help. Permission to use my own discretion with my team?...certainly." He tossed the phone aside onto a sofa, turned to say something to Tomek and stopped to retrieve the phone again; it would do him no good left on silent.

"Tomek, call the boys and have them head to Czekolada's, you're all working for me today. I need you to find out everything you can about what happened at the mine and who's asking what questions."

He rushed back into the bedroom and reappeared having splashed water on his face and slung on a smart shirt and blazer. He pocketed a tie and swept his fingers through his hair as he slid his feet into a pair of shoes in his entrance lobby. He was aware that he hadn't brushed his teeth nor emptied his bowels, as was his habit of a morning, but there was no time, he had to limit the damage.

Within five minutes they were sat out front of the cafe waiting for Justyna to appear to take their order but it was Bronislaw himself who made the delayed trip out to their table, his portly belly wobbling decidedly unhealthily telling of the café owners taste for his own product. It was rare that Bronislaw rolled himself out to his customers, preferring his perch behind his counter where he could see his television set mounted on the wall that gripped him so insensibly when custom ran dry. Tomek surmised quickly that Justyna was either off for the day or was late in, either way she wasn't there to take their order, not that Tomasz noticed as his head was embedded painfully into the screen of his Ipad.

"The German wants to know if the news reports about the research facility and what is being mined at the location are linked." It had come in in an email as it appeared the German was information gathering in the same way Tomasz was before having to speak in person.

"Well was it?"

Tomasz gave a look that Tomek read well enough.

"So lie. Tell him no. It's all just initial reports coming out at the moment, just speculation."

"You're right; the company will clear up the media mess."

"Your job is to control the money. If the mine is

down the company will need all the backing they can get to get it up and running again."

"It was hard enough to sell it to them in the first place; I can't see how the hell I'm supposed to redeem this."

"Tomasz, what will happen if you don't?"

Tomasz took stock of the question. What could they do? It wasn't as if it was his fault, he hadn't blown up the research facility, not to mention that he wasn't employed to broker these deals, that wasn't his main forte, he was only supposed to examine the contracts and reports and find the holes, but now someone had blown a whopping great big one right through his pension plan.

"Hey," it was Lenart pulling up a chair, "I got here as quick as I could, you caught me just as I was about to leave the house with the girls."

Tomasz launched straight in. "I need you to find out who would want to blow up the research facility at the Russian mine," then looking back to Tomek, "and when Wieslaw gets here have him search for any potential new backers who may see this as an opportunity. I need a plan B if I can't get all the players back on side."

"What do you mean if?" scoffed Tomek as Bronislaw nodded from the side of the table. Tomasz ignored him leaving Tomek to gesture back. "Usual, make it four."

"This isn't your fault, Tomasz, surely they know that."

Bronislaw wandered off slowly, the folded over grease on the rear of his white t-shirt blubbering back in towards the café like a walrus heading back to the sea.

"Of course they know but at the end of the day

they'll be after a scapegoat to blame and I've no intention of it being me."

At that moment his phone rang and he looked down dreading any number of names that would come up on its screen.

"But why would it be you?" argued Lenart.

It was Sergio. He hit the red button to cancel; it wasn't a call he could deal with right now.

"Last in first out?" came Tomek's answer to Lenart's question.

"Are they really that ruthless?"

"Are you kidding? Do you know who this guy is working for?"

Tomasz raised his head at Tomek, glad that his friend had taken note of him enough to understand his position.

"No, quite frankly I don't. Do you?"

Tomek shook his head and raised his shoulders slowly.

"Hell, do any of us? I'm not sure even I know, and officially I'm the only one on the payroll." At this they all fell silent. Enough was said.

13

She had barely made it back to her room when the distant blur of his name crawled back towards her: Luigi, an Italian she was able to converse fairly well with having recently brushed up on the language for her last job, not that they used many words to get down to it. He looked like a Luigi, and he performed as poorly as she'd expected, fumbling with the foreplay, climaxing too soon, and then rolling over to sleep. He'd pretended too anyway, maybe fearful of her walking out on him, all the while he had seemed nervous as though his wife was about to walk in on them, not that there was any sign of a wife, the room had the wording of a pamphlet so far as belongings was concerned: a single man on a short stop over. The ring told the tale well enough as he showed all the edginess of a man doing what he knew he ought not to; a tug of war battle with his conscience drying his mouth knowing the guilt would condemn him for years to come and affecting his marriage forever, even if she were to never find out and he were never to confess.

She could hear the false breaths he took as he fought to stay awake, maybe suspecting she would rob him, or most probably just scared she would walk out and he would never see her again, and if he was really unlucky she would have left him with a dose that would be hard to explain when he got home. She waited till his breath had slowed and that awkward drawing in through both nose and mouth that's so hard to genuinely fake whilst awake was well on its way and then she leant over him to see the rapid flutter of his eyes beneath his lids that told her he was dreaming on his way down to a deeper place. Then, and only then, did she creep out of bed and put on her clothes, the sexual buzz and craving having been satisfied, for the moment at least.

So poor was her mental recall at that point that she had forgotten her surprise at finding herself on her own floor of the hotel when he had led her to his room. He had tried to convince her to go to hers but that was never going to happen. She had walked all the way back to the lift by the time she remembered she was already on the right floor and had to backtrack to her door, by then his name was inching away and his face was shadowy. She remembered he was tall and thin and wore an ugly moustache and that his hair was wildly in need of a cut, but his features that lay beneath the stubble that scraped her cheek and thighs were clouds in the sky waiting to the wind to blow and remodel them.

She entered her room and went to the bathroom to shower off, slipping out of the dress and dropping her accessories to the ground as she went.

As the hot water flowed over her naked frame she dreamed of the day she had got closest to him. That day had been a test to see if he would make her close up, but in his pumped up air of self-confidence he saw only what he expected to see.

The company must have drawn his card long before knowing his time as an employee was past its use by date for they knew her desire to have him killed; the old shrink had known it all along.

They, as strangers, had danced a passionless tango together, she in her muscle packed tall frame reaching over him straining to tear out of her dazzling ball gown, her pounding breast squeezed tight against his chest as they both teased each other at knowing the job they were there to carry out but each daring the other to make their move first. He could have taken the first shot, but instead had shown a rare weakness and bowed gentlemanly to her virtuous form, *ladies before gentleman,* stepping back he allowed her to slip away up the stairs while he feigned a collision with an unsuspecting party guest.

She had got the job done, both hers and the company's, and they had both escaped. She remembered the smell of his breath and the firm feel of his shoulders, the chiselled jawline with the scar that buried into his flesh telling of the not so innocent charmer that lay beneath.

They were cut from the same cloth she and Jack.

She stepped out of the shower into the steamy room and wiped the mirror to gaze once more at her disfigured body.

Her body had changed much in her youth. The drugs she had been forced to take at the Manor House Hospital as a teenager had taken their toll and had their fair share of side effects. One after the other she had taken as they had tried to sedate and calm her at different points, experimenting on a course of treatment that she doubted had her best interests at heart: Ativan, Xanax, Serax, Prozac, Zoloft, Effexor, Diazapam were just some of the names she still remembered of the anti-anxiety and anti-depressant drugs she was regularly force fed. But it had not been those that had caused her body to mutate.

The bugs had been crawling about in her abdomen

for a good while and spreading through her, wriggling through her veins and swimming to her lungs so that she found it hard to take a breath. She had told them but they just upped her dose. The pain in her ankles and knees she told them were the worms trying to find a way out. She screamed at them to help her get them out but even the kind Scottish nurse that had told her about the worms that could grow in her stomach when she gorged on sugar didn't believe her. The headaches persisted as she banged her head against the walls allowing the blood to flow to let them out but there were too many. Her breasts, still small but growing rapidly with puberty, were tingling insatiably, her ribs expanding with the effort of her beating heart as she thrust out at the doors from hip bones that threatened to separate from her skin. Her bare feet and bloodied fists would have bound her in a strait jacket had she not procured a biro which she snapped to use the fractured plastic to dig at the irritation burrowed deep within her breast.

By the time the hospital staff came to her aid she had dug a deep bloody gash that forever reminded her of the wriggling worms beneath her flesh and deep within her abdomen, even now decades later she still felt the painful pangs of the ghostly bugs within her, but now she knew the pain for what it really was, a symptom not a cause, deferred from the real problem that had so conveniently secured her escape from Manor House.

Occasionally her body would twitch, the muscles being just a tad jittery, bopping out of her control. It would never last long and she would always stare at whichever appendage was affected (usually a bicep or a calf) with amused curiosity rather than any real concern. It was never enough to affect her performance and anyone observing would be blind to the dancing muscles that partied alone beneath her clothes like an epileptic at a funeral. There was no pain with the twitching but the frequency had increased. Just another symptom. She would have to get checked out but dreaded the diagnosis, and it would have to wait for now; she couldn't let it get in the way of her catching Talisa Hayes.

She often got the cravings: the tingling in her extremities accompanied by the nausea and shakes, dry mouth and headaches that went with the absence of her usual medication. To say she was off her meds would be an extreme understatement, for it had been at least fifteen years since she'd placed herself in a position to be prescribed any. She supplemented her cravings with illegal highs, pills she acquired on the club scenes and from wannabe boyfriends, drugs which she relabelled in her mind as her prescription medication along with the regular doses of sex and murder. These were all things Jack didn't need; he thought more clearly than her in a natural sense; where she had to focus and concentrate to formulate a plan he fell into pattern as though he were born to it. She chuckled at the thought - of course he was born to it!

They were cut from the same cloth were they not? She had studied the cruel ways of the world in the solitary confinement of a mental hospital, whereas he had studied the barbaric treacheries of life from a juvenile prison cell. Oh yes Vicky's education in the institution was very much in line with her brother's.

14

Sergio awoke to the sound of the door closing. His reaction was sluggish as he drew himself from the sinking warmth of a pillow that lay next to Maia usually stroking his arm from behind him after they had made love in the most passionate and energetic way since before the children had been born. He slowly drew up the blinds of his eyelids to take in the unfamiliar view, taking a moment to realise that he was in a hotel room with just enough light coming through the gap beneath the door to cast the stolid shadows of the wall and wardrobe that aligned to the door in a staring contest with the bathroom. He smiled to himself, still not fully awake to his surroundings but in that place between dreaming and waking where both worlds merge and the mind can't distinguish between the two and you almost dare to hope that you can choose which is the true reality.

He reached back with his arm to return the caress of his wife, his arm failing to find her, stretching far enough to find the cold edge beyond the cooling warmth where a body had recently laid beside him. He had turned around enough now for his head to be raised with his twisted body and his eyes to widen with a self-loathing horror to his predicament.

A panicked scour of the room ensured he was alone. The bathroom light was off but that didn't prevent him from tentatively opening the door and checking she wasn't there.

He sat on the bed with his head in his hands and his body flooded with guilt and shame. He wanted to confess; how urgently the impulse to declare his sins and beg forgiveness, but no priest sat on the stool of the confessional box of the bathroom on the other side of the wall which he faced. She would hate him he was certain of it.

Soon, he had no idea how long 'soon' was exactly, it felt like an age but he was sure his frantic mind was racing along a different time zone to the slow tick of the hotel clock, but soon his mind shifted, prompted by the distance sound of a door opening and closing - hers he assumed. He thought then of the danger he was in, and then of whether there was any way he could redeem it and use it to his advantage, but his thoughts were too clouded, his judgement already smudged by his masculine weakness. How could he tell what was the best course of action?

He reached for his phone and dialled the number he had for Tomasz thinking to take his direction. It rang once, twice, and then cut off. He looked at the clock and tried to calculate the time difference and loosely guessed it to be mid-morning in Poland. Another thought climbed into the window of his mind and he looked at the phone with disgust and threw it aside as though it were a spider crawling across his hand.

Hadn't he given enough ammunition to these guys already! They already owned his business, yet there he was about to hand over his marriage too. He mentally kicked himself for his stupidity and thanked his lucky stars that the call hadn't connected. He couldn't tell Tomasz; he couldn't hand *them* anything else to hold over him; they had enough in their arsenal already.

He dressed quickly, suddenly suffocating from the stifling air of the room, keen to be out in the open.

Outside the door it was deathly still and quiet so he drew the door closed behind him slowly so as not to wake the corpses lying in their tombs.

He walked towards the elevator, stopping briefly to listen at her door. He could hear the shower running within and knew whatever advantage could be gained from her was not to be sought now. He wandered to the lift and pressed the button, breaking the silence with the hum and ding as it rose from the ground floor.

The air outside was muggy but fresher than the swollen gland of the hotel that bulged his neck. He breathed deeply, sucking in heavily to his chest the sea air as it wafted over the low wall of the hotel garden. He stared across the road but there was little light to illuminate his view and the sparse traffic was too little to even allow him a glimpse of the waves breaking on the sand beyond.

He found himself a padded sun lounger by the far side of the pool far enough from the main building of the hotel so that he could lean back and stare up at the few lights widened with insomnia as he tried to work out whether her room was visible from this angle, but he couldn't tell and his brain hurt to try and figure out the angles of the interior corridors and where the rooms looked out over. There weren't even any stars to distract his thoughts as the clouds above hung thick with moisture telling him not to tempt a saunter too far unless it was to one of the all night bars - but he feared what that would bring as he'd done enough damage already.

A cat, one of the hotel's regular residents, meowed and purred off to the far side of the pool near the entrance to the lower annex of rooms that sidled the gym. He glanced across to see a hand trying to wave the scrounging moggy away and batting off its advances of desperate attention seeking, lacking the care and attention of a loving owner to comfort it. The low wall of the pathway boarder hid the figure that clearly didn't want to be spotted lurking, spying, by the pool.

Sergio sat upright, his attention caught and his interest sparked to something that could momentarily draw his attention away from himself and his self-inflicted misery. He perceived a head breaching the corner edge of the wall but a low level light glared behind casting the figure into silhouette. He fancied eyes were staring at him, and then they were gone, the figure running low, crouched down out in the open for a brief moment before reaching the safety of the annex entrance, the cat scattering away to the shelter of a distant bush across the garden.

It was a dark haired woman, he thought, or a young girl by the way she moved. He puzzled over who she was and what she was doing there, but the thought was brief.

As he pondered the empty space left by the faceless figure Maia's fury and disappointment began to rise swiftly to accost him once more, distracting his thoughts to pull him away from any intrigue to draw him into the treacle pool to drown in his own guilt and shame.

15

Wieslaw Raczynski lit another cigarette and took a long exhaustive drag that recoiled the singed paper back towards his fingertips with frightening speed. His breath seemed held far longer than his lungs could possibly expand before he slowly released the smoke through his nasal passage. He tapped out the ash into the wide glass oval tray in which he had only moments ago extinguished the last one. He lent back from the coffee table rubbing his eyes and shaking his head.

"We have been over this; we are just going round in circles," Wieslaw was clearly getting frustrated and tired with their lack of progress.

"I agree." In fact Cristian Lenart had mumbled something similar twenty minutes earlier as they sat in the comfort of Tomasz apartment to where they had adjourned their meeting, but their quartet had been deep in argument over whether or not to use their trump card against the German. It had been Cristian who had traced a regular payment from the German's financier's bank account to a family in Stuttgart. At first the payment had them stumped but a little more digging around about the parentage of the children uncovered that the current man of the house was not the father of the eldest child and that the mother had been a receptionist at the businessman's Stuttgart office, a fact that they were sure the German's Berlin based family were ignorantly unaware of.

A heated moral debate had ensued as to whether Tomasz should threaten to destroy the man's family in the hope of convincing him to reinvest his millions into an increasingly dubious endeavour. Surprisingly it had been Tomasz that was taking the moral high ground, supported by Lenart, while Wieslaw and Tomek took the aggressive stance of wanting to pull out every big gun they had. In the end Tomasz's logic held the top rung of the ladder as he argued that the sum at stake to be lost if the German invested in the mine alone could be crippling and he had his own board of stakeholders to appease and justify; what they proposed as a threat would end up having to be carried out if they were to retain any face and authority for the organisation, and so stabbing a sword into the heart of two families needlessly came across as a callous act. Lenart, having children of his own, had taken the voice of the children themselves and so was more than happy with the conclusion.

"We're not actually getting anywhere here," repeated Wieslaw, "and I don't know that we're going to." His voice had dropped to almost a whisper but every word was heard as the others fell silent around him. It was no use, they had come up with no financial resolution for the mine and it wasn't helped by the news (the images of which still played silently on the big screen behind them) that had broken at lunchtime that no foul play was suspected but that it was most likely an unexpected gas pocket that was struck due to the placement of the research facility which appeared to have somehow bypassed the official planning regulations in its construction. Clearly someone had been bought off in the Russian government for the project to be approved and so it was a natural assumption that scapegoats were going to be needed.

Someone somewhere was going to lose a lot of

money and someone else was going to have to take the fall for it. Tomasz fully expected to be facing both barrels when he failed to secure any financial investment.

"I don't need this at the moment, I really don't," muttered Tomasz.

"I don't think it will be that bad." Tomek was trying to be reassuring, but deep down they all had their doubts. "They will go easy on you I'm sure; it's not your job, and it's not what you were employed to do."

"I'm not convinced they'll see it that way. I've got all this crap going on in Mexico to deal with as well."

All three perked up at the mention of Mexico for it was the first Tomasz had spoken of it. At their interest, and in a moment of weakness at the need to confide in someone he gave a brief summary of his employing the Italian private investigator to trace an assassin paid by his employers who had absconded half way across the globe. He had probably said too much, in fact he knew he had upon reflection later on, but he had left out his reservations about the company's motives in this matter as well as the mine (to which they were all suspicious, as by now were half the world). He told them of having missed the call from Tomasz this morning and that he had missed a further two calls from London regarding the same matter this afternoon, but that he had verified his position with his handler, a Romanian named Stefan Gorst, who had confirmed that he was to focus on the mine crisis and that he could suspend his interest in the assassin until such time as he had anything more concrete.

Wieslaw's phone rang and he pulled it from his shirt pocket and looked at the screen. "I have to take this," he said prising himself from the leather sofa and stepping out of the room. He gave a curious look back at the group, his ear still half-cocked to Tomasz as though eager to catch every word that he betrayed.

Tomasz continued as Weislaw manoeuvred around the large glass coffee table out of the room. "My worry is that in ignoring the calls I've stuffed things up there and have missed vital information, maybe even jeopardised his safety, and yes before you say it," he said holding up his hand, "I know I could phone them back, in fact I tried calling the Italian but he didn't answer."

"I don't see what you're worried about if Gorst has told you to prioritise the mine stuff, it's not like either project actually comes under your job description." Tomek was quite forceful but he could see Tomasz wasn't convinced.

"I get what you're saying but this organisation doesn't work that way. There are no rules that they have to stick to, employment law doesn't matter and neither do contracts, you all know that, we've done enough bending of the rules ourselves over the years to know this is a ladder that has extremely greasy rungs the higher up you climb. Mr Gorst was quite specific in saying that Oliver Hand himself had taken a personal interest in the financial affairs of the mine and was scrutinizing things close up."

"Who's this Hand guy?" asked Lenart.

"A major player. One of the board. He's right at the top from what I can make out, or at least the top level that I'm aware of."

Wieslaw had been whispering into his mobile phone in a room just off the hallway but had stopped and was listening intently to Tomasz' exasperation at his predicament. He shook his stooped craned head in disappointment and re-entered the room but said nothing to the group.

"Well, it sounds to me," offered up Lenart, "that we better concentrate now on pitching your defence against this Mr Hand."

"Preferably without me having to fall on my sword," begged Tomasz.

16

There was a large part of Vicky Rivers story Giles Montgomery didn't feel comfortable writing down and was hesitant in including it in an emailed document. Unfortunately for Giles his attempts to reach Tomasz on the phone had failed and he knew better than to persist. From what he knew of the way the organisation worked and the different types of projects they embedded themselves in (all information of which he had gleamed from many an undisclosed source as he interrogated, interviewed, and counselled the company's patients) he wouldn't be surprised if they were all up in arms over this Russian mine explosion that was all over the news.

He reread the body of his text, his eyes peering over his glasses at the computer screen on his desk as his hand hovered over the send button.

It was without a doubt that Vicky Rivers was a messed up kid, or woman as she was now. Certainly she had a complex history of mental health issues and was beyond any flight of the imagination far from normal: a psychotic killer with delusions of,,,

He paused as he reread his own words

...with a God complex perpetrated by hate and incited by the desire for revenge for past hurts, and unfortunately inadvertently promoted by her own physician. He didn't go as far as to name the blame he apportioned himself but allowed his eyes to drift away from the document enough to let his eye wonder to another time in this office.

He had set up the meeting with the intent of trying to

undo his past mistakes and convince her that she was on the wrong path and that no god had ordained her to kill, yet he was no clergy, no pastor or priest with a dog collar learned in the words of biblical faith to draw on to back up his argument, so he relied on what he knew and reasoned that literary argument had gotten him into it maybe he could use something similar to get him out of it. 'Let no man talk of murderers escaping justice, and hint that Providence must sleep.' He had quoted it with an air of snugness that he was sure he would be able to launch a productive argument off the back of.

She had sat back in thought for a moment before leaning forward in her chair again with a sly smile skiing the icy jumps of her face. 'Oliver Twist?' she had asked to his surprise. He faltered in his pose; he should have known she would have already latched on to any reference to the subject.

'You're well versed in literature my dear,' he had stalled. Of course she had read it; the story of an abandoned orphan locked away in a hardened and distrustful institution, abused and neglected and misunderstood and bearing the burden of a criminal act committed by someone else, even the discourse of falling in with a crime syndicate fitted the story of her life; he supposed she envied the titular character's fortunate redemption and reclaiming of his lost life, maybe she still hoped the fairy tale ending was still a possibility. Looking across the table he knew that particular boat had sailed for her a long time ago. Compiling his thoughts he had resumed his original plan. 'You know the story, all the better. You know then that Bill Sikes was wrought with guilt as he fled London after killing poor Nancy, ultimately leading to him tie his own noose.'

'Yes Doctor, I too am well read. And if I recall it was Sikes' feelings of guilt associated through his relation to his victim that disturbed his otherwise incorruptible conscience, I however form no such attachment with my victims.'

'That's not true with all,' he countered.

'All but one,' she paréd, 'and there will be no guilt over him,' she had said coldly.

'But don't you see how so alike you have become your brother?' He had lunged with the comment but his strike had missed its mark.

Her brother had been the cause of it all, at least that was where it had all begun. Whether there was an inherited gene that made them both that way he would never be sure, but it was certain that her trauma had been the beginning of her mental breakdown.

Jack Walters, or Jonathan Jack Rivers as he had been known back then, was barely six years old when, during a night time episode of sleep walking, he had picked up a pair of scissors and made his way to the bathroom where his father was taking a shower and had stabbed him repeatedly before making his way back to bed. His older sister had slept through the whole incident right up until her mother, who had been out with friends, came home and discovered her husband dead in the shower. That had been the last time Vicky had seen any member of her family, having gone to bed a peaceful, happy young girl rudely awaken to be huddled out of the family home by police never to return. Her brother had been taken into protective custody and eventually securely locked away until his escape when he was in his teens. Her mother had committed suicide a short time later leaving Vicky all alone and rapidly withdrawing into herself. It hadn't taken long before Vicky found herself in permanent accommodation at Manor House.

Vicky had done well in those early years to overcome her difficulties and mistrust of people and it had taken intensive therapy to crack the outer shell that had formed around her mind. Then she had fallen ill. He was as guilty as all the other staff for having missed it. No one suspected the small tumour which had formed at the base of her brain. Once diagnosed the pituitary gland tumour was swiftly treated and a course of drugs administers to regulate the hormone overload that erupted from the overexcited gland. Her body had changed as a result of a reaction to the drugs: her muscles grew firm, her bones elongated into masculine structure, yet despite her strong arms and stolid legs she had managed to maintain genuinely attractive female facial features with strong cheek bones that were smoothed over with glisteningly buffed marble skin drawing round to slender ears and a firm unbreakable jawline that carved beautifully beneath bulbous puckered lips that most men would die for and most women would swear were enhanced. The end of puberty sprouted her frame just short of grotesque when the process stopped and her body settled down, but by then the damage had been done - not so much to her body but to her mind. She had been found hanging by a nurse she had befriended and was cut down and pronounced dead by a small select band of confidants.

No one in authority had suspected what had transpired at the time. Giles himself had no idea as he signed off on the paperwork as to why he thought the seventeen year old had committed suicide. No one other than those close to her had pieced together her fear of her brother's escape from juvenile detention and the likelihood of him coming after her. She thought her only escape was to feign her own death and disappear.

It wasn't till years later that Giles learned the truth and wondered at the risk and betrayal of the system that the staff at the hospital had taken. It had been convenient timing that they were aided due to the recent chemotherapy and drugs, it being assumed she was dead as her heart beat had slowed so much it was barely detectable. The disappearance, or rather the loss of her body by the time it got to the morgue so that it couldn't be fully examined, was a huge embarrassment and as she had no family to mourn her or complain of the loss it was decided it was easier to cover up the gaff rather than lose people their jobs.

Had Jack escaped at any other point in time the circumstances would never have allowed the course of her life to travel along the line it had - this he was sure she had also attributed to providence.

By the time their paths had crossed once more years had passed and he had found that she had dedicated herself to fulfilling her dormant desire, kept secret from all as her hate simmered in a pan of revenge and loathing of her brother. Through their sessions she divulged the multiple finely detailed scenarios she imagined as she allowed her creative mind to drift into a future imagined world where her retribution was enacted to her own intricate design

He lifted his head from the screen and pushed his glasses up higher on his nose, let out a deep sigh and pressed the send button. Whatever was happening with

Vicky Rivers now he doubted his report would help her predicament.

17

The boys filed out of the flat one by one and Tomasz shut the door behind them having already told them that he would meet them later on or call them if he missed them at the bar.

He had a few calls to make and couldn't afford the prying ears of his friends; he had told them too much already, not that he'd said anything too incriminating but it was enough for investigative minds to do some digging to reveal the elements of truth within his cryptic conversation. He hated having to be so careful but it was for everyone's good; the organisation didn't appreciate loose talk.

He walked back to the window behind the dining table picking up the handset of his landline phone as he watched for the boys to exit the building below and walk across the street to the Sphinx bar. He dialled a number, this was one he had memorised for necessity. The temperature outside was dropping, soon they'd be donning heavy winter coats and battling off the oncoming frost, something he expected to have to do now on the phone.

"Hello." The voice on the other end was abrupt and reigned in with an Eastern European accent very different from his own.

"It's Tomasz in Warsaw"

"Of course it is. How is Warsaw today?" His tone was curt and sarcastic. Of course he was in Warsaw, why did he always insist on saying it.

Tomasz made guttural noises of hesitation as he struggled to know how to begin the conversation.

Stefan Gorst saved him the trouble.

"So, it has been a difficult day for you Tomasz, sorting out our mess. I assume from your hesitation that you have reached no satisfactory conclusion?"

There was no hiding anything so Tomasz gave into it without trying to dress it up. "No. There is unlikely to be any recompense to the loss of investment and no other sources have been identified, we can proceed no further at this juncture."

There was a beat of silence on the other end. "Very well, thank you for your frankness on the matter."

"Mr Gorst, am I likely to be held responsible for this fracas?" He thought what did he have to lose by asking the question?

"Redeem yourself Tomasz, it's not too late. Mr Hand will expect to be appraised fully when he arrives in Warsaw?"

"He's coming here? When?" There was a clear panic in his voice which he failed to disguise in his surprise.

"He should be with you tomorrow. He is taking a close oversight of recent events. I'm sure you understand the board is rather concerned."

"Of course."

If you can offset your failure with some good news of events in Mexico, they are still in Mexico I assume? If there is good news there then Mr Hand may not feel that all things handed to the Warsaw office are bound to go, what is the phrase, tit's up?"

"Yes, as far as I know they are still in Mexico. I will get back on to it immediately."

"I know you will. Take this number down with the following instructions."

Tomasz stood back from the window and grabbed a pen and paper from the sideboard and scribbled down quickly what Gorst told him and then the line went dead.

It had finally come, the request he knew would eventually fall into his lap. He had allowed his hands to get too dirty so far and was now in too deep that he had no chance of getting out. If he made this call for them he was eternally damned and in their pocket.

They were no fools; they had dressed it up as his only choice to save his job. They'd played him by giving him a task that couldn't be completed, forcing his back up against the wall in order to buy his soul. Concluding the Mexico situation was now on his shoulders and if he handled it well he was in line to step up a level in the long run, or else be put out in the cold and forever looking over his shoulder.

He looked around his lavish apartment; there was no real question about it, he had acquired a taste for the high life and they had the means of ensuring he never worked again, yet deep down a tremor shook the tectonic plates of his conscience, a warning that not all was right with the motives of the organisation.

He resolved himself to make another call but not the one instructed by Gorst, his feelings of self-preservation were undermined enough to at least put it off until he'd found out some more information.

Giles Montgomery wasn't answering his phone. Checking his Rolex he guessed that the Englishman would have called it quits for the day as he tended to keep fairly regular daytime hours in his office. He pulled up his emails on his phone and scanned down for any from the psychiatrist. Sure enough one was sitting in his inbox. He opened it and read the summary and then scrolled through the attachment briefly. Most of the content he was aware of from her file but there were a few surprising notes in there about her brother and the manner of her escape from hospital as a child and her illness; a lot of it made sense to the person she had become and the saga over her brother gave him a new insight into the devious manipulation of the organisation that had employed a ticking bomb, ready to set it off when they wanted to eliminate one of their own: her brother.

He flicked back to the covering email. Giles stating that he wanted to speak to him on the phone, something he hadn't filed in the report. He weighed it up and thought it unlikely to delay his next call, besides, he had reasons not to delay now.

He punched another number.

"Ser...Luigi," he chirped, almost calling him Sergio against his better judgement; he needed to distance himself and dehumanise himself from the situation.

Luigi recounted that Vicky Rivers was still holed up at the hotel in Cancún and that he was still watching her. She didn't appear to be going anywhere but had been moving through all the crowded places quite frequently as though looking for someone. His voice had sounded strained, cautious about something. Tomasz got the distinct impression the Italian was holding something back. He gave him room to elaborate but nothing seemed to be forthcoming.

Tomasz proceeded to ask whether she had contacted anyone. The answer was a negative but he repeated that she appeared to be looking for someone. Male or female, he had asked. Could be either was the reply.

Hesitantly he spilled the last piece of the puzzle he had.

If Talisa Hayes was as dangerous as Tomasz thought then Sergio was going to have to be careful.

18

There were two reasons Sergio Vannucci usually pulled the moronic face where his mouth gaped open and his tongue lolled out as he chewed on it absentmindedly. Anything that caused him to stop and concentrate was generally the main reason and as such most people in both his professional life as well as his personal life had grown familiar with the pose that to an unknowing person may have come across as a little retarded. The second reason was rarer and often came off the back of the first, which was a nervous uncertainty. It was this nervous uncertainty that drew curious looks now as he stood in the doorway of the hotel restaurant as he watched the multitudes of greedy holiday makers gorging themselves on an early morning feast.

He gave his room number to the waitress stood by the door and she crossed off his name from the list and told him to find his own table and help himself to the buffet breakfast. There were a few people he recognised from the day before that he had seen lounging around the poolside or walking along the front, but mostly he found them hard to distinguish now that they were wearing more attire and their glistening bronzed flesh or beetroot slapped patches were covered up, even if it was only temporarily before they hit the beach or the pool again. He guessed some may be going on excursions to the Mayan sites or the activity parks that were scattered about the coastline but it was more likely that they would have left already for the long drives having breakfasted early.

She was there, with her back towards him near the

window half way through the large hall. She sat alone at the table and there were a couple of spare tables near her giving rise to his uncertainty. He stalled his decision of whether to join her or not by heading towards the coffee and filling his cup with a large black, hoping that she would shuffle off and save him the embarrassment of trying to open up conversation.

She was still sat there staring out the window thoughtfully cradling a cup of her own. He joined the queue for the cooked food but didn't take a plate as he just looked at the selection and bided for time.

He had spoken to Tomasz before leaving his room and had been instructed to maintain surveillance until someone took over. He complained at how long that would take and was assured that it would be soon, imminent even, although he hadn't been convinced by the hesitation in the Pole's voice once again.

When the phone had rung he had expected it to be Maia or Carmela and was thankful it was neither. He could keep shop with Carmela and avoid an uncomfortable discussion, although being perceptive and knowing him well she was sure to pick up on his evasiveness. Maia on the other hand, how was he supposed to talk to her? He would avoid that as long as possible and even the thought of going home he was at pains to delay. His words would say one thing but his heart was already betraying the guilt that was tightening around his arteries.

He had accosted himself repeatedly with the berated curse of *'Vanni, Vanni, Vanni,'* as though other words of his failings were insufficient.

There were some stark warnings in the call from Tomasz. Heavily he had laboured about this Talisa

Hayes. At least he knew now to look out for a female. His mind had flicked back to the girl watching him by the pool during the night and wondered whether she knew who he was; if she was connected to the company then she may well know he'd been hired to follow Vicky, and if the two met up (for whatever unknown reason) then Vicky would then know about him, and what danger would he be in then? It was a tangled web made so much more complicated by a reckless and foolish one night stand.

In the clear light of day now that the blood of lust wasn't pumping through his veins he saw her again for what she was: a lethal contract killer whom he was being paid to follow. He thought back to his night of loveless passion and wondered how she had managed to get under his skin enough for him to cross so many lines: professionally and personally it was all wrong. Even the memory of the sex was fading quickly.

He wondered whether she would acknowledge him if he sat opposite her or on a nearby table. He didn't think she had any inkling as to who he was other than a cheap lonely shag. If he spoke to her would she want more sex? And more importantly, would he reject it? He wasn't sure, his head said he would but in the heat of the moment... he'd caved once already. Would speaking to her help his cause in identifying this Talisa woman? Maybe next time she would take him back to her room.

He physically shook off the thought, almost spilling his coffee as he moved along in the queue. Follow her and see where she's going next had been his initial instructions, but now Tomasz was warning him to just follow her, to make sure he kept his distance and didn't engage in any way, to watch until told otherwise, and if he thought he'd been made then get the hell out of there.

He turned around to look at the continental section of fruits and cereals and stopped dead in half turn, his hands raised in mime, his coffee slopping at the sudden halt in motion. Whilst his back had been turned she had risen from her seat and was now directly behind him with her back to him. He didn't think she'd seen him, at least her body language wasn't telling of it. She bent and picked up a plate giving him room to step away and out of sight. She seemed to be piling up her plate which caused him to glance over to her table. Sure enough all her place settings were still intact. She must have only just beat him downstairs.

His mind ticked rapidly. For once he knew where she was likely to be for the next fifteen minutes at least, judging by the amount of food she was putting on her plate.

He took a sip of his coffee and then abandoned it on a nearby empty table figuring it was an opportunity not to be missed as he slipped out of the restaurant.

19

It had been one of those eerie and seemingly unusual events when, rising over the land in the east of a blood red sky with thin wisps of cloud and vapour trails hanging over an unusual biting ground frost, the sun peered out from the sliver of the concrete and glass horizon to spread slowly across the city skyscrapers placing all beneath in silhouette on its way to fall again, to dive into the refreshing sea.

That was the last beautiful sunrise she had taken the time to enjoy, sitting on the end of the pier at Santa Monica wasting the time away before she had been snapped violently out of it by Vicky Rivers.

She had taken the time to watch the sun rise again this morning, a few clouds colouring the yellow and orange of dawn, the rain having dropped its load inland during the night to make way for the next build up to sweep in from the sea.

She had sat watching the large tankers slowly cut their way down the Latin American coastline from her sandy perch on the beach. She didn't feel the pressure to worry - Vicky wasn't here for her, she was with him last night. Thankful that she was preoccupied with a male distraction during the night she had convinced herself that those hours were hers. Not that she understood their relationship. She'd seen him come down to the pool during the night and then go back up. He'd seen her but didn't give chase and Vicky hadn't come back down all guns blazing so she figured whatever his business with her it wasn't connected to

Vicky having chased her across the country.

So yes, she had taken the liberty of enjoying the sunrise, figuring each one could be her last. She would play the cat and mouse game with her nemesis later, watching her from her poolside viewpoint, staying out of her line of sight long enough so that maybe she would get bored and eventually assume she had left town. Maybe if the opportunity presented itself she could find a way of disposing of the bitch herself. Not that she was a killer, just the thought of it turned her stomach, but she had taken so much from her and wanted even more. How painful a death would she have at the hands of Vicky Rivers? A grateful death if it could be achieved at all, which she doubted.

No matter what she had to stay out of her grasp, or did she? Suddenly a new plan hatched in the back of her mind and she swept up from where she sat with a mind to set it in motion.

20

Tomasz had made his call. It was to a cell phone in the United States. With regret he relayed the relevant information and hung up. It was a man on the other end, an American judging by the few words spoken, muttering only the essential to confirm the order before hanging up. There was more chit chat from an abandoned archaic Morse telegraph post than from the bloodless assassin on the other end of the line.

He didn't rush down to the bar but sat stewing for a while, a pang in his stomach as the cancer of guilt rode into town on a horse named 'victim of success'.

Twenty minutes later he rode the lift down practising his jolly in control and lord of all face ready to command the crowd and dispense any hint of frailty and insecurity in his personality.

The Sphinx bar was indeed heaving and as he entered Tomek ordered him a pint and passed it along the line towards him.

They spent the good part of an hour whittling away coarse talk about girls and drugs, dragging in some of the hotties present for a pleasant fumble as they were more than happy to be included in the banter of such an exclusive high rolling group.

When the idle chat had died down Tomasz couldn't help himself any longer in wanting to confide to his friends. He wanted their advice, something for which he rarely sought and for which he had no one really to turn to. They had avoided all talk of the day's events but now he brought it forward. The others dismissed the girls seeming to sense it coming.

"So, what's burning a hole, Tomasz Sikora?" asked Lenart who was drawing dangerously close to an alcohol level that would have him chastised when he got home to his good wife.

"I spoke to Gorst." The three of them stood expectant if not a little ear battered as the Euro pop and cackling struck them loud like the padding of boxing gloves against a set of punch bags. "They've set me up, played me all along." The faces around him were blank. Wieslaw looked down to his shoes, an easy enough task from the way he was stooped. "They gave me the mine knowing it was all going to blow up in my face. I mean, I don't think the whole explosion thing was expected, I was just never expected to win the funding."

"What for? What was that to achieve?" Tomek sounded genuinely concerned.

"It doesn't matter. I now have to save face by having someone killed. That's the payoff."

"What!" spat out Lenart, his beer spraying forward into the circle but not far enough to hit anyone.

"Tomasz, maybe you shouldn't be talking about this. Let's change the subject," offered up Tomek trying to protect his friend.

It was a good idea which clearly Lenart agreed with as he started looking around for a subject to switch to.

Tomasz was clearly disappointed but went along with it as Lenart set eyes on what was happening outside on the street.

Politzi had pulled up in a regular blue and white and had mounted the pavement to accost a regular street drinker. It was a common enough occurrence and nothing special to look at as the two officers got out of the car drawing their batons ready to forcefully beat the drinker into the nearest alleyway. It was tough justice but effective policing as it kept most of the drunks (of which there were many roaming the city streets) out of site and hidden in groups in the back alleyways.

The sight of them sparked a memory in Cristian Lenart's mind as he spun jovially with a tale about their youth. "Hey do you remember that time we were making a getaway from that security guard and he landed on the roof of the car?"

"You mean the time Wieslaw was driving around looking for us after we got caught trying to hack the computers at that data storage unit?" recalled Tomasz.

"Yeah, whose idea was that anyway?" asked Tomek.

"Yours if I remember right," chirped Lenart. "It was a balls up from start to finish."

"We were lucky to get away with it," chuckled Tomasz.

"We nearly didn't," muttered Wieslaw, "as I saw it you landed across the bonnet and Cristian almost got crushed between our car and a parked car. Tomek only just caught up with us after I'd reversed out of the one way street and rammed another car out of the road."

"That guard almost had me. I was sure you'd drive off without me. If that guard hadn't fallen I'd never have got to the car in time."

"I saw the guard the other day. I meant to say it earlier but I forgot all about, you know what with all the...anyway he was on the door of Rinski's."

They all stopped and looked at Lenart.

"What were you doing at Rinski's," asked Tomek.

Rinski's was a lap dancing bar in one of the more

dubious parts of Warsaw. It was one of those clubs that every man knew of but none ever admitted going to.

"Come on you guys, my uncle lives that way, you all know that."

"Yeah, yeah, we believe you," offered Tomasz with a light air of disbelief.

"Anyway, going back to the guard, he's turned into a right porker. I mean I remember him being a heavy set bruiser which was why we were able to outrun him, right, but now he's all burly muscle and really overweight and looks like he's got a bitter foul temper like life dealt him bad."

"You sure it was the same guy?" enquire Wieslaw.

"Yeah, I'll never forget that face, sucking on lemons," he pulled a grimace of expression to demonstrate.

"Oh yeah, that's him!" Tomek laughed as they all had a go at imitating the sour look of the guard.

"And besides he still has cropped hair," added in Lenart between chuckles, "only now it's streaky grey and so is his goatee. You remember the tattoos?"

"The name of his kids on his arm and a dagger and death on his knuckles." Tomek shuddered with the memory of the grasping hands that had so nearly changed the course of his life.

"Well now they're stretched wide and grotesque."

"Tattoos, good idea at the time but no one thinks about what they'll look like twenty years down the line," smirked Wieslaw as though it were a righteous justice inflicted for not just letting them run.

The conversation petered out and Lenart took that as his queue to bale on the group having successfully steered it off course. He made his excuses and headed for the door with no one trying to convince him otherwise. Of all of them he was the one they secretly envied most; he had someone to go home to.

"Tomasz, you should go home too." Tomek was always watching out for Tomasz, looking up to him and hanging on his every word, thankful for having been let into his inner circle and ready to learn from his mentor.

"Yeah sure," was all the reply he got as Tomasz necked his glass and walked towards the exit shadowed by Tomek and Wieslaw.

"I don't understand this organisation you work for, Tomasz," mumbled Weislaw with a sozzled slur.

"You don't want to," Tomasz replied. "They deal in unscrupulous tactics, employing assassins to terminate their employee's contracts and the like." Wieslaw gave him a disbelieving glance. "It's true, that's what they've got me doing. You guys don't know how close you've come to guessing the truth at times. There is a secret global consortium that have, through science, sought immortality and universal control of space and time. It's straight out of the films." Tomek nudged him with a flick of his head up to his apartment but Wieslaw saw it and frowned at him to allow Tomasz to continue, marvelling how never before had he been so candid about his work. "They believe it's all achievable and they think that ancient world myths indicate that they do, at some point in the future, achieve their goal."

Wieslaw paused for a moment trying to make sense of the statement.

"What, time travel?"

"Maybe, Wieslaw, maybe. I don't think that's their main aim. I think it's that age old desire of mankind to live forever. They are the alchemists and warlocks of the day, using science to master immortality."

"I don't believe it," stated Tomek as he guided them across the road to Tomasz' block.

"That's your prerogative - it's up to you my friend what you believe. But I think they have achieved it already. Although this project ReSYEM had side effects and they lost control of their test subjects, so now they are trying to narrow down the formula and capture their wayward guinea pigs. That's what I think anyhow."

It was a conversation best not had over a couple of beers, and probably Tomek was right that it was best not had at all, but that didn't stop Wieslaw's mind from probing and trying to coax the information out of his friend and draw him into a moral debate as if they were sat around the tables of Czekolada's.

"So in a world of immortals, who decides who lives and who dies?" asked Wieslaw.

Tomasz turned as he put the key in the outer front door of his apartment block, his last words before he disappeared for the night. "They do," he said and shut the door on them both.

21

Heart racing and mind spinning Sergio quick stepped back through the lobby and hastily pressed the button to call the lift, his hand using the obligatory quad push with his fingers that everyone resorted to to call a slow moving elevator when in a hurry. It came and ascended the few floors at a pace that calmed his heart little but gave him enough time to set a countdown on his cheap digital Casio on his wrist; he set it for ten minutes which he convinced himself was enough time to get clear of her room, any longer than that would be pushing it and he had no desire of getting caught.

Now was the time to see if the money he had slipped José the bellboy had paid off. He had caught him early this morning which was why he was later down to breakfast than he'd anticipated. Of course the key-card he'd been slipped was as yet untested so there was a niggling doubt in his mind that the high price he paid was wasted.

The lift pinged and the doors slowly opened. He half trotted to the room, slowing upon seeing the maid's trolley in the hallway a little way up but no maid in view as she busied herself in an open doorway.

He reached for the key, noting the 'do not disturb sign' that hung from the door handle. He slid the key in the vertical slot and watched as the light flashed red. A refreshing wave of relief washed over him and he dared to allow his shoulders to relax as he took a deep breath. He gave another glance both ways along the corridor to confirm no one was watching then reluctantly tried again.

The light tittered on red and he dared to smile before it fell to green with a click. He yanked the handle down and pushed open the door as naturally as he could without turning to look at the maid he sensed stepping out to attend to her trolley at that precise moment.

With the door closed behind him he knew he had little time but probably had more than he expected. He pulled his mobile phone from his pocket and opened up the camera app knowing the quickest way to document the room was to photograph everything to examine later.

The bathroom was to his left: it all looked as expected, a range of toiletries laid on by the sink. Nothing shouted out at him. Click.

There was a sliding wardrobe to his right: hangers with a few items recently purchased hung morbidly waiting to be invited to the ball. Above them on a shelf was a spare pillow. Click.

He slid the other door to reveal a kettle and tray of cups, saucers, and a selection of teas and coffee, sugar and biscuits. He had similar in his own room only his wasn't untouched as this appeared to be. On another shelf was a room safe, its door shut but not telling unless upon further inspection if it was locked. He made a mental note to try and open it on the way out if he had time. Click.

He made his way deeper into the room, crossing to the window to check for a view down to the restaurant but there was none; he could make out the pool and the sea beyond but nothing that could alleviate his nerves as to how much time he had. At the very least he now could tell her room from the ground. Click.

The bed was made, tightly tucked in in military style

with the appearance that it hadn't been slept in. She was better at housekeeping than he as he reflected on the way he had abandoned his thin sheets with guilty disgust this morning hoping the maid would change them completely. Click.

A small duffle bag sat on the table next to the television. It was zipped closed so he carefully opened it to peer inside. There was a tangled net in the darkness which took him a moment to identify. It wasn't until he removed it from the bag that he realised that it was the underside of a wig, its long brown locks curling beneath in a web having been discarded hurriedly in the bag. Beneath the wig were folded items of clothes, he delicately lifted them out and placed them aside on top of the wig trying to remember their precise position in the bag. There was a book, or rather an album within which he withdrew and placed on the side. It didn't surprise him to see a hand gun cowering in the darkness of the bottom of the bag. He knew better than to touch it. Click.

He opened the book and quickly realised it was an album of photos and newspaper cuttings. A family photo seemed to hold pride of place on the opening page and from the period dress of the four figures immortalised as parents and children he gathered the photo had been taken in the '70's. Click.

He turned the pages and marvelled with an air of disturbance at the subject matter of the newspaper cuttings that were interspersed with photos of a girl in various poses and varying styles. In some she was happy, in others sad and taken from a distance as though she were unaware, the type of shot a stalking paparazzi might catch from across the street. In one shot the girl, who looked young and petit, hung from a lamp post smiling broadly. Click. In another she appeared to be sat on a beach crying in the rain. Click. Yet another she looked solemn staring out of a window with rain on the window pane confusing the viewer as to whether a tear lined her cheek or not. Click. In one she was walking hand in hand with a man - Sergio recognised the location as Niagara Falls, not somewhere he had ever been but its iconic imagery was unmistakable. Click. There were many others but he feared for the time to study them. Click. Click. Click.

He began to flick through the headlines of the articles that had been pasted in with the photos. They were all of a similar vain. Death had signed them all with an editorial hand of singularly triumphant praise. Car crashes and train wrecks, missing planes and explosions. In many the death toll was few but in too many the numbers were too horrendous to recount. He shook his head knowing in his heart that he was in a way skipping over Vicky Rivers' CV and that this was a catalogue of her chase to find this girl Talisa Hayes. Bile rose in his mouth and he felt a need to scrape at his tongue at the thought of having slept with a gorgon as grotesquely murderous as his very own Medusa. Click. Click. Click.

Beep beep. Beep beep. Beep beep.

His phone alarm started him from his thoughts and he quickly looked at the time as he shut off the alarm on his phone. Damn, that had gone quick. He closed the album and placed it back inside the bag carefully over the gun and then put the clothes and the wig back in before re-zipping the bag. His eyes scoured the rest of the room as he backed away trying to gather any more information on his retreat. He hadn't checked the mini-bar or the drawers or her bedside table. All things that were too late and he was pushing his luck as it was.

He put his ear to the door. He could hear the maid further along the corridor sounding as if she had proceeded no further. There was no other footfall to be heard so he slowly pulled down on the handle.

There was sweat on his forehead as he exited the room and moved towards the safety of his own room.

"Hola," said the maid as he passed her.

"Hola," he replied with a forced smile. Getting to his room and fumbling for his key with his right hand while the phone he still held in his left. He slid the key card in the door and it turned green but he didn't pull down on the handle, instead he was frozen in horror at the realisation that he no longer held in his possession the key to Vicky's room. He had placed it down on the table by the television when he had opened the bag and in his panicked haste had left it there. A hundred curses came to mind at that point but no curses prompted a solution to the problem as a tingling thickening deafening cloud closed in around his head blocking out the ping of the elevator. Eventually, fearing that he looked like a man stood at a urinal struggling to let the flow run clear, he turned his head to look down the corridor. There she stood at her doorway staring at him, her lips curled into a smile. She winked once before her demure figure slipped into her room.

"Ah hell," he gasped in his most exasperated Italian. He swiped his card again and almost collapsed into the room.

PART THREE

TRUST

1

The assassin arrived in Mexico with the air of a desperado, a swarve American with slick sunglasses donned in a crisp tight suit but with a cold Russian demeanour with a firm clenched jaw and prominent cheek bones that revealed tense muscle as he chewed, his thin pursed lips barely moving with the motion.

For all intents and purposes he had no name and the one he travelled by on this occasion was far removed from that his mama had labelled him with at his birth and it didn't even draw close to the name he had chosen for himself and answered to when he dared to let down the facade of steel caging he protected himself in.

He carried no luggage, not even a small carry on as he stepped off the plane, clearly intending his trip to be short or else intending to secure whatever he needed upon arrival.

He passed through passport control with the minimum of eye contact but enough to not arouse suspicion. He had it down to a fine art: there was a level of acceptance between rudeness and intimidation and he found even the most scrupulous of border guards could be intimidated. Even if they stopped him what could they do? His papers were clean, he carried no weapons or contraband and the only thing of malice was his face, and if they didn't like that then the US consulate would probably take the offensive somewhere down the line. Besides this was Mexico: murderers crossing the boarders were common place, only few were in his league.

He crossed to the closest car hire counter and ordered a basic car, paying cash for the deposit from a roll of heavy notes that were folded round inside his trouser pocket. He had enough for this expedition but had access to more if he needed it. He left an imprint of a credit card for the final balance on an account that matched the name on his passport, but by the time any irregularity showed on the card he would have been long gone.

He walked the short distance to the car and smoothed down the short blonde quiffs as he looked in the mirror and put on his sunglasses. He would stop off at a chemist on route for some wash out hair dye; his hair would be black by the time he arrived at his destination.

As far as leagues of super criminals went he was in an elite group, an expensive group. He took on very few contract jobs but when he did he commanded a fee with six zeroes trailing behind it and his targets were usually those where nothing was to be left to chance, and often it was one of his own he was having to take out.

He had never met his target. He had heard of her of course. 'The Viper' or 'The Vixen' she was sometimes called, not that he cared much for names. It was faces he remembered, those changing faces he was careful to zero in on, those features that couldn't be disguised. He had burned the image of the photo that had been texted to him onto his mind; she was striking and sure to stand out even if disguised. As usual he'd been told nothing of the why, just the who. Though what he knew of her he could guess at the why.

He calculated his route and set out onto the main coastal road south out of Cancún. He had to take a moment to acclimatise to his surroundings before heading back into town towards the hotel. It wouldn't do him any good to be made too soon and her with the advantage of knowing the lay of the land and most likely expecting the visit. Besides he had yet to purchase his tools, and here in Mexico they were easy to come by.

2

Sergio had little time to examine the photos he'd taken on his phone but upon a brief reflection was assured by two things: one - he now knew what Talisa Hayes looked like, and two - Vicky Rivers was a total psychopath responsible for mass murder and not just the odd contract killing. Why someone in her line of profession would carry about such an incriminating résumé he had no idea, maybe it was just her way of mapping Talisa's activities, but whatever it was it was foolish and highlighted to Sergio just how obsessed by this woman Vicky Rivers had become.

As he pulled out of the car park trying to be careful of Vicky not seeing him in her rear-view mirror he wondered further as to how much more dangerous Talisa Hayes might be considering Vicky had failed to kill her after so many obvious attempts. He resigned himself to checking the pictures later to see if he could gain any more information but for the moment he didn't want to lose sight of her, not now that the job was nearing completion and home was a flight or two away.

His mind had already been working overtime trying to assemble a believable story of woe and difficulty that would account for his distant and possibly erratic behaviour when he got home. He was a good liar when he wanted to be but not where Maia was concerned, she could normally see straight through him and could read the expressions on his face that he didn't even know he'd dressed in.

The sudden information from José had cost him dear but he was thankful for it anyway. Had the bell boy not called his room to tell him she would be leaving the hotel in her car he would have been sat around the hotel all day not knowing where she was and fretting that she might launch upon him at any moment.

As they drove south along the coast road they passed Puerto Morelos and carried on towards Playa del Carmen. His initial panic that she would spot him trailing a few cars back subsided as he allowed himself more distance so long as he could see her tail far enough off along the straight stretch of road. There were traffic lights controlling various junctions and an elevated section of road where he worried he might get stuck too far behind and miss her turn off the road but he found he caught up with her easily enough as though maybe she had slowed for him.

He had rehearsed his defence for when she challenged him. In his finest bashful Italian he would cowardly admit that he was smitten, infatuated with her having eaten only once of the forbidden apple, that being here alone he wondered whether he could see her again to taste that fruit once more, but being a married man didn't know how to approach her and so had followed her in the hope of catching her alone to speak to. It would make him look ridiculously hopeless, and probably creepy, but he figured it was a common enough personality type to be plausible. He dismissed his initial worries about her accusing him of being in her room as he doubted she would have gained any proof and if she had found the extra key-card she would have had little time before leaving to try and investigate where it had come from. Yes there was an outside chance that she might just guess that it was him, but he would deny it all the way and just play ignorant. Besides, this was Mexico, it could have been anyone.

Of course there was another scenario that played out in the recesses of his mind, playing in the shadows like an annoying child just rising above the din of silence of a waiting room as he or she played with the metal hoops and plastic rings and stickle bricks laid out on a low table for their entertainment. What if she knew? What if she were luring him out? Or worse still, what if she assumed he was the company man sent to deal with her, because that's really who he was waiting for, right? Wasn't it? And if she was knowingly off the grid then surely she'd be expecting a visit of that kind.

He slapped the child silent and continued to sit in his waiting room behind the wheel of his car. Even if she did kill him, he wondered, would Maia ever find out about his betrayal?

3

As Vicky Rivers drove along route 307, the Caratera between Cancún and Tulum, she had no idea she was passing a fellow assassin on the other side of the road heading back to her hotel to kill her, instead she drove innocently by Puerto Morelos and on passed Playa del Carmen and through even further passed Akumal. At Tulum she took a right onto the 109. A straight road that led directly to the historic site of Cobá. The whole journey would take her two hours door to door and she had passed a number of likely tourist buses on route that could contain her prize, but she couldn't be sure of any of them. All she could do was push on to her destination and hope to spot her among the crowds.

She knew of course that she was being followed, but in the distance she couldn't make out who drove the hire car, a company employee most likely keeping tabs on her, she assumed. She had slowed down a number of times to allow enough distance so she could keep him in her sights; better to know where he was than have him sneak up on her. She hoped to ID him if he managed to stay with her for the duration of the journey.

She hummed a familiar tune in her head unaware of it running concurrent with the thoughts spiralling in a whirlpool as her boat threatened to capsize and flip her out.

You drove me, nearly drove me, out of my head
While you never shed a tear
Remember, I remember, all that you said
In truth her mother had never said anything to her

beyond that night; not a word since she awoke to the nightmare around her. Maybe she feared that she too, her own loving daughter, was afflicted with the same disease of death that had haunted poor Jack in his sleep.

Poor Jack nothing! He deserved what he got, my only regret was that I took so long about it and didn't make him suffer longer.

You toyed with him enough! He was your brother.

And they were my parents!

Vicky sank into the memory of her mother with the unclenching grasp of a nine year old, adoring her and smelling her perfume as she rocked in her arms.

The car swayed and she snapped out of it.

Well, you can drown me in the river

Tears for the river

I'll weep a river for you

Sure you did. Cried yourself straight into the looney bin. If you hadn't died you'd still be there now!

I'm not crazy!

Keep telling yourself that honey. I bet Jack thought he was sane too. He was a better killer than you, you know!

Like I care.

If you don't care why did you always compete for his jobs?

We were on the same circuit; we had the same employer.

But you compared yourself to him.

I hated him!

You emulated him. He was the only family you had.

He killed my family and took everything.

That's why killing him didn't fill the void!

"Shut up!" she yelled at the windscreen in front of

her. The voices went away on command as Giles Montgomery stopped arguing with that other voice in her head, that angry, bitterly twisted voice of hate.

So what if years of steroids had altered her appearance and kept her strong, working hard with her fitness and flexibility along with whatever cosmetic appliances she could muster to enhance her youthful looks and regain, if only part, of her lost youth.

Her mind failed to register the change in thought process as she began to justify her behaviour in other areas of her life.

So what if she didn't look her age as she tipped across the border of her mid-forties, she had the stamina and passion of a woman barely stretching into her thirties. Many a man was fooled, even after she'd serviced their needs. José was for sure.

Some older women tried to carry off the earrings and piercings, with their shades of bottle blonde ponytails, but their saggy necks and blotchy skin gave them away as wrinkles loosely hung from untoned muscle. She on the other hand had escaped the map crossed crow's feet and evaded the saggy cheeks that put her on a par with those of a much darker complexion whose age was often hard to distinguish, not to mention of course the lack of tired eyes brought on by years of sleeplessness and stress that children brought along, with boobs that turned south without firm support and an extra padded widened rear that just looked wrong on the saddle of a bicycle as it was swallowed up by the jaws of the butt that their husbands no longer stared after or tried to pinch, yet having let themselves go still wondered why the men in their lives strayed or didn't pay them so much attention any more, digging them in the ribs when a younger slimmer model caught their eye and turned their head.

José indeed had seen her as that younger model. A young fresh hot blood Mexican with a hard on for the ladies and in a prime position to exploit what he could offer and sell it to the highest bidder. Fortunately for her his rates were cheap, for her at least.

José's convenient tip had come early that morning as she breakfasted, or rather on her way in for breakfast. He had passed his information with a polite call of, 'Seniorita?' to which she had answered for him to mutter his news and then be dismissed with a lick of her tongue and a glance at his crotch and an instruction to come to her room later. She could see he had gone hard at the suggestion and had limped away to hide his embarrassment.

He would go to her room later but what he would find would most definitely not be what he expected.

The information he provided she chewed over as she ate breakfast, it was short but compelling: a single lady by the name of Hayes had booked an excursion through the hotel to visit Cobá for today. The bus she would have boarded would have left already.

She didn't owe José any more than what she had already paid him when she had allowed him to deliver her single carry bag to her room when she had arrived at the Playa Mujeres. She could have carried it herself but knew she needed to align herself with someone for information.

She didn't have to pay cash, and rarely did she if she could avoid it; she had other commodities. She could, and did, pay in other ways which to most would be degrading and little more than prostitution, but for her it was a pleasure and a form of payment she was most willing and forthcoming with, enticing in the young hotel worker as she had sunk to her knees upon drawing him to her room to engage in forbidden the pleasures that would buy her the information she needed. It didn't stretch so far as buying his allegiance for she knew the corruption of society, and the minds of such a culture were loyal to no man, or woman, and that the price of information was only as high as the next man's purse.

She had learnt that harsh lesson many years ago in the depths of Nigeria when she had been paid by the consortium to take care of a tribal leader who had crossed a line in his own thirst for power as he expanded his territory to overthrow farmlands belonging to a neighbouring ruler. It was a common occurrence in the heart of Africa where small tribes expanded or merged and a prominent leader emerged with the potential following and support of a rebellious people, who for whatever reason, whether it be political or religious, sought the stance of rebel uprising against an already corrupt establishment; the corrupt always fought the corrupt and the worthy rarely grew a strong enough voice to stand up against it. On that occasion the tribal leader and would-be rebel leader in question was destined to be cut short in his prime as the lands he sought were now under the auspicious control of the consortium who had acquired them in secret after a geological survey had unveiled a potential cache of a much sought after ore needed for scientific experiments carried out in a facility in Illinois. That facility no longer existed, another compound destroyed amid speculation of illegal and dangerous research carried out by high financed corporations with the unofficial backing of a number of governments. Heads rolled then, as they were bound to now with the Russian saga unfolding in the news, not that it was her problem - she wasn't paid to deal with that.

Back in Nigeria she had been paid to hire a guide to the remote tribal lands and to take care of the problem. It should have been simple enough had the guide not been already paid by the tribal leader, Mobasi his name was, to mislead anyone who came looking for him on the promise of higher payment. It had turned messy when she realised she had been duped and had been led to a holding cell in a remote house where no aid was likely to reach her. In any other circumstance she may have been able to open her mouth or her legs and screw her way out to a better bargaining situation, but in the heart of HIV Aids riddled Africa that in itself could have been a death sentence, and yet to remain tied up, a pretty white face, being an open target to gang rape was equally not an option. Still her charm had worked in her favour as they underestimated the ruthlessness of a single female with the tools and know how to free herself and seek revenge. Mombasi had died that day, and so too had twelve of his men. There would be no doubt who ordered the hit nor why, and even Vicky had come to the conclusion that her capture and violent reaction had all been part of a long term forecast set out by someone somewhere sat in an office staring into a crystal ball predicting and manipulating future events to the company's gain.

Before leaving Nigeria she had learnt the ways of corrupt society well enough, that no one could be trusted no matter who you thought you had in your pocket or how much you thought their services were worth. Loyalty meant nothing in places like that, and here in Mexico too the pockets were deep and treacherous, but she knew this upon arrival and so trusted no one, in fact she expected to be ripped off and double crossed and so trusted only for certain what she could see with her own two eyes.

And so she followed José's lead, but tentatively, expectant of all things and of none.

4

There are those awkward moments when nature rolls up the crescent wave to find the sand is gone and devoted duty has replaced it, not with the fine coarse shingle but with a wall of hard granite rock, when the flow of the warm tropics splashing against the rock of immoveable mountain stubbornly refuses to budge under the weight. Nerves of fear, or even excitement, threaten to escape to spoil and betray in an emotive event, bursting forth in an unsolicited gush of bodily containment where to be caught short would be unforgivably embarrassing.

Such was the plight of Alejandro Munoz as he stood guard at the entrance of the Mayan heritage site so popular with tourists the world over. It was his duty but he needed to move and dared not, not just yet.

The site drew a crowd not only due to its size, encompassed and embedded in the deep forest of the woodland with its ancient city sprawling over a distance of five miles in a circumference even he had yet to journey, and he had worked here for nigh on eleven years since being made redundant at the car manufacturing plant in Merida, but what drew the crowds mostly these days was that the pyramid of Nohoch Mul that sat back against the trees beyond the great twin lakes of Macanxoc and Cobá was the last of Mexico's great pyramid sites left open to the public to be climbed upon. All the other Mayan sites now had preservation orders on them forbidding the trampling of curious feet damaging and defacing the ancient stone architecture; it was cheaper to preserve than to restore and being fenced off hadn't harmed the tourist trade so far. It was only a matter of time before Cobá would fall to the same fate and have its base roped off and a security detail posted under the shade of a security box not unlike the one he sat in now.

He sat with crossed legs, one foot tapping the ground impatiently, one hand holding his abdomen which was bloated beyond its normal paunch and painful with the weight that threatened to burst the internal bag, that bladder sack that could contain no more. The mere sight of liquid now worried his mind so much that he had removed his bottle of water from the counter and placed it out of sight behind him.

The mid-day sun had almost peaked and still foolishly the coaches arrived. It was not the best time of day to visit any outdoor site in Mexico; early morning or early evening were considered best when the air was cooler and the light cast shadows of the miraculous and mysterious, the ghosts of an ancient way of life whose descendants still proudly promoted as they clung onto their heritage.

Two more coaches had pulled into the car park and a small number of cars, all of which meant that he couldn't yet leave his post until he had issued the entrance tickets and secured their 38 pesos and advised those travelling without a tour (those on the buses knew where to get a guide and most likely had one pre-arranged or a regular one they liked to use) about using a local guide and its cost (to be negotiated individually). The cars would already have been relieved of their 10 pesos at the car park entrance by Rodrigues who sat in a similar wooden booth. At least he didn't have to spend his time trying to explain the lay of the land and the extra facilities where they could hire such as bicycles and carriages (a two seated cart pulled by a local on a push bike) to traverse the cleared paths that stretched out between the valued ruins of the city. When he had first begun in the job he had found it frustrating trying to negotiate all the differing languages to the point that he gave up and sold the benefits of the guides instead; these days a hand rack had been placed outside his stall, the national tourism funding having stretched to information leaflets printed in various languages for the customer to help themselves without his need for interference rendering his job now simply as money taker.

Fifteen minutes he calculated it would take for this hoard to pass through his gates as he watched them enviously sauntering about the car park, some stopping at the various gift shops, some at the lake look out where the zip wire tower stood awaiting those brave and adventurous enough to swing over the lake itself. A small queue was forming at the main gift shop opposite and he knew why; after a long coach ride they often rushed straight for the nearest toilet. The one in the shop was clean enough but the pressure was there to buy if you used it. There were cleaner and newer lavatories just inside the entrance of the main grounds themselves but the tourists wouldn't know that unless their tour guide had informed them of it prior to their arrival.

The temptation was there not to wait, to abandon his post, or even to empty his bottle and turn his back, who could see him below the waist anyway?

Slowly, too slowly they came to his stall and paid their money and with a strained face he handed over the small white stubs emblazoned with the blue inked photo of Cobá's pyramid and stamped with the day's date. The coach loads passed through and the first of the cars that had hung back to avoid the crowds approached him. His smile was waning. He had drunk too much as the day was rising and the crowds were teeming and now he was desperate to make the short journey to the washrooms within.

There were more stradlers in the distance but he could wait no longer. He pulled across his shutter and abandoned his post but the walk even out of the stall was too painful to bear as he stopped short beyond the back door and stepped two or three paces towards the trees behind and unzipped his fly.

Urine burst forth with the stench of bitter coffee steaming onto the dry earth at the base of the tree that sheltered his daytime abode. He smiled with his eyes closed as the pressure was alleviated from his waistband allowing him to spread his feet a little wider to avoid the possible snaking pool that was likely to slither back towards him. His legs apart he broke wind with a ripple of thunder that could probably be heard in the car park, not that he cared, not until he opened his eyes at least.

As he looked down to zip up he sensed a figure to his left stood staring at him. He jumped back startled and embarrassed. A tall striking woman stood before him leaning against the corner of the enclosed stall. She could have been Swedish he guessed going by her wildly spiked blonde hair, or German going by the strong and harsh jawline, an Amazonian of Aryan descent, but it was the piercing eyes painted in behind a swath of point black eyeliner such as the Egyptians wore that glued him to the spot so that he failed to notice the spillage catch up to the edge of his boots and hug them lovingly as it circled round the sole.

She made a gesture with the tilt of her head as if to ask, 'have you finished?'

Alejandro nodded bashfully.

She had something in her hand which she held forward with her arm fully outstretched but just far enough away that he couldn't make a grab for it. It was a photograph of a young woman. He studied the face. She looked familiar; he thought he'd seen her pass through, if not her then someone very similar. He nodded slowly and cautiously, not totally sure of himself and feeling a little more than intimidated at being caught short under such unusual circumstances.

"¿Hoy en día? ¿Esta mañana?" she demanded.

"Sí," he said without hesitation, not feeling he could afford to give it any further thought.

She pulled back the photograph and rolled back around the corner out of sight. He edged slowly after her confused as to what had just happened but she was gone. He favoured that he caught a glimpse of her jogging in through the gates to the entrance of the hidden city but she was too swift for his eyes to focus over the distance.

Alejandro made his way back into the booth, his mind swirling about what that had all been about and hoping that he hadn't just caused some trouble for the girl in the photograph who in comparison looked sweet and innocent and unable to hurt a fly. A slight shudder ran up his spine at the thought of what the blonde woman could and would maybe do to the girl she was seeking and he made up his mind there and then that if anything happened he would deny ever having laid eyes on either of them as they entered.

He resumed his seat, taking a gulp from his water bottle as he did so, the heat of the day now not being the only thing to make his pores open to dowse his cotton uniform shirt.

A tall thin man with a moustache and busy hair approached the counter and asked for a single ticket. He had an Italian accent and his face was pleasant and smiling. It was a pleasant exchange for which he was thankful following what had just happened out back. The tickets and money swapped hands and the Italian went about his day, pausing to light a cigarette before entering the park, leaving Alejandro agitated and watchful for who would leave the woods that day or whether la policía would be called for some drastic occurrence beyond his control.

Once again he set his mind to deny all.

5

Oliver Hand was an upright upper class Englishman whom for the last twenty years had spent little, if any, of his precious time in his native land other than to broker the odd deal in the cold offices of Threadneedle Street, or more recently Canary Wharf, or to clasp hands with the bureaucrats and politicians in Westminster who needed a prod occasionally to prevent them blocking the desires of the consortium.

The consortium itself had no name, not officially that anyone would dare to mention, yet it was known to most simply as 'the company' or 'the organisation' or 'the consortium' depending upon to whom you spoke, the terms being interchangeable and recognisable as meaning the same thing to those in the know. They were a most powerful elite of individuals all serving the same goal of united politics and finance: a united Europe, a global economy, a singular secular religion, a world democracy controlled and maintained by the wisest and richest, the most powerful and selfish. They purported openly to have the world's interest at heart, that under their philosophic rule none would go without and all would be taken care of and everyone would be deemed as equal. There were obvious comparisons to communist rule and fears for the decline, or even purposeful eradication of religion and free will under such tyranny, yet despite this the group gained large amounts of finance and following by those wealthy enough to manipulate and legislate the laws of the land, keeping the rich richer and in control and the poor submissive and fearful of rebellion. Nation after nation financial instability rocked the security of once sturdy governments, and uprisings within formerly firmly held strongholds of dictatorships broke forth into long drawn out civil wars, all distractions planned out and propagated by the puppeteers of the consortium who strove to rewrite the world's infrastructure with the aim of being global princes, ruling under the auspices of the immortality gained through science and a control over time and space procured through the same.

Billions of dollars were invested heavily into scientific research into what they as a group believed were true, for they had seen it prophesied throughout history of their coming age and of their own interference in the poles of humanity's timeline. They were the gods of old that had shaped the religions of the past and would command the future age. So they believed.

To the ordinary man they would be deemed religious nut jobs perhaps, whose misreading of history and artefacts was skewed by their immense wealth and ego, but to those who to all intents and purposes lived in a financial bubble so disconnected to the real world, that one percent of the world's wealthiest, their cause was infectious and compelling, and beyond that it was respectable and worthy of investment and a bowing and bending of the rules every so often to accommodate the cause.

Oliver Hand was one of those elect few who hoped to attain that prized immortal position in the heavens. Plenty had gone before him with an air of authoritative assurance only to be disappointed, but he was living in an age where the results were beginning to shine through. Only recently they had opened a wormhole through space and time - unfortunately it was unstable and the mechanism to control it had fallen from their hands and many other matters of security and other worldly stability had hence been raised, especially when the main research facility in Illinois had been destroyed.

Then there were rumours of ghosts from another plane controlling the ethereal realm they had deemed themselves the ephoral judges over. It was a rumour they dare not challenge as the mystique behind it seemed to bolster their status as being ordained instruments of power over the Earth.

The ReSYEM Project's success was just another indication of their growing power and near grasp of their ultimate goals. Never before had they been so close to achieving immortality as they were now. The process had to be refined, a chemical process was still lacking to ensure its stability but the research was continuing in earnest and expanding to further regions where the natural compounds were readily available to expedite the research time, for all at his level were keen for a stable result for there were two of the board whose age had almost passed and whose physicians had proclaimed their last days as counting, these two were willing to sample of the unstable compound and forego the painful risks that came with trials. Selfishly they were held back by the governing board who in their own spiteful ways sought two lesser men to share the throne.

They all knew that should they succeed their immense lust for power would set them at war with each other eventually but each had agreed on the pursuit of discovery of ancient lands and far flung civilisations, fulfilling their roles in history as the Zeus and Yahweh, Ra and Odin of a lesser year before returning to seal the future fate of humanity.

So they believed, and so to this end they strived with all their wealth and power at their disposal, manipulating all in their path.

Oliver Hand sat and waited. He was a patient man who took great diligence in scrutinising the extremities of a problem when things went cataclysmically wrong. The Russian mine had gone wrong in such a way. One such loss was acceptable but this was the second research facility to have been lost to an explosion in so many years. The consortium was haemorrhaging funds and too many backers were losing faith in their ideals. In short they couldn't afford many more mishaps.

Warsaw was one of his least favourite places to visit. He disliked the colder climates and preferred his offices in the Far East; he held an office in Hong Kong and one also in Singapore where he found eastern mythology and religious beliefs more conducive to being swayed in the direction of his own ideology. Still Warsaw was where he had chosen to promote a new lieutenant into their ranks, to allow him, an aspiring young manipulator of business and scrutiniser of policy, to prove himself. Unfortunately it seemed his judgement had been misplaced. It wasn't that Tomasz Sikora had failed in securing the funding - he had never been expected to achieve such a task. It wasn't that he had mishandled the Vicky Rivers situation - that was still playing out as predicted and would soon come to a tidy conclusion, and for his part Tomasz had played his role impeccably. The area of disappointment however had come with the news that Tomasz Sikora had proved disloyal - he had questioned and doubted his instructions and queried the motives and manner of his employer. What Oliver Hand had come to see was whether this disloyalty was a danger to their goals and whether it needed to be neutralised or whether Tomasz Sikora could be persuaded to be brought back in line with the corporation.

Oliver Hand leaned back in his chair in the hotel conference room he had requested for the meeting. He had heard what his confidant had to say and knew too of his ambitions to climb into the role that Tomasz Sikora currently filled - that was never going to happen, the man simply didn't have the skills, but so long as the carrot was hung above his nose he kept looking up to something he would never reach and that satisfied his purpose. He cared little for friendship and the disloyalty between friends, except to note that disloyalty bred and the man before him was already too foolish enough to know that he had cast himself out of the league by proving himself untrustworthy.

"So'" Oliver Hand leaned forward slowly and said with careful consideration, "he has spoken openly about his doubts about the company, eh, our motives and our methods, and has revealed details, no matter how sketchy, to a select outside few, eh?"

The other man nodded in agreement that that was the basis of what he had just reported in greater detail.

"I see."

Oliver Hand looked to the shadow of the man stood outside the room, one of his security guards awaiting his orders. He would get an order soon enough and would carry it out with the utmost discretion.

A folder sat on the desk in front of Oliver Hand, its contents were empty but that wasn't its purpose for being placed on the desk. He moved it now with the slow caution of one not wanting to alert another as he gripped and raised the pistol that harboured beneath it and shot coldly into the distance in front of him. The shot rang out causing a slight flinch from the shadow outside the door but not enough to cause him to abandon his stolid stance.

Oliver Hand placed the smoking gun back down on the table. Unlike most of his contemporaries he liked to take care of his own business personally; if anyone was going to play Zeus it would be he and he alone!

The unsuspecting body slumped from the chair in a lifeless heap, a single bullet wound slowly spilling blood onto the laminate flooring from where Tomek Bednarczyk lay dead.

6

The mosquitos buzzed about her ankles as soon as she entered the shade of the jungle and she immediately regretted not planning carefully enough. She gathered enough from the pamphlet to know that she wasn't all that interested in the minor ruins near the entrance, and she cared little for the ancient ball courts that hid further in that were used as climbing frames by the grey rugged iguanas that stood camouflaged on the ashen stone until such a time as they felt the impetus to scatter at speed with their front legs flinging wide whilst their rear was propelled from side to side across the dust of the jungle floor.

She hung back from the group she'd followed in and feigned a brief interest as if to observe some of the immediate ruins near the entrance before making her way towards the guide come tricycle taxis lined up awaiting a fare. There were about six lying in wait under the shelter of some trees but none touted for her business but waited patiently to be approached. Pleasantly surprised at not being pestered she strolled up to the nearest, a young man maybe in his late teens, slim but strong in muscle (she guessed from the constant peddling of passengers to and fro in the cart he hauled behind him). His complexion was dark and his eyes slightly slanted and his hair jet back and she favoured him to be one of the local Mayan descendants from the builders of the lost city that had been swallowed by the land that closed in around them. She pointed to the picture on the pamphlet and begged the question in her strong Irish lilt if he'd take her to the pyramid. He nodded and gestured to her to take a seat behind him and off they went.

It was a surprisingly pleasant ride as she listened out for the sounds of the birds hoping to see a Toucan but not too disappointed at the lack of appearance. Huge multifaceted butterflies danced from tree to tree fluttering across the path before and behind her carriage as her chauffeur pumped with his strong thighs to cover the mile and a half of dense woodland that had been cleared along the original city roads to create a wide path for the tourists to reach the fabled sites in safety.

Her first glimpse of the pyramid was awe shattering as she broke from the trees into the open space at the foot of the 138 foot pyramid to the clamour of brusque battlements of a coachload of brash American's egging each other on in a race to the top.

Talisa thanked her ride and paid him with a smile as he then cycled to join his other comrades sheltered under a tin roof waiting for the American's to come back down and beg a ride so as not to get caught walking back in the midday heat.

She too stood back and watched the American's as they jostled for space among the giant building blocks that formed the steps, some using the rope that lined the middle from top to bottom to pull themselves up, others stepping wide of the middle and stretching their legs high for reach onto the next step. For most it was clearly an effort as they stopped to pose for photographs or to just take in the midway view.

She decided to wait till they came back down before beginning her ascent. Climbing would be difficult with her short legs and she had never been one for having an audience in such sporting trials. There was a shaded waiting area with plaques of information about the historical site which she decided to educate herself upon as she killed for time.

The whole thing was a test to see if they would appear together as she tried to figure out whether there was anyone around her that she could trust. She had consulted with José, the bell boy that seemed to have a finger in every pie as he sidled up to all and sundry with his cheeky smile and willingness to please. She had asked about what sites were good to visit but weren't too swamped with tourists. She wanted a place that was easy access to get to but where she could easily see a face in the crowd if she needed to. After taking his advice she had booked in the excursion at the hotel's tourist desk hoping that he would feed it back to the psycho bitch that was chasing her. As far as she could tell Vicky hadn't yet spotted her hiding in the shadows right under nose, but the other guy had. If they were in cahoots together, and she was pretty sure they were, then they would arrive here together and she hoped to spot them from a distance, a distance of 138 feet up where she could easily evade anything thrown up at her. If they didn't turn up together then the mystery of who he was hung tauntingly in her mind as to whether he was friend or foe; it had been so long since she'd had a friend that she dared not put too much hope in it.

***

He took a deep breath and closed his eyes. "Are you sure?...So why was that never in the report?"

There was a long pause on his end as he listened intently, nodding occasionally his understanding as it all fell into place. "Yes, I understand. Thank you." He went to hang up the phone but stopped himself abruptly. "Tell me, doctor, does the...er... does the company understand the implications of what you've just told me?... I see. Thank you."

Tomasz hung up the phone and quickly dialled another number. He had to let Sergio know what he was walking into. Talisa Hayes was a time bomb just waiting to go off.

***

Sergio walked the path following the crowds hoping to spot Vicky in amongst the bus loads that had arrived just before them. He had lost sight of her as he waited patiently for the man in the booth to get his act together and stamp his ticket.

He swatted at the mosquitos as they buzzed at his bare legs and he regretted then not changing into the thin linen trousers that were in the boot of the hire car. An iguana ran curiously in front of him, close enough to kick it away if he wanted to, and he marvelled at how tame these reptiles had become around the frequent human visitors.

He clung to the edge of the tourist group, a mixture of English and German, and tried to blend in, suddenly aware how unprepared for this excursion he was having no hat or deet, the latter of which rose to his nose in plumes of spray as the group reacted to the firm signs of the little blood suckers zipping out of the shadows on a hunting expedition having spied the big game enter the park.

Vicky wasn't in the first group that he could see so he edged away slowly to get a view of the path ahead.

He thought he caught a glimpse of short blonde hair weaving through the trees up ahead and quickened his pace. He got to the point where he thought he'd seen her only to find a pair of mating butterflies, bright yellow in colour waltzing along the path.

The mudded ground was dry but smelt slightly damp and he wondered whether anything ever dried out completely under the thick canopy of the trees. He followed the path until he came to a slanted block of rock the length of two tourist buses. At a point a small carved piece of rock jutted back towards the slant forming a hole in the stone. He stepped back to try and figure out the purpose of such a structure and then realised that behind him stood another exactly the same only facing the other and partially crumbled in places and hidden by the encroaching trees. They reminded him of an aqueduct only their purpose didn't appear to be for the flow of water. He could picture himself running across the diagonal surface from one side to another and then wondered whether it was some sort of pavilion or stand for a sports arena. He didn't know how close he was as he backed away missing the sign printed on a wooden plaque explaining that it was the ball court the Mayans used for sport.

He reached a crossroads where the paths split and the sun broke through the thick leaves that sheltered the fluorescent blue morpho butterflies as they beat their wings through the sparkling rays of dust that fell across the path. It was drier here and there were less mosquitos. He'd had the presence of mind to at least bring a water bottle with him, not enough for the heat of the day but it would suffice for the moment. He unscrewed the lid and sipped sparingly.

A sign pointed in one direction stating Cenote, and in the other it stated Nohoch Mul. He knew what Cenote meant, he had seen enough signs for them on the drive from Tulum and had read about them in the guide book in his hotel room: they were the natural pools, mostly hidden underground, that drew divers the world over to swim in their natural beauty, some went for miles underground and many others were shallow but surrounded in beautiful landscape settings. He hadn't visited any himself and doubted he would get the opportunity as he kept reminding himself that he was here to do a job.

He had no idea what Nohoch Mul stood for but figured it was a better bet than following a path to the pool. Now alone on the path with no distraction the edging fear of who he was following and why crept up on him again and it came to mind that no one knew where he was. He reached for his phone thinking that he should inform Tomasz of his whereabouts, especially if someone was coming to deal with Vicky - *am I really going to step aside for them to kill her? Does that make me complicit in her murder?*

He shook off the thought violently, his tangled hair bouncing with the movement - *make the call, find her, go home!*

He looked to his phone and dialled the number. A high pitched whine rang back at him. He pulled the phone from his ear and looked again at the screen to discover that in the wilds of empty jungle, even at a famous historical site, there was no reception.

7

The shade from the stubby tower at the top of the pyramid had been drawing in towards her feet at a rapid pace. Talisa now crouched low in the entrance to the top of the great structure - a low wooden door fit for a dwarf but gated off with metal bars to block the way of tourists, a lip of stone that protruded from above the gate was her only shelter from the blazing sun.

She had already checked out the other side of the structure that was hidden from view in all the pictures shown to the public. It was no surprise to her to find that the rear of the pyramid was roped off as its crumbling rocks fell into the mound of earth and trees which had grown up on that side making its ascent treacherous and near on impossible to navigate.

She readjusted her cap to cover as much of her face as possible without shielding her view and dabbed at her neck with her sleeve. There had been only a few stragglers on the giant steps as the waves of tourists ebbed and flowed with the coaches that brought them. Most people didn't stop for long, a few lingered to take in the amazing view of clear blue sky meeting a carpet of jungle as the trees knelt for miles in every direction in worship of the monument she sat atop of. From this angle it was amazing to think that it couldn't be seen from the distance of the road so protected was it by the jungle. Of those that lingered a few gave her curious glances but in return she made them feel successfully uncomfortable enough to abandon any desire they may have had to stay.

She had used her time to plot the quickest route down, judging the size of the steps with the ease in which others descended. The climb up had been hard going as she had raced to the top not wanting her back open to attack for any prolonged period of time. She had used the rope to pull herself up as she steadied her feet and stretched out her short legs on the steep rocks.

Another wave washed in now and she studied them from her eagles perch knowing that none would be able to spot her crouched so low. There was no one of interest wandering through with the crowd as they slowly circled below and stopped to take their photographs of the imposing structure. They spent a good few minutes examining from afar the thing they had come such a distance to see before the first of the group struck up the boldness to climb the first step. Once he was three or four steps up it seemed to signal to the rest that it was safe and ok to climb and before you knew it the slow race had begun again in earnest, though hard going in the midday sun.

Sometimes she marvelled at how acute the mind could be and such a time was now as two things peeked in perfect sharpness in her mind simultaneously. The first was the ambling figure of the Italian breaching the woods and staring in wonder as any other tourist but also searching the crowd before him looking for someone. The other was the sound of exasperated breath and hands on rock as feet kicked away at the creepers of undergrowth that threatened to ensnare behind her.

Talisa bounded from her hiding place and peeked her head swiftly but cautiously round the sharp edge of stone that was the cap of the holy temple. The blonde head rose up from a body on all fours, that of an albino panther viciously snarling its hatred as it clawed its way to the summit.

Talisa wasted no time. She hadn't expected an assault from behind, had thought her plan fool proof and that Vicky wouldn't be able to spot her from below and if she did she would have had the advantage of seeing her first.

Damn she was good!

As she leapt for the first steps down she concluded that she had underestimated her opponent yet again and that Vicky must have second guessed her every move.

She bounded down the first half dozen steps with ease but then felt the breeze of the assault behind her as the long legs of her opponent took the advantage and swept after her, skipping stones as she jumped distances Talisa dared not fly. She reached the halfway mark where oversized Americans were puffing and panting and stopping in confusion at the two banshees wailing down on them. Talisa misjudged a step and went colliding into one of them knocking them both down. Vicky too collided with someone but her collision was on purpose as the fairly muscular man was in her path, instinctively he struck out in defence as they both clasped one another's clothing, grappling for balance as they tottered on the edge. It was enough to slow Vicky down and had she not been in a hurry to deal with Talisa she would have dealt a more permanent blow to the fellow in her way.

Talisa meanwhile had tumbled over the figure that had blocked her way, he having had the speed of mind to grab the rope to stop his backward descent leaving Talisa to bounce over him to fall hard on the rocks below and to continue bouncing in the long hard road to the bottom.

Talisa looked up from where she lay battered and in agony. She had got down quicker than expected but it had cost her some broken bones, she could feel them trying to mend themselves as she stared up at Vicky who stood half way, holding the rope as though waiting to see whether she would still try to make a run for it.

Talisa had no doubts and she wasted no time. Not looking back she gained her feet and ran for it. The Italian blocked her way, hands out and pleading but she didn't stop to listen to what he had to say but noted that he wasn't actually trying to stop her either.

She bounded up the path away from the pyramid in the only direction that led out of the park. The sound of a bicycle bell racing behind her was the first and only thing she swerved and swung around for. One of the taxis boys, having seen her plight, had come racing to her rescue. Without slowing too much he beckoned her to get in as he raced her along the path towards the entrance.

As she sat in the back of the shaded carriage she allowed her body to heal and listened for the heavy thud of footsteps chasing behind or the clattering of another bike but neither came.

It took no more than five minutes to reach the entrance and she leaped from her seat without waiting for the stunned rider to stop. He yelled something behind her, whether it was out of concern for her to see a doctor after her fall or demand for payment she had no idea, she blocked her ears to it and kept on running. She ran into the open car park and to the first car that stood victim to her. The window was half down, a regular practise to allow the hot air to escape. She slipped her arm in and lifted the catch and fell into the driver's seat, pulling the door closed behind her. She had two minutes at most she calculated before Vicky caught up with her. She checked the usual places for keys in the unlikely event that they were in the car as she wasn't sure how long it would take her to hot wire it. As she flipped the visor down she couldn't believe her luck as they keys dropped down into her lap.

Talisa was tearing out of the car park like the devil was on her tail, the image of Vicky racing into the open behind her filling her rear view mirror with the Italian trotting out of breath behind her.

8

Tomasz Sikora's head was pounding. For a few moments confusion reigned as to where he was and why he felt paralysed. He tried to recall his last memory but found the murky waters being dredged still heavily battered by the storm raging overhead.

No longer was his head resting on the pillows of his super king-size bed in his apartment, although a fragment of a dream recurred a muscled hand across his mouth and nose and a cloth with a strong odour of chloroform.

A chair now held his back rigid where the mattress had allowed to curve his spine in comfort and his hands and feet felt secured tightly to the frame by plastic cable ties. He tried to pull his hands forward from their position behind his back where they pulled at his shoulders but he felt the too tight plastic cut into his wrists drawing blood it would seem not for the first time.

He had no sense of time; even with his eyes closed he sensed the curtains were closed and the room was in relative darkness shut out from the rest of the world.

I'm dreaming. Go deeper. Sink back to the pillow.
And he did.

The next time he awoke the smell of chloroform was far distant but a fresh sting of a needle felt as though it had pierced a vein in his neck. The headache remained, only stronger this time, but whether it was to do with the drug he'd been administered or the swollen fractured jaw he felt drooling blood and saliva he couldn't be sure. He tried to open his eyes but found that one of them was swollen shut like an airbag had expanded on his face and he had neither the strength nor the inclination to lift himself from it.

With his one good eye he could make out the silhouette of a smartly dressed muscle bound heavy.

You again. I was hoping you'd left. Has your boss arrived yet?

The words echoed in his mind but failed to speak as he whispered to himself to be quiet, his mouth having caused enough damage already.

"My apologies for my tardiness, Mr Sikora." The voice seemed to echo through the room as it bounced off the walls of his living room and disappeared, lost in the open space between the dining room and his bedroom. "Jonas here has been a little heavy handed in his treatment of you for which I offer no apology for he reacts badly to a loose tongue and the insubordinate resistance of cheek. What you find humour he deems as aggression, eh. I'm sure you understand, don't you, Mr Sikora?"

The voice was that of an Englishman, pompous, authoritative, and ultimately commanding of the situation.

"Mr Hand," Tomasz slurred as the smaller second figure stepped into view before the drawn curtain holding back the day, "I don't understand."

"No, no, of course not. Very few understand the implications of their actions, if they did they wouldn't act so flippantly even among their most confided compatriots, eh? Do you not think so, eh Mr Sikora?"

"I... I don't understand," he again drooled wanting to wipe at his chin but once again feeling the cut of his wrists which pulled his head up sharply from its stoop at the shockwave of pain that fled up his arms to his shoulders into the back of his head.

"You know our business, Mr Sikora? Of course you do, you have grown fat off it of late, have you not?" The Englishman swept an arm of display around the room to indicate his wealth. "How many corners were cut on the build control to expand such a property? You must have paid the council well to turn a blind eye. It is such a shame, you could have gone far, eh." He said this last statement as if to himself as if with genuine disappointment. "But alas you know too much of our business for one with such a loose tongue as yours.

"You disappoint me," he said with a step forward and drawn breath, "I had expected more of you going from your credentials. You could have gone far with us Tomasz, but you look at files you have no business looking at and you question motives that don't concern you. To an extent that cannot be overlooked. The nature of humanity is a curious beast is it not? Trust, however, is the back bone of our business. We do not tell tales. We do not confide in those outside of our circle. To do so is to undermine our goals. To widen the circle is to widen the risk. Loose tongues lead to loss of finance. Loose tongues lead to suspicion. Loose tongues lead to the birth of enemies who would otherwise be ignorant of our very existence."

"Please Mr Hand, I only questioned about Vicky Rivers." A tear was trickling down his cheek, a river surfing the swollen mound that bulged beside his split nose merging with the sea of red to dilute it with its salt.

"Do not cry Mr Sikora, it is not befitting of you. Let me ask you, what was there to question with Miss

Rivers, eh?"

Tomasz couldn't think, he was confused as he struggled to remain conscious above the pain.

"There was nothing for you to question, Mr Sikora. There was nothing for you to look into. There was nothing for you to talk to others about."

"I'm sorry, I just...I just... it didn't feel right."

"Ah, Tomasz, you're not paid to feel, you're paid to examine the data and to follow instructions."

"But there was something in the data," Tomasz grasped at the straw as being his only defence, "the data showed she was chasing someone."

"Yes indeed, but still that was of none of your concern, eh?"

"But Talisa Hayes, you know about Talisa Hayes?"

"Of course, my dear Tomasz, in a way you could say we created her, but still she is and never was any of your concern."

Tomasz slumped his head back down with a slight shake, a reluctance of the truth he knew was coming.

"You know how this must end, eh, Mr Sikora. Goodbye Mr Sikora." With that Oliver Hand took a slow step around Tomasz and left the apartment.

Tomasz closed his eyes and waited for the inevitable, the impact of a bullet into his forehead like the impact of an unseeing locomotive riding full speed along the tracks as he knelt head forward braced for its impact.

He heard the heavy steps of the faceless goon before him and felt the needle once more inject the cold serum into his blood stream. The last thing to filter into his mind being the flick of a knife and his restraints being cut free.

9

The cloud seemed to blow in from nowhere as it lifted over the small buildings and trees of Tulum and Akumal littering its light smattering of rain upon the windshield. Within minutes the sky had grown darker and the rain heavier as it littered heavy droplets that bounced indiscriminately off the shell of the car and the fractured tarmac of the road alike. Initially he had ignored the need for wipers but the downpour suddenly grew too great to ignore and the blurred roadway hazardous as headlights sparkled in place of the sun of only moments ago. It was likely to be a short passing; heavy storms were common at midday but lingered only briefly over the coastal road as they blew inland in search of higher climes to drop their load, saturating the thirsty jungle.

The rain made it hard for Sergio to make out the cars in front but at a squint he could just trace the frame that shimmered with Vicky's tail lights.

His phone had sprung to life as he had passed a small town between Cobá and Tulum but by the time he'd retrieved it from the pocket of his shorts it had rung off. It had been Carmela and he found himself split with emotion as to whether he was sorry to have missed the call. He longed for a friendly voice right now but would settle for a voicemail if she left one. She didn't and he found himself disappointed. He had tossed the phone onto the passenger seat aware that her call was not the only one it registered as having been missed while he was in the mobile desert of the Mayan ruins.

Now driving along the sodden and unfamiliar road a good hour's journey back to Cancún his phone rang again. He glanced across to the passenger seat. Again it was Carmela. He reached across for it, taking his eyes of the road briefly, his hand on the steering wheel swaying the car slightly across lanes obliterated by the rain. The horn of a truck creeping up unlit on his blind side shouldered him back into lane and he abandoned his reach for the phone. This time she had left a message.

Talisa's eyes were watering, not that she noticed, her face was so cold she hadn't felt the warm trickle of tear line her puffed rosy cheek. The air-con was still blowing out cold air despite the sudden drop in temperature with the rain outside. In her mind she was formulating a plan but she needed to be quick for it to work. It would be painful but the odds were in her favour and ultimately, she reasoned, it would be less brutal than what Vicky might dispense upon her. The only doubt was in getting Vicky close enough in closed quarters without her knowing her intent. It was a long shot.

She remembered seeing the hardware store along the road before on the drive down and hoped that she was now on the right side to stop for it, if only she could see it in time through the rain.

Vicky almost missed the turn off she had been that close to hugging Talisa's tail. She screeched to a sliding halt inside the forecourt and caught the startled look of her prey who had leapt from her car already. They both gave a cautious look to the blue and white parked up with its solo officer sat in the driver's seat. He gave an anxious and troublesome look towards Vicky which read 'don't make me get out into the rain lady', to which Vicky raised a hand in apology for her reckless driving hoping he would take it as her failing to cope with the conditions of the road.

Talisa ran inside, both knowing there was likely to be another police officer sheltering within the store. Now wasn't the time or place and they both knew it.

Sergio missed the stop altogether, cursing in his usual cry of self-loathing of *Vanni! Vanni! Vanni!,* and cruised to the rough edge of the hard shoulder a hundred meters further up the road where he hoped he wouldn't be so conspicuous when he needed to pull out again. He thought about reaching for the phone again but was scared of missing his cue to drive on as he studied his rear-view mirror for any sign of cars pulling back out into the road. Instead he thought of Vicky bashing past him and sprinting along the path away from the pyramid which he was saddened only to have gotten a momentary glimpse of.

He reflected on how she hadn't seemed surprised to see him, nor even acknowledged his presence as though she knew he was there all along and couldn't care less as she raced blinkered like a horse out of the trap. She could run fast that was for sure and he could only chase her a little way before he gave up, out of breath and dizzy. Fortunately at the outburst of so much frantic running the curious taxis' came cycling laughing at him being outrun and in jest offered him a ride, but by the time he caught up with her she was already racing for her car.

In his mind he likened her activity not too dissimilar to his own, with the exception of the killing. Like a crocodile they both lay in patient ambush waiting till their prey was close enough to leap out of the water, letting it feel comfortable by allowing it to come back time and time again until they struck, only Sergio usually struck with a camera lens whereas Vicky struck with a knife and used those vicious teeth of the reptile. His confusion was not knowing at what she was striking and why.

He shuddered at the comparison, disgusted at likening himself to an assassin such as she.

The rain began to ease a little and a hint of blue rose above the trees to the right of the car, not that it brought any comfort for she would be bound to spot him sat waiting at the side of the road as she exited back into the traffic.

He raised his water bottle to his lips, not out of thirst but for something to do, his bladder feeling the early twinges of being full but he ignored the sensation; surely they'd be back at the hotel soon enough.

As the rain drizzled down on the face of Talisa Vicky could make out the police officer walking beside her chirpily assisting her to her car carrying supplies of what looked like industrial toilet cleaner and lime sulphur insecticide. The officer looked directly at her and she busied herself as if adjusting her make-up in the mirror while they loaded the materials into the trunk of the car.

Vicky flashed back to a news report she saw, at least she thought it was a news report, the images seemed too real in her memory as if she'd been there at the event of a bitter woman snapping at a young girl, a girl who had done little more than look with curiously at the disfigured stranger who was soon to become her assailant who then proceeded to throw acid in the young girl's face scarring her once natural beauty forever as a reminder not to mock the appearance of others.

Did she do that? She couldn't quite remember.

Was this what Talisa had in mind? She doubted it. Talisa had other ideas and Vicky's mind wasn't so far gone to fail to mix the ingredients in her head. She knew what those products could create and she had no intention of giving her the opportunity of mixing them in her presence.

Whose bloody car is this anyhow ya daft cow? she quizzed herself as she reversed under the watchful eye of the two police officers.

She gave a sly smile to Vicky as she pulled out onto the road knowing she had to hit the gas hard to gain as much of an advantage as she could. The rain was easing which would make the going quicker if she could just cut across as many lights ahead of her as she could and thrash the crap out of the tin bucket she was driving.

The fuel gage said she had enough to make it back without another stop. She prayed Vicky's wasn't so plenty.

She cursed herself for the umpteenth time for missing the step on the pyramid that caused her so much pain and almost got her caught; she thought she had planned the route so well in her head.

She had a sudden and overwhelming desire to cut

her hair as the chemical scent from the trunk of the car played memories of peroxide wafting up to her nostrils in vague recollection of a previous disguise, it leant her mind to another scent too, that of bromide she associated with her treatment at the hospital that wasn't, the cyst panging her insides in reminder that not all things heal. A flash of memory spat into her mind as she recalled the almost comatose girl she used to share a room with, a paranoid schizophrenic the nurses had said, they kept her dosed and sedated most of the time, occasionally coming to to whisper some random gem of far flung thought from whatever universe her mind usually occupied, raving for her to get out and escape the experiments they were conducting on them all. Whenever she had trouble sleeping she would slip across to her bed and sneak a couple of her pills to help her cope and knock her out from her own entombed reality; the nurses never noticed and the girl herself cared little, if she noticed at all, and eventually it became a memory blotted out with so many others as she hid the trauma and the truth of what they had turned her into.

She punched down hard with her foot at seeing the traffic lights ahead change and just scraped through unscathed, her petite figure reaching up to the rear view mirror with a viciously evil smirk at seeing the car behind being forced to screech to a halt.

"Damn it!" Vicky yelled as once again her path was blocked by traffic. There was a police check point higher up on the raised section by Player del Carmen and so she had dropped down to the slip road that ran parallel but hadn't counted on the numerous traffic lights and speed humps that controlled the traffic towards the residential and shopping districts.

"Why, you stupid cow? You should've known!" She thumped the horn, not for any warning but out of sheer frustration of her own foolishness. She was getting sloppy and not thinking straight.

Are you sure you want to do this Vicky?

"Shut up Giles!" she yelled at the voice that echoed in her head.

Don't be like old Ahab.

She shook her head. She'd had this ghostly conversation before with the old man Montgomery pleading as like poor frustrated and fearful Starbuck with the old stubborn captain to turn tail and head for Nantucket. She taunted him in return that he, like Starbuck, was impure of thought and willing, lusting for her heart to be pulled and squeezed dry, for she was certain too that murder and mutiny had crossed the crest of his mind concerning her, but cowardice be the stronger motivator and stilled such thoughts; the stalling of an aircraft falling silently with the updraft battering its sails, its passengers sat with eyes pinched awaiting and praying that its captain take control and command of his vessel upward before the swell of land or sea leapt up through the clouds to meet it.

Why chase the whale you cannot kill? You foolish girl!

You read but you do not learn!
You look but you do not see!
You chase but you do not catch!

"You don't understand!" she yelled back. "This is Providence. This is what I was born for. This is my destiny."

Richard Plantagenet craved what was rightly his at the cost of his head hung at the gates of York. Agamemnon, sacrificed his daughter to gain favour with the gods for the war, because Menelaus believed it right to chase after his Helen. What will you sacrifice? Who will you deceive like Jacob of his brother's birth right? What of your arrogance like Hannibal of his charge across the Himalayas against the mighty Rome, or Scott taking on the battering breath of the Antarctic. You have lost your bearings, like the Argonauts flailing around in the dark of Doliones and slaying their king.

"What, you think I should do to myself as Cyzicus' wife?" she screamed abhorrent, unaware the conversation was in her head.

You are no Jason and will return with no fleece! bellowed back the doctors voice.

"I told you before old man, get out of my head!"

A series of horns tooted loudly around her snapping her out of her argument to see that she had stopped the car violently in the middle of the up ramp back to the main coastal road, the car behind narrowly avoiding a collision to her rear.

"Stay out of my head old man," she said more quietly to herself as she punched the pedal with her foot once more.

She swung onto the busy road forcing a path in the traffic, not knowing how far ahead she had allowed Talisa to get and caring little for the Italian she knew skulked somewhere behind. She refocused her mind on the task at hand and set a goal to overtake everything on the road.

What happened to your brother Lisa?

"Shut up!" she cried with a genuine tear streaking her face. This time it was her mother's voice who begged the question, the only voice of reason she'd listen to, but she was too lost to her anger.

10

In the world we live in there are good and bad by the multitude, often, however, we may only see one side or the other. If we surround ourselves with people of one persuasion then often we will look through life with the morals and status in life which that side brings, to then stand in judgement of misunderstanding of the other. For all though there is a choice, and at some point in our lives we make it, hitting that fork in the road and staring down the path that totters along the cliff edge whose sign posts announce: Hell, or prison, or bad boy, or silent rogue; as opposed to the other path paved with imagined gold, or at least of a shiny metal to reflect its glory, its sign reading: Heaven, or happiness, a good life, or a good person. To begin with the signs to these paths might not be clear: the wind might have blown the dust across the path to blanket the sticky tar from the gold, or mud, or dare I say it, blood may have been smeared across the sign making its letters unreadable. Either way we make a choice, but the desert land in between is not impassable and despite the distance we can choose to step off our chosen path and trudge across the barren lands to choose the other path before our current one runs out, trusting our sense and our judgement, or even the guiding of an unseen force or hand, maybe the whispering of a still small voice. The choice remains ours so long as the clock is ticking and the gong has yet to be struck.

Tomasz Sikora had made his choice. He had chosen to surround himself in his later years with the bad boys of society, and so those he trusted in were as untrustworthy as himself, some emulating him as good in their distorted view of their own path and surroundings, while others manipulated him from their position further along the same rotten trail.

Wieslaw Raczynski and Cristian Lenart had too made their choices as they followed their fellow friend, like sheep to the slaughter, giving little thought as to where it led. For both the journey across to the other path was not a great stretch of their legs as their eyes adorned and even cherished parts of that glorious life that they hadn't quite abandoned hope for. Cristian Lenart in particular would often glance across the plain at his family with one foot in the dusty desert and the other firmly stuck in the gloopy mud of the path that clung him to his misguided friends.

Neither knew as they sat at their usual spot outside Czekolada's of the fate of their two friends: Tomasz and Tomek. Neither knew that things could have turned out differently had they made different decisions in life, or surrounded themselves with a circle of friends to whom the poor judgements and criminality was an alien thing; people who lived in ignorance of such things but not without trials and problems of their own, only theirs were of a more innocent nature of what circumstance threw at them.

Justyna placed down their coffee cups on the table, smiling broadly and no doubt wondering why Tomasz was not yet among them, wiping the spillage on her white apron as she turned her back to re-enter the shadowed interior of her life. Vicky (had she been there) may have noted the sloppy lipstick marks on the cups where they hadn't been washed thoroughly by the dishwasher.

But Vicky Rivers wasn't there - she didn't need to be. There were enough bad people in their circle that span around the outer rim of the black hole that would eventually swallow them all as the gravity of their deeds weighed too heavily to repel them from the sun. Had they stopped to look to that glowing orb and away from the darkness they may have had a chance, but for all it was a decision for another day.

The explosion rang out high and loud shattering glass further up the street towards the C&A and the Atlantic cinema and the St. Andrew's Palace Hotel. People stood in the street outside these buildings were knocked to their feet by the sudden impact of the blast, unhurt except for the odd splinter of flying glass but shocked to the volume and tremor in the air.

The two friends, who sat innocently enjoying a coffee at Czekolada's waiting for their friends to join them, both stood, both judging the distance of the explosion and its direction, both staring at the other in the familiar knowledge of what buildings stood in that direction, and more importantly whose home.

Justyna ran out along with Bronislaw pulling up his pants over the flab of his behind to face the shattered debris that could still be seen falling as people lifted themselves from their places of relocation.

Neither men, nor any bystander preoccupied by the blast that rippled along the street noticed the black car that had silently rolled into position outside the coffee shop, its window lowered and the barrel of a silencer that slightly protruded from within.

A zip of shots flew out across the air unnoticed by the clamour and rising shouts of distress as the two men flinched and spasmed in a shocked jig to the silent march of death as they fell wordlessly to their table.

The car rolled away just as unnoticed as it had arrived.

Justyna would turn uncomprehending and too late to make any difference to their fate, and she would scream a delayed and fearful scream once her eyes had adjusted and met with her mind to finally make sense of the scene of her fancied friends.

11

The car park was full thanks to the two great big coaches that laboured heavily their exhumed breath into the otherwise saintly air of the resort. One was parked blocking the entrance to the hotel reception in the car park itself, the other was on the street, half mounted on the pavement with its rear too far over the driveway to permit anything but a Mini to squeeze by and risk peering out beyond the tail of the bus, even Nemo under the fin of his father's fear had a better view of the dangers awaiting him in the ocean outside.

Sergio could see that he had little chance of fitting into the car park; a quick glimpse along the drive told him there were already frustrated tourists lined up waiting for the first available space. Instead he swung his hire car around the front of the coach waiting on the street and mounted the pavement on two wheels not too clumsily from the front garden of the hotel.

How far behind he had fallen in the chase he had no idea but he knew he had fallen back way too far when he pulled off the main road at Playa del Carmen and got caught at the traffic lights too many to mention. He had no choice then but to head back to the hotel and just hope they were there or were heading back there soon. He wondered whether Tomasz' man had yet to arrive.

He locked the car to the hypocritical shake of a head from the coach driver as if to say 'you can't park there' and then walked down the narrow drive to the main hotel entrance. It was a nest of ants running back and forth. José and his colleagues were busily hauling cases from trolleys and lifting them into the belly of the whale or into the hump of the smaller taxis whose pot-bellied drivers stood doing the minimal with cigars dangling as they joked in Spanish with each other in what were no doubt sleights aimed at deaf ears. Beyond them the reception was overwhelmed as the attractive and always smiling and helpful to please girls behind the counter, with their perfect make-up and balanced hair, made a case of not being flustered or over worked as they systematically checked out the coachloads who on mass had decided quite by accident to all leave it to the last minute to settle their accounts.

Clearly there were outbound flights due this evening which also meant that another bombardment of pink flesh was to swarm the nest now being vacated and was likely to arrive as soon as the staff had caught their breath.

Sergio backed out of the driveway and walked across the road to the beach. He didn't need the crowds, the rush of faces, the noise and clamour, the chase of death he didn't rightly understand - there were things he needed to do: he needed to sit and be still, reassess his life and his direction, he had people in his life he could trust and who trusted him, but he needed to figure out how to cut out those who didn't belong there.

He sat down on the sand and scratched at the new mosquito bites that now adorned his shins and allowed his tongue to loll as he reached for his packet of cigarettes and took time before making the calls he knew he had to make.

12

Talisa had made it to her room with no sign of Vicky on her tail. She had done well to lose her so far behind and suspected she'd tried for a short cut that had failed. She hauled the large plastic containers to the lift without anyone battering an eyelid, they were all too busy, one tourist even offered to help her carry them, an offer which she accepted with an attitude of thanks, the lift doors closing on her schemes and her secured load.

She placed them down in the centre of the room and closed the curtains so the room was dark and then sat for a moment to best think out how to trap her.

In her dreams it had never panned out this way. Never was she the one holding the cards, having the tactical advantage. Her dreams always consisted of running with the innocence of a child, an innocent victim being chased through indistinguishable city streets unsure of her pursuer or pursuers - hidden masked faces hunting her with some unknown malice, a helicopter above watching her as she runs into a faceless tower block and gets into a lift which stops on a high floor as she tries to get to some unknown saviour on the roof, someone who could take her away from the nightmare horror of the chase that had engulfed her life, but as she grasps for safety and stretches out, daring to smile with joy at the hands reaching towards her to aid her escape and pull her home she is suddenly tugged back and all is lost. She is dragged back to the lift, her feet not touching the ground, no wind drawing back against her face as the rooftop blurs and she is stood alone in the ambivalence of a frame of continual flux whose boundaries have no walls and whose mind has no control and where rules do not apply. So there she would stand alone within the prison of the four walls of her cell block, the doors of the elevator firmly sealed and the counter above the door slowly lowering from its hundreds as it began its descent - and then the brakes would disengage - and she was plummeting. Too soon the numbers reaching single figures as she gripped at the sides and closed her eyes knowing the pain would come but that, being immortal, she would live through it. But the numbers didn't stop as they fled into minus figures and the rules of the dream refused to apply to the reality she imagined.

So many times she had dreamt the chase, fleeing from rooftop to rooftop running from building to building, from city to city. It wasn't always a rooftop, sometimes it was a mountain or a cliff face or a famous tower, but wherever the location there were always the same ingredients: she was always pursued to a height, always by hidden figures (never by Vicky but knowing she would be there in the end to exact the final judgement), always hands reaching out to save her before she fell into the cloudy mists of imagined vision.

Who would judge Vicky when it came to it? Who would judge her crimes?

Innocents were convicted unjustly all the time, condemned without trial, shot for being the wrong colour, bombed for having the wrong faith, sliced for being of the wrong persuasion. She thought of an aging priest she'd once read of serving a lengthy prison sentence for not paying his local taxes, and of the neighbour sentenced for assault after chasing off the gang terrorising his and his neighbours children, of the teacher who lost their job and career to the spite of a malicious and unfounded schoolchild accusation. Where was the justice? Where was the justice and the trust in the system when people like Vicky Rivers could roam the world killing indiscriminately and be protected by the long reaching arms of a criminal conglomerate, the same who wielded their power to steal lives and experiment and play god, not caring or even giving a thought to the lives of those beneath them and the effect it had on the person?

No, in her dreams it all worked out differently; in her dreams she always fell, always got dragged back, always plummeted into an endless abyss. But there was a comfort in the dreams, her familiarity with the expected pattern meant she felt she had a little control as the realities of her dreams merged with her waking world around her giving her a slight control over her own destiny, and with this growing power she dreamt that if all went well she would strike the head off the Medusa and then mount her path to Olympus to scatter the gods who reigned there. For in their plans they had overlooked her and the threat they had created for themselves.

She stood in the centre of the hotel bedroom waiting. Soon she would strike out with her rod of vengeance on all those who had harmed her and created the abomination she'd become.

13

The early afternoon sun was so strong that you would never have suspected that there had been a recent rain. Sergio dug his toes deep into the sand and lent back on his elbows with his knees bent and his eyes squinting into the sun as he hung his head back.

He didn't want this feeling to end, the unpressurised solitude of relaxing on a beach under a hot sun with no one to answer to and nowhere to be.

It was a fleeting feeling, a mirage cast in his mind by the sun, a waking dream sent to refresh and revive his weary mind. He would enjoy it anyway, it may be the last pleasure he had left. He knew full well that to enter the hotel after having followed, and been seen to follow Vicky all morning was not going to put him in good stead with the warrior queen who no doubt would have abandoned all thoughts of their sexual tryst last night and be questioning his true motives and identity.

Blocked in on all sides he felt as if the walls had moved to encase the hotel, the airport, his office and home, each a trap of emotion in his mind as he sat on his sandy bed of denial wishing he'd never answered to the name of Luigi when Tomasz had first called. It was too late now and life in all its comforts that he had worked towards was close to being lost.

He put his water bottle down on the sand and reached for his phone, having put off the inevitable for too long and dialled the Polish number stored in his phone. A harpsichord of disjointed tones clanged loudly in his ear followed by a message in Polish which he couldn't understand. He hung up and tried again. Again the same disquieting response. He checked the number before trying a third time but once again the tone seemed to suggest the number was somehow disconnected.

He scrolled down the log of his missed calls to see how many times he had missed Carmela. Four times she had called and left messages twice. He pressed and held the icon for his messages and listened intently to what she had to say. His eyes widened with each word and his head shook with realisation, not that he could do anything to effect the result. The message was of two women, Vicky Rivers and Talisa Hayes, two women who were probably in the building behind him and whom he had no desire to go anywhere near.

He hung up the phone and opened up the photos he'd taken in Vicky's room.

There was a photo of the bathroom - he zoomed in on the toiletries scattered among a number of medication pills he couldn't quite distinguish, but it tallied with what Carmela had warned in her message. A can of Lynx deodorant spray looked out of place next to another make of roll-on deodorant and he wondered whether the spray contained something other than deodorant: CS spray was what came to mind but he moved on quickly to the other pictures.

He eventually made it round to the family photo. *'It was killing her brother that had triggered it,'* Tomasz had told her. It was all in the report.

He moved on to the pages of the album. Names of the dead were mentioned, too numerous to count, but nowhere could he find Vicky's or Talisa's. There were suicides from famous sites, bomb explosions at rallies, on trains, and in buildings. Small articles of famous and influential people accidentally killed: a former astronaut killed in a jet-ski accident; politicians lost to a downed plane; bankers embroiled in sex games gone wrong. In each story there was no link except maybe in the mind of the author of the album.

'Her brother's name was Jack Walters, she killed him, but she was already diagnosed schizophrenic before then.' Carmela's tone was of concern, verging on panic, clearly wanting him to drop everything and come home for the sake of his family.

Intermixed were other stories: a French man named Jean Paul who had survived the plummeting depths from Niagara Falls; a woman who survived when her car plummeted off a bridge into raging waters in Dublin; a skydiver's miraculous escape when his parachute failed to open. There were more but the zoom of his camera failed to pick out the details.

'She's highly intelligent but completely mad. Tomasz called the office and told me to warn you. He said she compensates for the life she never had by imagining scenarios and places she's been. He said you had to leave. Sergio you have to leave!'

Interspersed with all were cut outs of Talisa Hayes posing: in one she hung from a lamppost on a busy Irish street, in another she held up her hair with a pout at a facial close up, heavily donned in make-up, in yet another she stood conservative in a tweed skirt and blazer, a smart yet innocent office attire that played on her youthful looks and gave her a coy schoolgirl appearance yet a sharp no messing business woman look. There were others - plenty of others, changing faces of styles and moods in stature and breadth the very opposite of Vicky, and on first glance you could be mistaken for thinking they related to the articles that they were stuck in next to. He examined them closely, glossy photographs, professionally taken, and in most cases cut from magazines.

'Vicky was her mother's name. Her real name is Lisa Victoria Rivers. I referenced the name Hayes, it means 'Fire'. Sergio, call me as soon as you get this and come home as quickly as you can!'

Sergio looked up from the phone thinking, the panicked voice of his trusted Carmela bore in it good advice. If Vicky Rivers had a sudden desire to kill someone then he had placed himself within her perimeter for striking distance with every justifiable motive.

Sergio prized his butt off the sand as he sloshed the remnants of his water bottle to the back of his throat and stood, propping the empty bottle on the stone edge.

The last place he wanted to go was back into the hotel behind him but as he looked back at it he knew he had to retrieve his passport from his room which meant he was likely to have to cross her path, or at least pass by the threshold of her door.

14

Vicky entered the room candidly. She could smell the strong vapour poured into the bin in the middle of the room, not too far in that she couldn't see it from the door, just lying shy of her side of the bed.

She kicked open the bathroom door but it was empty. She thought about pulling her gun from its tiny holster but decided it wouldn't be necessary. She knew what was coming. Talisa was making a stand, but first she wanted answers.

"Where are you bitch?" she scathed with hatred, her voice carrying through to the balcony where the door was open slightly blowing the white netting inwards in a gentle flap. She cautiously made her way towards it, her hand by her thigh as though ready to draw at the tattoo of the Colt inked into her flesh. She peered slowly round the bed - no one there and no room underneath for anyone to hide. With her fingertips outstretched and her head pulled way back out of reach of the door she tempered the net to the side for a view of the high balcony - it was empty save for the white plastic table and two chairs. She closed the gap of the door and turned around.

Talisa Hayes was stood boldly staring up at her blocking the passage to the narrow hallway that ran passed the bathroom to the door and the only way out of the room. Vicky figured she must have been hiding in the wardrobe.

"You're not fast enough to run for the door," Vicky warned her.

"I'm done with running," came the reply, the Irish

accent punched with a bitter bite that warned Vicky to be cautious.

Vicky drew down to her left thigh and slowly pulled up on the strapping that bound the jagged edge to her flesh and silently rose it close to her cheek and licked the flat edge of the blade.

"I like to use a knife when exacting vengeance so that I can feel the blade sink in, you don't get that with a gun."

"Vengeance? What have I done to you?"

"You breathed and then refused to die."

"You can't kill me and you know it. I'm what you live for."

Vicky hesitated and she gave away a slight shudder in the blade.

"What, do you tremble? Are you all afraid? Alas, I blame you not; for you are mortal, And mortal eyes cannot endure the devil. Oh, thou dreadful minister of hell! Thou hadst but power over this mortal body, this soul thou canst not have; therefore, be gone."

"Don't quote at me bitch! You think you're clever, I've got a million death quotes buried up here," she tapped her temple with her index finger. "I'm done playing word games! I'm not scared of you!"

"No? Then why try so hard to kill me?"

Vicky's lip trembled. Despite her brave words she was unsure of herself. The small figure of the woman before her held the gravitas of a bridge troll forbidding her to cross. Not that she'd wanted to leave the room, not until now anyway. This was what she wanted, to be close, in striking distance, but now it was here something felt wrong - terribly wrong. She needed to get out of the room. Her mind was flitting through scenarios wondering how to escape, like Odyseus trying to figure out how to open the cave door and bypass the giant, hoping she wouldn't have to get close enough to strike out the blazing eye of her cyclops, the furious Polythemus in female form.

How had things got so reversed in her mind so suddenly?

"What you want to leave? Now you want out?"

Talisa was reading her thoughts, examining her weaknesses. Unbelievably standing her ground. No one stood their ground before her, not even Jack.

"No you just shot him point blank. Cold. Calculating. Your own brother!"

"Get out of my head."

"You know the funny thing about Jack," Talisa continued, "is that he might have changed, probably would have. He came looking for you you know? He wanted your forgiveness, wanted to make amends. But you were long dead by then in the hospital and he blamed himself, figured it was his fault, that you were another victim of a little boy's butchery."

"Shut up! You can't know that!"

"That's what tipped him over the edge and turned him into a cold hearted killer. That's what convinced him he was a born killer leading him into the path of playing the executioner, the path you followed and emulated."

Vicky slammed her eyes shut in denial.

"What you think you can kill and it not play on your conscience?"

"So what, the company created you to kill me, is that it? Gave you access to Montgomery's files? Have a good read did you?"

"Don't flatter yourself. They think you're as barking mad as I do."

Vicky shook her head. She didn't understand. Despite it all staring her in the face she still didn't get it.

15

He cut through the pool entrance to the hotel detouring to the toilets in the main lobby rather than using the ones nearest the pool.

He was busting. A day of racing about following Vicky Rivers meant that he had drunk only enough to keep him functioning all day. He had missed breakfast in his rush to search her room. He had missed lunch in his rush to keep up with her at Cobá. Had it not been for the bottle of water he had taken with him he would be faint right now. His mind told him that he hadn't drunk enough fluid to have a full bladder and that he had already expelled more fluid from his body in sweat than he had taken in, yet that heavy urge was there and if he was going to make a quick dash to his room for his passport and risk bumping into her again he'd rather not do it with a full bladder.

Of course he was nowhere near as desperate as the ticket guard at Cobá had been who, totally unbeknown to Sergio had lapsed into a state of barely recognising his surroundings by the time he'd burst forth from his cabin. Sergio was acutely aware of what was around him as a heightened sense of self-preservation took over his urge to use the washrooms and note every slight movement and shape around him in case Vicky should be lying in wait for him.

It was this acute sense that caused him to spot the figure sat perusing a copy of USA Today in the lounge bar just inside the doors of the pool entrance. His back was to the wall giving him a good view of the pool, the lobby and the elevators. He wore dark shades and a cold stare which, even without seeing his eyes, told that he wasn't reading the paper. He was over dressed, too smart, too crisp, not what you'd expect of someone on holiday. He didn't look relaxed. He was working but not a holiday rep or a hotel employee, his features were too chiselled to break a smile for the hospitality industry. Ordinarily Sergio wouldn't have noticed him, but now he did as he walked passed and he couldn't help but note the raised head and the lowering paper and the push up from the comfortable armchair as he went by.

So he ducked to the further toilets to see if he would follow him all the way wondering whether he would get to relieve himself in the urinal or whether this guy was going to make him piss in his pants.

The metallic frame of the elevators bounced enough reflection of the heavy Caucasian figure and the marble floor echoed his steps, things he would never have noticed before. He was on edge. The whole Vicky/Talisa thing had thrown him of balance, it was a curve ball he hadn't seen coming which added an extra ripple of disgust and regret to his night of passion as he thought of how lucky he had been to see the night through and still be walking around now - but if he stuck around much longer that luck was likely to run out.

He pushed the heavy door of the men's room. There was a mirror that bounced back the urinals to anyone in the lobby that could see the open door. It was a pet hate of his: having no secondary door installed so that the world outside could watch you pee if the door was open. This time it didn't matter though. This time he was glad. This time it was security. He walked up to the urinal and unzipped his fly.

The door opened shortly afterwards but long enough for him to be in mid-flow. He didn't turn to look, just kept peeing. Whoever had come in behind him didn't need to use the toilet but had walked straight to the sinks not the urinals or the cubicles. There was a picture on the wall above the urinal and Sergio could just make out the shadow of figure reflected in the glass.

He heard the tap running behind him and then the pull of paper towels from the dispenser. Sergio finished and zipped up, turned slowly and walked over to the sinks and stood two away from the heavy set guy so that there was a space between them. From the rear he could see the shear muscle of the solid frame beneath the linen suit jacket. Sergio washed his hands trying not to make eye contact but the other guy was taking his time, deliberately as though trying to get his attention without speaking. Sergio looked across at him in the mirror as they both rubbed their hands with their paper towels. Blank eyes stared back at him through the darkened lenses as his hands dropped to hitch up his trousers from the belt, a deliberate move which brushed back the flap of the jacket to reveal the butt of a black handgun snuck in a holster at the groove of his hip.

Sergio didn't want to see that, wished he hadn't, but he had, he pretended not to as he raised his eyes quickly and caught the stare again in the mirror. The figure nodded, turned and walked out.

Sergio let out a breath not realising he'd been holding it ever since walking to the sink. He took a moment to splash water on his face and dry himself again. That was it. The handover was complete. Now he could leave.

He stepped out of the washroom. The hitman was nowhere to be seen.

16

"Do you honestly not see it, ya daft cow?" Talisa was staying strong, stronger than she expected to be at this stage in the proceedings. She kicked the bin and watched the thick odorous insecticide slop within. The smell was almost unbearable but Vicky didn't seem bothered by it, hardly seemed to notice it even. Surely she knew what it was for? These were the things she dealt in after all.

"Yew can't kill me you iron maiden. They plugged me full of drugs so that my skin will tear and burn and my flesh will split and me bones break but I'll keep coming back no matter what you do to me."

"I'll see about that. I'll rip out your guts and tear off your head before you make it to the door."

Talisa laughed. Vicky wasn't paying attention, or she was playing ignorant. Couldn't she see that she had no intention of going for the door? She kicked the plastic bin again.

Vicky looked down and sniffed. Talisa could almost see the vapour burning inside her nostrils.

"What do you see Vicky, your life slipping away?" There was a smile on Talisa's face as she said it. For once she felt that she had the upper hand.

"I see lots of things that aren't there," Vicky replied, but Talisa didn't understand the comment.

"We'll both die in here," she said reaching for the big bottle of industrial cleaner sat on the bed. It was full and heavy, the cap already loose and ready to pour. "The thing is when *you* die *you* stay dead."

"That is a dream also; only he has remained asleep,

while you have awakened; and who knows which of you is the most fortunate?"

Talisa tried to place the quote. She hated these games. She had played them before. She'd taught herself to play knowing her brother liked to quote and she'd practised with...

"With who?" Vicky asked. The tables were turning, Talisa could feel it. Vicky was gaining strength again, playing games with her mind.

"I love that book. It taught me a lot about patience and control, and Providence. Can't you place it Talisa?"

Talisa held the bottle over the bin sensing Vicky was about to pounce.

"Don't you dare take a step further!"

"I just wanted to see the sawing of truth in his eyes when I pulled the trigger. I seized the moment and relished it, only unlike Dante my execution of vengeance was prompt rather than a long drawn out stripping of riches and power and humiliation." There were tears in Vicky's eyes as she spoke but anger in the voice that came back at her.

"What you think killing your own brother quickly was an act of compassion?"

"What would you understand? You can't even see the room you're in. Look about you Talisa, whose room is this? Whose car did you drive back here from the ruins in? Whose money paid for what you're holding? You want to know why you missed the step, why do you think?"

"I'm nothing like you!"

"You're so right. We are so opposite I can't believe I denied it so long. That old bastard Montgomery warned me about you."

It was Talisa's turn to not understand as she shook her head. She knew Giles Montgomery, of course she did, it was him she played the quotes with, it was him she'd seen...

"But I'm not like you," she muttered.

"No. You're skinny and weak. A puny little stuck up scab who needs to get laid. Look at you, you're everything I'm not! Everything I despise! The epitome of..."

"What you're afraid to be?"

They both stood across the room staring at each other, a familiar tune rolling a tear along both their cheeks but blotting out the words that were no longer necessary.

"On the steps of the scaffold death tears off the mask that has been worn through life, and the real visage is disclosed." Talisa's lips had mouthed the quote, saved up in the recess of her mind long ago for just such an occasion as this as though read direct from the page of Dumas, but it was Vicky's voice that echoed the words as the hallucination died and her hand poured the liquid into the bin.

17

Sergio exited the lift, cautiously peering around the metal sidings and listening to the heartbeat of the corridor. He heard nothing. It was dead. His feet padded softly over the carpet as he crept almost tiptoe round to the wall edge to view the long line of doors that elongated in a terrifying tunnel of traps like a scary ride at the fun fair, treading the path of the haunted house forever expectant of something jumping out at you.

He hugged the inner wall careful to hurry passed Vicky's door on the way to his own. He heard nothing inside except the pulse of his own blood pumping through to his head as he held his breath. He reached his door, slid his key and entered quickly.

He let the breath out in a big exasperated sigh, paused to take stock and then rushed around the room grabbing his things and shoving them into his overnight bag. It was all a tight fit now as he'd acquired new things in his short stay. He decided to change quickly. It made sense; he could wear the bigger bulky clothes for the trip home and it would leave more room in the bag. He gave a last minute idiot check of the room to ensure he hadn't left anything behind. Checked his passport was in his pocket - if he got jumped he could afford to lose everything else. Satisfied he aimed for the door. His plan was to check out, drive to the airport and hand back the keys to the hire car and then book the first available flight back to Geneva, or failing that to Heathrow and get a separate connecting flight from there. At least waiting at the airport would feel more secure than waiting around here for his flight.

As he stepped out of his room there was a figure in the corridor blocking his path to the lifts and stairwell. He thought about using the emergency fire exit stairs behind him, not knowing where they would bring him out, but he was curious.

The hitman stood there staring at the door - Vicky's door. He was stood opposite it with his left hand raised to his ear and was talking softly. It took Sergio a moment to realise the man was on the telephone.

The hitman glanced over at Sergio and the blood drained from his face as he stood indecisive with his bag in his hand not knowing whether he should slip back into his room or head for the fire exit. The bulk of the hitman ruled out any passage in that direction and besides he wanted nothing to do with what was going down.

They locked eyes and the hitman motioned him forward with a tilt of his head.

Oh crap! thought Sergio and almost said it out load. He had no choice, what else was he supposed to do? If this guy wanted him to go forward who was he to argue?

He slowly stepped forward noticing a pungent aroma rising to his nose the closer he got. He hadn't noticed it before because he'd passed with held his breath but now it was unmistakable, a choking reek of rotting eggs.

He could hear the voice of the hitman, softer and gentler than he'd expected but with the deep low tone that his body denoted. There was a chirp of conversation from the other end of the mobile rising passed the man's ear. As he drew close enough the hitman held out the phone for him to take.

Tentatively he took the handset and slowly raised it to his ear. One eye was on the hitman who was calm and still as a statue donned in dark sunglasses. The other eye was on the closed door to Vicky's room. The smell was coming from there - and it was strong, almost to the point of making him gag. He knew there was no danger, not to him anyway. If Vicky was in her room then she was no longer breathing.

"Ciao," he said nervously reverting to his native tongue and not certain of what language he should be speaking.

"Luigi?" It was hard to tell from the one word but Sergio thought the man on the other end to be English and from the name he used he was a company man. He wondered what had happened to Tomasz.

"Sí."

"No doubt you are wondering as to the smell from the closed door before you. It is hydrogen sulphide gas, a potent mixture of chemicals so I'm informed by the gentleman stood with you. One breath in close quarters and your life expectancy would be no more than thirty seconds, eh.

"It would appear Miss Rivers has saved us all a lot of trouble. My good man with you there has agreed to stick around and verify the facts and of course ensure there is nothing to incriminate the board in her timely demise. Men like he must be paid for something, eh?"

Sergio looked across at the hitman and grunted a reply in the affirmative. The smell seemed to be getting stronger and was beginning to burn the back of his throat. He followed the example of his cold hallway companion and kept his breathing shallow and slow.

"By all accounts from what I understand," resumed

the Englishman, "you have proved yourself very resourceful and trustworthy, eh! You have a history of being able to intuitively identify problems in advance, eh? Conveniently we have a vacancy for someone with your skills, dare I say it, you may go far with us."

It wasn't what he wanted to hear, not by a long shot. He thought of the freedom he had hoped for and his dreams for his business and security for his family; he had sacrificed a lot over the last few days and would be going home treading carefully over the immoral cracks in the pavement of his life that he had chiselled in there.

"The gentleman has an envelope for you." At the mention of this the hitman removed a small white envelope from the inside pocket of his jacket and handed it to Sergio. It felt thick and padded. He didn't open it. He didn't need to. It was a large amount, in dollars he guessed.

"Your duty with us is completed - enjoy your journey home Mr Vannucci." The phone cut off and he held it out from his face uncertain, looking at the screen to ensure the call was ended. It was. He handed the phone back and the hitman stood aside to let him pass.

It was all over. He could go home.

He wasted no time in rushing to the lift. There was a dead girl behind the door, someone he'd slept with only last night, and now she lay dead only feet away. He shuddered and impatiently pressed the call button, bile was in his mouth and the image of Vicky Rivers was imprinted on his mind.

18

He awoke crying, again. He was depressed as usual, nothing new for a manic depressive. A broken bottle of booze was on the floor next to him, he looked down at it, at the sharp edge with the thin trace of dark red blood dried across its curve. He shook his head. He'd been here before, many times, always hoping this time it would be different.

He reached out to grab for the glass with the aim of a street bum caught in a drunken stupor slumped in an alley surrounded by the discarded rubbish of the restaurants that the rats gladly fed upon. How he got there wasn't important. He was there - for now anyway. He'd move on today, or tomorrow, or whenever he felt the pressure. No one looked at the hobos and the tramps, no one cared if they lived or died. No one cared where they came from or why they were there.

There was a gun on the floor beside him just hiding under his thigh out of sight but not out of reach. He shifted his weight and felt the cold pressure that pushed up from the concrete. It was comforting to know it was there.

He squeezed the glass in his hand until the pain brought his senses round and then he tossed it aside and stared after the freshly drying blood that now covered what was there before. He could feel the thick liquid warming the palm of his hand as it dripped away from him on gravity's path.

The alleyway was dark and dank and no one was there to see his tears as he winced in pain. It was a pleasurable pain now. He had gotten so used to it that he now thrived on it. Longed for it. Missed it when it wasn't there.

He reached down with his clean hand and swept away the rain coat that draped across his folded legs and pulled the small revolver from its hiding place. It was only a .22 calibre but it should be enough to do the job. He swung the chamber out. Only two bullets left.

He burst into tears again. He couldn't take it anymore - too many years, too many lonely, painful years. Such a miserable life. How long before someone comes? How long before someone questioned the copious amounts of blood on his shirt?

The pain was fading and its loss hurt more than the cut of the wound itself. He cried out in a loud wail thumping the gun in the palm of his hand hard to his forehead daring it to inflict damage.

Damn them! Damn them all for what they've done!

He turned the gun to his temple. No, he'd tried that. He put the barrel in his mouth, cocked the hammer back and pulled the trigger.

The sound of silence had been shattered by the thunder crack of the shot, but in this part of the neighbourhood shots rang out all the time and few battered an eyelid. The familiar night time sounds rang out again and in the distance the faint wail of a siren blazing through the streets could be heard.

A short while later, no more than seconds he imagined, he awoke crying again. The alcohol was wearing off but the depression and longing for an end was still there. He looked at the broken glass and then at his blood stained hand. The flesh was smooth and unbroken. On the floor near his leg was a gun. He picked it up and swung the chamber out. Only one shot left. The siren was getting closer. He had to move. He couldn't let them catch him.

THE END

VICKY RIVERS

Two men on a collision course: one, a ruthless gun for hire, and the other a gangland crime boss. Both men are damaged souls seeking redemption but will it come in time before the killing begins?

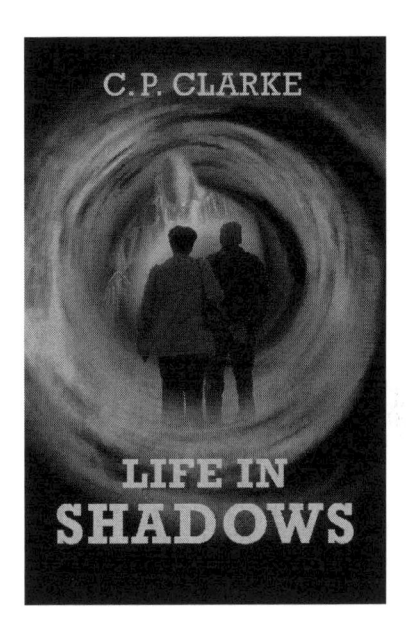

A search for faith, treasure, and an escape from the demons of a man's soul.
Simon is an assassin running from the horrors of his past on a journey that takes him to a strange new world that he is desperate to escape.
Alan is tormented by the mystery of an accident that should have killed him and fearful of the dark figures pursuing him.
In the shadows of a world beyond the two men meet - their fates entwined in an eternal battle of forces beyond their comprehension.

As eminent scientist, Dr Gerard Gill, is on the verge of a discovery that could change the realms of physics, and ultimately the world, he finds himself recruited by a dark and powerful organisation who wish to control his research for themselves - research that holds the secret to the disappearance of a couple years before and a deadly disease that has left a trail of destruction across the globe.

If Dr Gill succeeds he could be opening a doorway through space and time that he might never be able to close.

The book is a collection of 13 biblical accounts told from the perspective of some of the lesser known characters in the bible.

Printed in Great Britain
by Amazon.co.uk, Ltd.,
Marston Gate.